HE IS KNOWN AS

EGO

A Superhero Epic

2nd Edition

JAIME MERA

Dedication

I dedicate this book to my beloved family and friends. The world of science fiction is not for believing as true, but to see possibilities and the imagination which inspire us to live a better life with courage, faith, hope, and love.

Published books:

A Superhero Epic Series

Creator (2004, 2014)

He is Known as Ego (2006, 2014)

Guild Without a Name (2014)

The Galaxy is Ours (2014)

<u>Non-fiction</u>

Jesus and the Paint on the Wall, What Do People Live For? (2012)

Preface

□ □ □ □ □

Before the dawn of the 21st Century, the human race had accomplished great historical feats. They had survived thousands of years of upheavals—social and economic shifts, wars, political revolutions. However, what historians failed to look at were the patterns of things affecting the present and possible future. In the end, humans faced a critical period when they had to choose between civil war or acceptance of what many people called "super humans," "mutants," or "freaks of nature." But the choice was more than acceptance about nature, more than about flesh and blood, more than about mutations. It was a choice that also concerned the supernatural, the unexplainable, the beginning of human evolution, drastic transformation, divine intervention… No one really knew what it was all about, when it all started, or why some humans were especially gifted or cursed.

They were super beings that came not from another planet but from the house next door, who lived among all of us, waiting for a time when the world would not hate or fear them. They waited for the long-past stories about wizards, dragons, demons, and gods to become folklore before finally coming out. In the end, it was bound to happen. Late in the 1980s, one superhuman emerged out of hiding and led the way to a new era of society. He called himself Neutronium. It was a time when the world needed a person that would battle injustice and crime, could fly faster than the speed of sound, brush aside bullets off his chest and pick up 100 tons with one arm. Neutronium was that special person who led reform and changed the face of the Earth, changing the perception about what people used to call "mutant freaks" into what are known today as "superheroes."

Neutronium was truly the all-American superhero. He was a born-leader with a knack for politics and an undying zeal for truth and justice. In the end, he set the standard for heroes to emulate. It was because of his legacy that the world accepted superheroes in their everyday lives. But like any other good force, there was a strong opposite force: the Super Villains. The majority of society embraced superheroes, while evil and unscrupulous people embraced super villains with plans of conquest, acquiring power, or committing heinous crimes. It was a battle of good versus evil, which started with Neutronium as leader of the Emerald Legion, the first superhero group in the world. But Neutronium suddenly died, which was a major setback for the Emerald Legion and people fighting for justice. The glory days for superheroes, however, did not end there—while those were very dark times; nations rose up and superheroes took the challenge of fighting for freedom, truth, and justice.

South America and Australia became superpowers overnight, while a new superhero group emerged in the wake of the Emerald Legion's setback. It seemed evil was going to prevail until a group called Energy, Fire, and Light (EFL), declared themselves America's official second superhero group. It was a small group, but a very powerful one, with members answering only to themselves. They kept the peace for many years while government organizations got stronger in response to the increase in crime, terrorism, and the threat of super villains. While the forces of good were established, evil super beings continued to grow and develop a clandestine network unmatched by any organization in the underworld of villains.

New superhero groups were being born every year with almost all of them dying off or disbanding due to conflicting group differences, limitations, scandals, or legal red tape. Evil was at bay waiting to explode and engulf the world. Not even the EFL could tip the balance of power toward the side of good. But hope emerged when a third superhero group, the Eternal Champions, came into existence. They came together in unique conditions under the leadership of Richard Octavian, known to the world as Creator. A string of unlikely circumstances somehow formed the most adaptive and influential superhero group of all time. The four superhumans, an artificial intelligence, and human allies fought crime on the streets with unmatched efficiency. This is their story, as they become the driving force and guiding light for the side of all that is good.

List of Characters

Richard Octavian / Creator – Leader of the Eternal Champions

Becky Ellington – Head veterinarian for the Octavian Farm and supporter of the Eternal Champions.

Cindy S. Owens / Mirage (Samantha Brooks) – Disciple of Joshua

Elizabeth A. Octavian / Isis – Member of the Eternal Champions

Erica – Member of the Eternal Champions (Super Artificial Intelligence computer)

John Goodman / Mindseye – Member of the Eternal Champions

Larcis G. Draven / Night – Member of the Eternal Champions

Robert Dilinger – Head security guard for the Octavian Farm and supporter of the Eternal Champions.

Susan M. Goodman / Pandora – Member of the Eternal Champions (second-in-command)

Joshua Marks (David Bernard) – All-Powerful Superhuman

Jonah Stiles – Special Advisor to Cardigan International (Weapons Technology Corporation)

Pamela Wilkins – Head Doctor of the Asian Department in Kansas City Zoo

CPT Bradley Middleton – Leader of the Special Security Detail and Division Leader in SIA

LT Christopher Harper – SIA, Special Security Detail Team Leader

Randolph Maximilian – Director of the Special Investigation Agency (SIA)

Mark Farnell – Computer genius, expanded Super Artificial Intelligence technology

Glenn Seber – US Federal Marshall, Seattle Office

Jean Lorenz – Director of the Counterespionage Agency (CEA)

Jared Erickson – Special operative for CEA

Natasha Erickson – Sister of Jared and special operative for CEA

Andrez Pobles – South American Councilmember of the Federation

Diego Gonzalez – South American Councilmember of the Federation

Eduardo T. Ramirez – South American Councilmember and Founder of the Federation

Estabon Ramirez – South American Councilmember of the Federation, and Captain of the Starship Andromeda

Jose Begestano – South American Councilmember of the Federation

Commander Alejandro Javier— Second in command of the Starship Andromeda

Quatris/Scott Emerson – Leader of Energy, Fire and Light (EFL, superhero group in NY)

Hellfire/Rick Alexander – Member of EFL (second in command)

Starfire/Rebecca Emerson – Member of EFL and wife of Quatris

Starlight/Lynda Alexander – Member of EFL and wife of Hellfire

Ego– Being from the hexametric dimension

Nowhereman – Being from multiple dimensions

Contents

Chapter One

□ □ □ □ □

RESEARCH CENTER

Yimen Research Center, Elyria, Ohio, November 7, 2006

Cindy sighed deeply as the countdown clock started at 120 seconds. She sat on a clear plastic chair trying to recover her strength as the room's floor and walls shifted width wise expanding to 50 feet. The floor and walls eventually stopped moving as laser beams glimmered across the two sidewalls, creating a colorful web-like maze through the center of the room.

Cindy was almost naked except for the scant cover on her groin and nipples. Her golden, flowing hair was cut short. The tests required her to be completely nude, but she knew cameras were monitoring her every move. Her shyness and innocence would not allow her to compromise her modesty, especially at her age.

She leaned her head back and stared at the ceiling. Cool fresh air entered her lungs as she relaxed and concentrated on the task at hand.

"You're doing great Cindy," a female voice announced from the control room. "We only have to complete one more run before we can call it a day."

Cindy's face tightened as she strained to relax. "Why can't we finish all the simulations?"

"I'm sorry, Cindy, but we have a tight schedule to follow. Dr. Leman will be here soon and won't allow his experiments to be held up, especially by us."

"I thought we were all here to help people?" Cindy said. She knew the research center was dedicated to solving the problems of the world, conducting studies on medical to environmental concerns for the improvement of the Earth's ecosystem and the human race.

"I'm sorry, but the kids will have to wait an extra day," Erlene said, Cindy's personal medical researcher and supervisor.

Cindy covered her face with her palms and let out a soft moan of frustration.

"How about this," Erlene said, "what if I get with Dr. Rieder and see if we can use the room later tonight, maybe after midnight?"

Cindy thought about all the children and teenagers in the world who need help to overcome their immune deficiency syndrome diseases, and somehow, thinking of all those children's faces eased her impatience. Information from the experimental simulations would allow scientists and doctors to develop a synthetic super antibody to replace damaged or nonexistent T-cells in ill patients. The simulations had worn her body out severely, but fortunately, she would now be forced to take a break before completing the last four out of 143 simulations with her parents' consent.

"Do you think he will let us finish tonight?" Cindy asked with a wide grin, correcting her posture upright on the chair.

"I will try my best, but I cannot promise you he will."

Cindy took a quick breath, and stared at the countdown clock, then smiled. "Good. I'm ready now."

"Okay, remember to pass through the red lasers without phasing and then phase through the green lasers. You have to move slowly, or we won't be able to read your metaphysical adjustments. Okay?" The countdown clock hit ten seconds.

Cindy stood up and disappeared into thin air.

The thermo monitor in the control room displayed Cindy's heat signature as she walked across the room. "That's a good girl. I still have you on the thermo sensors. Can you bring it up one more notch?" Erlene asked as Cindy's heat signature likewise disappeared.

"Way ahead of you," Cindy snapped.

"Very good, Cindy. Now walk slowly into the beams." An ultraviolet monitor vaguely displayed Cindy's silhouetted movement as Erlene adjusted the biophysical and ultrasonic sensors from her console. Gigabits of data fed into seventy-eight databases in a matter of seconds as Cindy passed through the red beams. Technical readouts on Cindy's DNA displayed a wondrous process of photosynthesis.

"You're doing great, Cindy. Now start to phase," Erlene said. Cindy phased out, spreading her molecules apart, allowing the air and light particles to pass through her very soul. The monitors went blank as Cindy passed through the last green, then blue laser beams.

"Cindy, I lost you. Are you sure you didn't walk too fast?"

"A snail could have beaten me to the other side. You have the right settings, right?" Cindy asked as she dematerialized inches away from the last beam.

"Okay, walk back into the green laser beams and stop," Erlene said, adjusting the monitors several times.

Cindy phased out again and walked into the beams. Nothing but a blank screen appeared on the monitors. Cindy became almost translucent, visible to the naked eye, but was still phased out from existence. "What about now?" Cindy asked.

Erlene saw Cindy's ghostly image through the control room window, but no monitor except the video camera could detect her presence. Cindy walked into the red beams to no avail. Erlene's composure sank as data stopped feeding into the databases or her monitors

Erlene thought for a moment and then sighed. "They're on the right settings. It seems your body has adjusted to the new stream of particles. I don't think we will be able to do anything for a while until I can get stronger or get more flux pitch detectors. I'm sorry, Cindy."

"That's okay. I can wait a few more days," Cindy said, slightly frustrated.

"I'll wrap it up here," Erlene said. "Why don't you go and change in the ready room? I'll join you in a few minutes, okay?"

"I don't have much of a choice, huh." Cindy materialized and left the room, trying to stretch out her arms in an attempt to relax her frustration away.

Minutes later, Erlene entered the ready room, which resembled a standard locker room found in any five-star hotel. Carpeted floor, nice white clean walls, wooden locker doors, and plush cushions on the benches and rolling chairs.

"Well, Dr. Leman has moved in already. I will talk to Dr. Rieder in an hour and give him the bad news. In the meantime, I suggest you get some rest."

Cindy listened to Dr. Summers as she tried to brush her long hair forgetting the barber had cut it a day ago. "So, is Dr. Leman having as much trouble as you're having with me?" Cindy said and quickly put the brush in front of her face holding it up with one hand as if the brush didn't work. She blushed slightly as Erlene talked.

"Trouble–nonsense, Cindy. This is science," Erlene said. "It's not perfect, but it does get results. Can you imagine what would have happened if Thomas Edison gave up after the first ten out of over a hundred failures on many of his experiments? We wouldn't have the light bulb or many of the rubber products that we so casually take for granted today. You have to have faith, Cindy, and trust in science. We will make this project work."

"I will try to have a little bit more faith in science." Cindy smiled.

"Okay, kiddo, it's time for you to get some sleep," Erlene said.

Cindy dabbed skin lotion on her face and arms before securing the locker. With Erlene, she walked out into the hallway and into the elevator that went up nine floors to the living quarters. The guard remained at his post in the elevator while Dr. Summers ensured Cindy was safely in her room. Erlene bid Cindy goodnight and then went upstairs to speak with Dr. Rieder to give her report on the test results.

Cindy's room door automatically locked from the outside. At times, she felt like a prisoner, but according to the Foundation, it was a measure established to keep other patients from possibly hurting one another with uncontrolled powers or diseases. In addition, she agreed to act as a patient although she was really a volunteer. She was not allowed to speak with her parents, but she did have a few amenities like cable television and a small kitchen, which other patients had to work hard to get. At this point, she really didn't care. The long hard day's work taxed her body once again. She quickly took a warm shower and jumped straight into bed, trying to forget about the experimental failure. Cindy quickly fell to sleep as her body rejuvenated.

Less than an hour later, she emerged from deep sleep as her stomach and leg muscles cramped up, causing her to cringe violently into a ball. Cindy screamed in pain as she grabbed at her stomach and one of her legs. The immobilizing contractions ebbed in less than a minute; allowing her to stretch her legs and concentrate on breathing naturally. But she was still reeling from nausea as she felt the life force leaving every cell in her body.

The simulations in the past had weakened her before but never like this one. Cindy wondered what could have caused her this feebleness. She had been forcibly hydrated for the past three days and felt very strong until five minutes ago. "What's happening to me?" she thought, trying to figure out what was wrong with her since the last series of simulations were very similar to the previous tests.

Cindy lay in bed for a few minutes, recovering enough strength to sit up against the bed's headboard. Minutes elapsed as the pain and nausea gradually diminished into some sort of a drunken stupor. She slowly swung around and placed her feet on the cold tiled floor while holding onto the headboard with one hand. The room video camera light was on, but no one seemed to be monitoring as no attendant came into the room to help. Cindy waited patiently as she noticed her locked room door. Still slightly dizzy, she labored over changing into a pair of jeans and her favorite blue sweat top. Cindy called out aloud, asking for help, only to hear nothing in return.

The Complex was far from silent many levels above. Horrific shivers perforated throughout the faculties' fatuous and spineless workers. Doctor Castello froze in fright as a zombie with jagged bloody teeth snapped at his neck and face. The zombie's thorn-like scabby skin rubbed against the doctor's exposed skin, savagely injecting wasp-like stingers into his body. The doctor's body shook violently as poison from the stingers moved through his circulatory system and a chunk of bloody flesh was torn away from his neck. The shock was sudden, the blackness was forever.

The chief psychiatrist's body crumbled onto the floor alongside his staff members. The Complex stood silent as corpses lay motionless throughout hallways, offices, bedrooms, laboratories, and sealed security rooms. Not a trace of blood or signs of mutilation could be found on any of the several hundred people who worked and lived in the Complex. The once-humanitarian vision of life was now a vision of death.

Cindy's door automatically opened, letting in a void of silence into her room. She slowly made her way up to the distant elevator, calling out for anyone. She tried to open the dorm-room doors, but all were still electronically locked. She would have phased through the doors, but it could have meant disaster given her weakened state if she unwillingly materialized halfway inside a solid object. She finally made it to the elevator. The familiar security guard in the elevator lay dead below the elevator controls. The red camera lights on the center's monitoring system faded away as lifeless as the human operators.

Cindy stood in the elevator staring back and forth at the controls and the dead security guard. She eventually built up the courage to take the security guard's access key and enabled the elevator to proceed to the lobby. The elevator rapidly went up four stories, stopping on the first of three levels above the ground. In seconds, the elevator doors opened to the lobby. At that same moment, the power went out and immobilized the elevator doors. She could see four more dead bodies faintly visible in the darkened reception area.

Who could have done this horrible thing? Cindy fearfully thought and trembled.

She forgot about the passing of time as logic played tug-of-war with her worst fears. Surely, she was not the only one still alive. She turned invisible and walked out into the reception area. The elegant and very expensive French mosaic interior design and furnishings seemed dark and gloomy with a thick air of death overshadowing the once beautiful setting. The power outage left emergency lights blazing a path to the building's side exit. Cindy bolted across the large room and opened the glass-paneled double doors to one of the four courtyard exits. The cool outdoor air eased the tension for a moment, only to be overwhelmed by a scene of a devastated estate. There were several buildings lighting up the night sky as they brilliantly collapsed inward from what appeared to be massive red flames.

"What's going on?" Cindy was screaming as she realized that the entire Complex had been swallowed up by hell itself.

Do not fear Cindy, no harm will come to you, a soft voice spoke inside Cindy's head. Cindy nervously looked around for the source of the voice, but found nothing.

I am Joshua. You have been deceived by the same people you thought were your friends.

Cindy fell to her knees as visions of past events raced through her mind. Dr. Erlene Summers, Dr. Ronald Castello, Dr. Jack Rieder, and many more of the people she knew and didn't know were revealed to her as if she were in the middle of their conversations, even their thoughts. She even saw through all the lies about the purpose and intent of the Foundation.

The Complex had been contracting its services to the

highest bidders, developing new weapons and security systems along with conducting genetic experiments on superhumans and other animals.

Cindy could hardly believe what was being forced into her mind. She wondered why she had not gone insane as years of memories of over a dozen people dashed before her in a matter of seconds. Then, the vision she thought could never be true mentally flashed before her eyes. The man and the woman she had loved all her life were now dead, along with her brother and sister. Odd waves of painful agony and comfort fell over her as fast as the other visions. All those memories—the funeral service, the endless sessions with her psychologist, the battles with her own demons—came and went to her in a flicker of time.

"Daddy, Mommy!" Tears ran down her cheeks. "Who are you?" Cindy screamed, knowing only Joshua's name and voice.

I'm your true friend, as are the three out of thirteen others who still live in this Complex, Joshua answered.

In an instant, the image of three other people flashed in her vision as she was trying to get up. She knew that there was actually no one in front of her, but the people seemed so real as if they were just standing right next to her face.

The first was Randy Omar, a wiry man in his late twenties standing a little over six feet. His sandy blond hair, military-style haircut, and muscular build showed evidence of some previous military experience. Then there was the African-American Alicia Tarmen, with her very long braided hair, beautiful face, and slender body could have easily given her a fruitful career as a super model. Lastly, there was Lee Frost who, like Cindy, was in his early teens. The youth's composure, however, was not like any other teen, but more like someone who had lived half a century. His dark brown hair was also styled after an army ranger who seemed to be in the middle of extensive combat training.

Cindy tried to imagine the kinds of things the three people before her had gone through in their past and here at the research center. They were a mystery to her, but they oddly felt like family. She was sure that if Joshua wanted her to know about them, he would have told her in the visions he stuffed into her brain; but for now she was happy just to know she wasn't alone.

'*Why us, Joshua?*' Randy asked without elaborating.

Joshua spoke, '*All four of you are not responsible for the atrocities this place has committed. All of you are pure in heart and only victims of deception. The four of you are special with superhuman abilities, which can be used for good. I have seen the future and know that each one of you must live to fulfill what I call destiny.*'

'*And what if I don't believe in destiny?*' Alicia asked.

A faint mental smile could be felt as Joshua replied, '*Destiny is what you make of it. Some of you will do things that are far from saintly, but believe this: You are free for now. They will eventually come for you and some of you may die. I have given each one of you added abilities, which will help you in your quest to survive in a world full of hope. Go into the world, fight injustice, and live as best you can to the fullest with love and happiness. Destiny is being fulfilled as we speak whether you believe in it or not.*'

'*Where do you fit in all of this?*' Lee asked.

'*I have powers beyond comprehension, but I will not force my absolute will on the human race. I will be around when the world needs me most. If you need me, call on me when the time is right and I will help you. Consider yourselves as brothers and sisters. Should you meet each other in the future, remember that no matter the circumstance, you can and must trust each other with your lives, for you are all one family now...*'

'*They will be here soon to see this place disappear before their very eyes. I will show them the power they have been searching for all this time. Now, quickly leave this place and be free before they arrive.*' Joshua concluded the mental conference as the images each person saw and heard slowly faded away.

Cindy took to the air, flying as fast as her powers would allow, distancing herself from Joshua's final destructive wrath on the Complex. She slowed down for a moment—she had never flown in her life. Joshua must have given her the added ability or taught her how to fly using her own innate powers while he was in her mind. Whatever happened, it didn't really matter now. Cindy's depression and apprehension steadily vanished as the truth about the Foundation and death of her family trailed behind her.

Cindy heard a dull boom behind her. She quickly glanced back and saw a faintly visible beam of thin light shoot straight up into the atmosphere. Chills ran down her back as she tried to imagine what Joshua could have done to the Complex. She looked away and focused ahead, flying faster than she ever thought possible. After a few minutes, she descended into a thickly wooded area. She was tired from using her powers to fly and stay invisible. See looked across the empty road and hoped someone would come along. It wasn't ten minutes later when a pick-up truck came down the road truck heading north toward Canada. She stowed away in the back of the truck without alerting the driver. The wind was chilly, but no matter as joy overcame her knowing that Joshua would always be with her; feeling truly free with a clear purpose in life to fight injustice.

"Thank you Joshua," Cindy mumbled, becoming visible as she fell into deep sleep.

Yimen Complex

Mr. Stiles stepped out of his Bell Ranger helicopter, quickly scanned the area, and walked out to meet the emergency quick reactionary force team leader. The company of mercenaries stood in full SWAT-type battle gear ready to fight an unknown force. "Report!" Stiles commanded.

"Sir, we have secured the perimeter of what used to be the fence line, sir!" the team leader screamed over the din of the helicopter swirling rotors.

"What?" Stiles looked out into the rolling hills only to see large and small holes in the ground. "Where are all of the buildings?"

"Sir, they're all gone!" the team leader quickly replied.

"What do you mean they're all gone?" Stiles was shouting as he strode to one of the larger holes in the ground.

The hole was roughly the diameter of half a football field

and extended down into a dark abyss. Spotlights were trained on the hole only to reveal sprouts of water and sewage mains pouring out. Stiles stared at the excavated walkway leading to the entrance of the now destroyed building. The sharp and clean separation of the building from the ledge chilled his spine.

"Sir, everything is gone. We can't find any traces of survivors."

"You won't find any," Stiles snapped. "Cut off the water and electricity. Get the holes filled in. Get rid of all of the evidence that this place existed. You have twenty-four hours."

"Yes, sir!" the team leader yelled and ran off barking orders to his men.

A slim, elderly woman in a black knee-high skirt and matching coat walked up to Stiles. "It looks like you have seen this before," the woman said. "What could have done this?"

"No, this is the first time I've seen this, Betty," Stiles said almost absently. "But the question is not 'what,' but more like 'who.'" Stiles responded trying to place names with faces in his memory of the people who worked in the Complex.

"What? You mean to tell me that someone did all of this?" Betty exclaimed, disbelieving.

"Yes, it was one of the patients." Stiles walked slowly around the area, pondering the prime suspects.

"I know that the patients admitted here were gifted, but nothing like this. This is a display of power that surpasses anything anyone has heard of," Betty said.

Stiles thought for a moment. "It seems he has surpassed any superhuman I know. Now, we're surely going to pay dearly with him loose."

"Who's loose?"

"Joshua," Stiles said, his face grim.

Betty vaguely remembered the name, Joshua Marks. "But how? He was only rated as a level six telepath, wasn't he?"

"No, he was a level nine telepath," Stiles said, and in his mind, he remembered his personal interview with Joshua Marks.

The office was sterile of any loose objects as Joshua sat strapped to an intentionally reinforced heavy chair. Two telepaths stood behind Stiles as the interrogation ran for forty minutes. Joshua, half-dazed from sedatives, answered remarkably well despite absorbing half a liter of muscle relaxers, hallucinogenic inhibitors, risperidone, and lithium. Joshua was in his mid-twenties, and his long, wavy black hair and flowing beard framed his face. He was given a haircut only once every two months because the caretakers thought Joshua might use the barber's utensils against everyone in the room.

On first glance, Joshua seemed harmless, but he was the most dangerous patient in the Complex. He was the ultimate weapon, which the Foundation had nurtured and kept captive in vain attempts to duplicate his powers for world domination.

"Tell me again, Joshua. Why are you going to help with our research?" Stiles asked.

"If I help you, you will keep my wife and daughter safe,"

Joshua slurred.

"Yes, that's right. But remember, I am the messenger, not the executioner. I am here to help you. You do believe me, don't you?"

"You are the messenger and you're here to help me," Joshua mimicked without missing a beat.

"Good. You will start undergoing the Q40 treatment tomorrow. I will be back in three months to check on your progress." Stiles stood up to leave. By the door, he heard Joshua's clear voice saying, "Jonah."

Stiles tuned around, and saw the deadly certainty in Joshua's eyes. "There will be a day when no one will be safe."

Stiles felt the reality of Joshua's statement, paralyzing him for an instant. He wanted so desperately to ask for forgiveness, knowing he had taken a step too far beyond the drawn line of right and wrong. The two telepaths kept a vigilant scan on both of them, so Stiles quickly withdrew his thoughts, hoping Joshua would one day forgive him for not trying to get him and his family out of this evil place.

"I know," Stiles said, and walked out of the room.

"Sir?" Betty regarded the devastated scene with awe and curiosity, but did not question Stiles any further seeing his troubled state of mind.

"It's time to go," Stiles said and started toward the helicopter. Betty quickly followed and wondered how Stiles would report this to the board members as soon as they arrived in Chicago.

Cardigan International Research Center - Chicago, Nov. 8, 2006

The secure conference room in the middle of the Cardigan Building seated fifteen members presided by the chairman of the board, Mr. Huggins.

"Ladies and gentlemen, please believe me when I tell you that we cannot go looking for Joshua," Stiles was saying as he concluded his report on the destruction of the Yimen Research Center. "He will retaliate with deadly consequences."

"We captured Joshua before. We shouldn't have a problem now, especially since he's a clear threat to us," Mrs. Landings said.

"We have forty special operation teams suited for this task," Mr. Pines added.

The board members started a frenzy of plans on how to solve the problem with Joshua.

Stiles could not believe the ignorance and stupidity of the people before him. "Don't you understand?" Stiles roared over the babble of noise, and he almost jumped out of his chair, pointing at the pictures on the heads-up projection of the newly-created holes. "Joshua took ten buildings out of the ground like they were nothing. He didn't use teleportation or a machine."

"Look at those photos. He even bothered to leave the ground above the lower levels not connected to the upper levels, intact. Not to mention half a mile's worth of sidewalk. Look at that—the sides of the holes are perfectly smooth. Joshua has telekinesis and that's exactly how he did it. Do you know how much telekinesis it would take to make an object move so fast that it would be vaporized, not to mention ten buildings which is three times the magnitude of the same building we're in now?" Stiles paused; he saw the board members gaping in awe. "We cannot capture him again, we lost that ability when you all had his wife and daughter killed!"

"Doesn't Joshua have a weakness for drugs?" Dr. Owens interjected.

"He was heavily sedated before he escaped. He has been able to overcome the drugs and the six security guards who were constantly watching even while he slept. His powers come from the life force of others. The very people that were in the Complex gave him the power to destroy it." Stiles explained with a dumbfounded look on his face as he tried to comprehend why none of the board members were listening to him.

Don't worry, Jonah, these fools have no ears or eyes for understanding, Joshua said inside Stiles's head. Joshua's voice shocked him; he gasped for air as fear struck his heart. Joshua was here and by the looks of all the board members' faces, they also heard Joshua.

Maybe you all think that you can find me and kill me, but I assure you that that is not going to happen, Joshua continued.

All of the board members stood up as if being controlled by an invisible force. They all floated up and circled in the air above the table, just inches away from the ceiling. Stiles didn't try to get up or run away; feeling his body was paralyzed.

None of you know what you are dealing with, so I will make it easy for you. I am a merciful person and will allow you to live. *Do not take my show of mercy as a sign of weakness or your opportunity to continue to do wrong. In fact, look at it as a second chance to correct all of the evil you have done.* Joshua paused as if waiting for someone to respond.

"What do you want?" Mr. Huggins muttered in fear, being able only to move his lips and tongue.

I want you to stop all of the evil you are doing and work to help people. Your Foundation is capable of good things, so do what is right. If you don't, I will be watching and believe me—you will wish you died today. Now, I want all of you to look at each other closely. Joshua commanded.

The board members looked around the circle of eyes and saw fear in each one of them.

You have heard Jonah here tell you what I did, so take everything for what it's worth and do what is right. You can choose evil and a slow death, or good and a long life. I would prefer you choose life. The choice I leave is up to each of you. Joshua said and let go of his hold on everyone.

The board members all fell on the conference room table with only two managing to stand on the table while the rest were sprawled out on the table with Dr. Philips falling off onto the floor.

Stiles sat relaxed; he knew Joshua was not on a mission for revenge. He thought quickly as the board members got back into their seats as Mr. Huggins tried to bring back order to the meeting.

Half of the board members sat quietly, possibly in fear of

Joshua knowing what was being said, while the other half started yelling accusations at other members for letting Joshua get away or the Foundation not being able to control their experiments.

"Order! Everyone!" Huggins yelled and slammed his hand on the table. Everyone calmed down, but the room was still far from quiet.

"Mr. President, we can't let this freak run this organization. We have a mentalist of our own who can handle this guy," Mr. Connelly, head of special research, said.

Stiles tried to remain calm. "I suggest you leave Joshua alone and concentrate on what he told all of us to do."

The board members stayed quiet and pondered what Stiles said. Mr. Huggins stared at Stiles. "I think we understand the severity of the situation now. Thank you for your report. You are excused now." Huggins motioned Stiles to leave the room.

Stiles knew this was an unwanted passive stance, which meant they were helpless, and had to do what Joshua commanded or face the consequences. The only problem was they would lose billions of dollars, and money meant more to them than their own lives.

"Can you really understand?" Stiles said, and indignantly stood up and left the room. Betty, his personal assistant, trailed him.

"What do we do now, Mr. Stiles?" Betty asked with a trace of fear in her voice, while they walked down the hallway away from the receptionist and conference room entrance.

Stiles looked sternly ahead as he walked and wondered why Joshua had given him a second chance to live a just life. "I'm going to get as far away from here as possible and hope Joshua keeps his word. I suggest you do the same."

"I don't understand, Mr. Stiles," Betty asked, not comprehending.

"They're not going to leave Joshua alone and will probably try to find and kill him, knowing he is capable of destroying their little empire... The miserable fools are playing with a god who has the power to send them to a place far worse than hell. Those idiots!" Stiles gritted his teeth as he walked into the building's private elevator up to the rooftop helipad.

Chapter Two

□ □ ◻ □ □

RISING FAME

Eternal Domain, Octavian Farm, March 12, 2011

A fluxion of power temporarily jolted Erica's main memory banks as the self-diagnosis ended. The weekly ritual of maintaining the databases clear of viruses, intrusion programs, and non-conflicting operating systems was quite a task but necessary to protect against the best of hackers and other super corporate computers now more prevalent on cyberspace. The New Year had come and went with great joy at the Octavian Farm. Susan and John were ever more so in love as the first day they married. Liz and Richard looked forward to an extended family with the addition of a soon-to-be-born baby boy within the next seven months. Larcis, as usual, was hopping from relationship to relationship. The super artificial intelligence, Erica, had taken a strong liking for Susan and her almost double personality of Queen Omia. Susan was able to play many intellectual games of trivia and riddles with Erica, which would astound even the best of Jeopardy champions. The farm was generating a sizable profit, which made the Eternal Domain's cover that much easier to manage. Yes, crime fighting was as natural to the Eternal Champions as living a normal upper middle-class lifestyle.

The morning started with an early schedule of maintenance on the horse farm and reading news updates. Richard dawdled on the Battle Room sofa, monitoring the daily tabloids and reputable papers for evidence of extraterrestrial activity. The induction of Susan as Queen of the Argonian Empire rekindled many of the questions he had always been curious about. It was obvious there were hundreds of races in the galaxy that traveled the stars, but none had attempted to invade Earth. The possibilities of alien influence on Earth in the past, present, and future worried him. Susan told him the Argonian Empire had existed for over three thousand years. In its wake, the Earth was primarily left alone to evolve under the envelope of protection from conquering alien races and natural cosmic disasters. The soothsayers said Earth was destined to change the face of the galaxy, but there were no details to the event as Susan only alluded to the significance Earthlings had in the large scheme of intergalactic peace.

Richard knew the Argonian race to be very disciplined and honorable, but he also knew they weren't perfect. The display of treachery by Elexsuia, Princess Navia's second-in-command aboard Navia's star cruiser, mirrored one of the many characteristics in human society. It was comforting to know Susan was now a decisive factor in Earth's future. His mind drifted off, wondering if some of the superhumans on Earth were aliens or descendants of aliens.

Richard quickly changed his attention to the latest police and news reports highlighted on the Battle Room master screen. He looked on with added curiosity as the stainless steel hawk struck once again.

"Erica, are there any incidents of the hawk trademark outside of the US?" Richard asked.

"Negative," said Erica. "The trademark is oddly based in the US a total of six times to be exact."

"Oddly?" Richard said to himself and pondered on something. "Can you please show me the details of the robberies in chronological order." Richard instructed hoping to see a visual pattern by the thief or thieves.

Erica instantly displayed the contents of each robbery on the projection screen. Richard looked at it intently.

"The first robbery was a case of petty theft involving $125,000, seven years ago. The second theft that same year equated to $325,000. The third occurred three years ago with the theft of newly-cut diamonds worth $250,000 and $400,000 in hard currency. The fourth heist occurred two years ago with the theft of jewelry worth half a million dollars and $350,000 in hard currency. The fifth heist occurred last year with the theft of an Egyptian statue artifact of a sphinx weighing 600 pounds, worth thirty million dollars. The most recent heist equated to $300,000 worth of jewelry, $600,000 in hard currency, five million dollars in treasury bonds, and five large deposit boxes."

"Where did the robberies take place?" Richard asked after listening to Erica and reading the information on the screen.

A diagram of the United States with colorful relief came up next to the screen expanding it to 150 inches horizontally. Six yellow dots appeared and across the country, not in any particular pattern. "The California robbery took place on a money truck."

"I take it that there were no witnesses or fingerprints," Richard said.

"Correct," Erica said. "The guard inside the truck was knocked out with a blow to the head caused by a hard blunt object. There was no DNA evidence from any would-be assailant left in or around the truck. All three guards were mind-scanned by the SIA, confirming that the guards were not involved."

The California heist was the second of six robberies. "Why did you describe it as 'oddly'?" Richard asked.

"The robberies were successful. However, it would have been easier to accomplish half of the robberies in Egypt and the United Kingdom before the gems or statue came into the country. Perhaps the thief or thieves do not have international connections or don't want any in the chance that the connections will leave a trail to their whereabouts?"

"But why change the MO?" Richard pondered, noticing the only constant event out of all of the robberies was a progression of more money value stolen per theft.

"Do you mean, why change the method by doing something different for each robbery and take a chance of slipping up?"

"Yes, but it seems they're too good to be caught."

"How do you know it was more than one person?" Erica said.

"One person may have taken the sphinx, but it's not likely," Richard offered, thinking hard. "I am sure it took more than one person to handle and organize the thefts. I also think the thefts maybe a prelude to an even bigger burglary."

"Unlike you, Richard, I don't have a gut," Erica said. "But if memory serves me right, you have not been wrong since I've known you. So I will have to side with you on this one."

Richard smiled. "I didn't think you would ever give up so easily being the Devil's advocate all of the time."

"Advocate I am, but not the Devil's," Erica said, grinning.

"You proved my point." Richard smiled. "But, back to the subject. It really doesn't matter. We need hard evidence. I want you to compile information on any money transfers from banks and companies to the banks in question and then go over any possible links of not just robberies, but unaccounted-for money, lost money by the banks in question, or any other banks under suspicion of possible corruption in the past and until now. I have a feeling it was an inside job with more than a few thieves to make it work." Richard instructed, laying out the plan of attack for one of his many projects the two crime fighters had initiated in the past fourteen months.

"It will take me a few days," Erica acknowledged.

"Good, I have other things to think about," Richard said. He started to make a sandwich snack at the kitchen bar overlooking the Battle Room.

Elizabeth Octavian came out of the elevator into the Battle Room with a wide grin. "So, how is my husband this morning?"

"Great! Now that you're here, my beautiful lady," Richard smiled as he cut his sandwich in half from corner to corner. "Do you want a piece?"

"I would never pass up one of your concoctions," Liz said and accepted half of the sandwich.

They sat together on the black sofa in front of the ninety-inch screen. "So, what do you want to do besides exercising the horses and cleaning the barn?" Richard asked.

"Well, it's obvious you are trying to avoid our engagement for today," Liz said. Richard had promised to teach her martial arts.

"Hmm…and what engagement are we talking about?" Richard half-wittedly avoided the comment.

Liz eyed him. "You promised to teach me Kung Fu."

"No," Richard said. "I promised to teach you martial arts, not just Kung Fu, but I'm not sure if now's a good time."

"You know, just because I'm pregnant doesn't mean I can't kick your butt," Liz retorted.

Richard smiled; she had no chance in hell of hurting him even if he were sleeping. "Okay, but you will promise me that you won't go crime fighting once you're five months out. Alright?"

Liz looked at him lovingly, smiling as she chewed on his sandwich. "Alright. But only because you can make any type of food taste great."

"Once we're done here, we'll go."

"Oh, there's no hurry. John and Susan are still in the Danger Room."

"How long have they been there?"

Liz shrugged. "I don't know. I think they started at around seven this morning."

"Hmm, let's go see what the two love birds can do."

"Oki-do." Liz jumped out of the sofa.

Eight levels down from the Battle Room, the training control room doors opened. Larcis was at the controls trying hard not to mess up the electronic components.

"Good morning, Larcis," Richard greeted as he strode into the room.

Larcis looked in Richard's and Liz's direction, confusion—then frustration—on his face. Larcis Draven was the super fast energy projecting superhero of the group. He was tall and had an excellent build along with his handsome face, which made him the object of many girls' dreams at the University of Miami campus. He was the second member to join the group and had been Richard's sidekick for a year now. His ability to fly in ultrasonic speeds made him a valuable and unique asset.

"You have to take a look at this, Boss," Larcis said, slightly awe-stricken.

Richard looked out into the Danger Room platform. John was standing along the far end of the room while Susan fired a barrage of fist-size fireballs. The salvo was impressive, especially since Susan never had the ability to create or control fire. The ceiling's minigun turrets a little over six feet in diameter and three feet thick, popped out all over the room, as John started to dance around as he dodged Susan's fireballs. Streams of lead blasted across the room in and around John from six different turrets.

Richard was the only one who had used all miniguns for practice in the past, but it seemed John was now willing to get hit by the 20-mm armor-piercing rounds. To his surprise, none of the rounds made their intended target as John placed a light green force wall in front of him, stopping the thousands of mushrooming projectiles. Larcis turned off the miniguns once he saw their ineffectiveness.

A large pile of metal scrap pellets lay around John. Susan mentally grabbed John by the neck and flung him backwards against the metallic wall. John seemed to struggle for a second or two, four feet off the ground, only to break free from Susan's telekinetic hold and land on the floor with both feet well planted.

The Danger Room alarm came on with a loud buzz. "That was great, guys, but time's up!" Larcis said on the intercom.

"Very impressive. Have you been holding out on me, John?" Richard interrupted on the loudspeaker.

John only nodded as he took a bow for his performance.

"Why don't you come in, Richard?" Susan said.

"Sure, why not?" Richard gladly accepted the challenge.

Susan and John moved to the center of the 60 x 50 meter Danger Room as Richard entered on the far end. Richard's hair instantly grew a few inches longer and turned brown, shades materialized on his face along with the classic black slacks and brown vest on the rest of his body; in seconds, he turned into Creator. "So, what will it be? One on one, or two to one?" Richard loudly asked.

"We'll see how you do with John, before you include me." Susan smiled as she moved out of harm's way.

"Hmm, okay." Richard smiled.

John got into a ready stance, not knowing what Richard would come up with to try and embarrass him.

Richard casually started to walk toward John, trying to get within arm's reach of his opponent. John relaxed and flew into the air with hands together above his head. A small glow of light beamed from his hands. The entire room brightened as John unleashed a beam of white light directly at Richard's chest. Richard stopped in his tracks, bracing himself for the impact. The beam burnt part of Richard's vest as he concentrated on his target. There was very little knockback from John's attack, but no matter—Richard found a weakness.

In a flash, Richard unleashed a highly concentrated, almost translucent telekinetic projectile at John, hitting him in the stomach. John felt the powerful blow as it kicked the air from his lungs. John's body streaked backwards, hitting the ceiling and far wall of the Danger Room. Susan giggled as she saw her husband painfully get tossed around like a rag doll.

John knew now it was a mistake to take to the air in a confined room as his head stopped buzzing from banging on the hard metal ceiling. John fell toward the floor as Richard ran to meet him. A few feet before hitting the ground, John regained his flight, planting his feet on the wall and pushed with all his might against the hard surface.

Richard did not anticipate John's maneuver to drive into him like a human torpedo, but he was used to surprises. John soared at Richard with unbelievable speed only to hit Richard's right shoulder as Richard managed to side-step to the left, grabbing John's right arm redirecting him into the ground. Richard went down with John in a spectacular display of professional wrestling showmanship.

Susan covered her face as John's head made contact with the floor, resounding a dreadful echoed thump around the large room. Larcis and Liz's exclamations of pain could not be heard in the sealed control room as they watched John make contact with the metal floor.

Pain and anger ran through John's head and body as he dematerialized and slowly stood up. Richard walked away from John, noticing he had spread out his molecules.

"Good, so things can go through you. And I thought I was seeing things when the miniguns were firing at you," Richard said as he distanced himself from John's ghostly image.

John focused and shot out a salvo of telekinetic blasts in Richard's direction. This time, Richard did not wait to be hit, but dodged eight out of the nine semi-visible projectiles. The ninth attack hit Richard on the leg, causing him to twist around and fall to the ground.

John instantly took advantage of the situation and poured out as much telekinetic energy as he could muster at Richard's head. Richard raised his arm in front of his face, taking the impact of the attack, but the force threw him across the floor.

Richard, a little dazed, instinctively jumped to his feet and continued to dodge John's multiple attacks.

Susan, Larcis, and Liz watched with interest as Richard systematically dodged John's attacks with great and graceful difficulty. John rapidly tired as over thirty blasts seemed to miss their intended target with frustrating proximity. John let up, giving Richard what he was looking for—an opportunity to close in for the kill. John wondered why Richard was now running toward him, knowing Richard could not touch him as long as he was dematerialized. To John's surprise, Richard threw a telepathic blast of anger in his direction. Even though John was used to mental attacks, Richard's attack was exploiting his exhausted state. John could only freeze in pain as the blackness of unconsciousness took over.

The battle was over. Susan ran up to John and revived him. Liz and Larcis entered the Danger Room as Richard walked around recovering his strength from what he would call a refreshing battle.

"That was outstanding," Larcis exclaimed. "I didn't think you could beat him, Boss."

Richard stopped in front of John and Susan. "Do you know why I beat you?" Richard asked John, like a coach talking to a rookie player.

"I didn't attack you properly?" John's mind asked.

"That would have helped, but no. You can be powerful and fast, but to beat me, you must have the endurance to go the distance. You let me wear you down... But look at the bright side, you did great and I'm proud of you."

"I'm proud of you, too," Susan comforted John.

"Well, that's enough for you two. It's my turn to learn from our fearless leader," Liz said.

"Maybe next time, I can get a shot at you," Susan said with confidence.

"Maybe?" Richard doubted; he knew he was not going to let Susan get that chance, being probably the strongest in the group now that Queen Omia was an added part of her power source and knowledge. "One thing, though. You two are like magnets that attract cosmic energy, making you stronger. But how did you get those new abilities?"

"Susan and I are able to alter our cosmic energies into whatever we will it to do. Susan, of course, is much better at it than I am, and much stronger," John proudly explained.

"Interesting," Richard said, pondering the possibilities in future battles.

"Okay, let's clear the room," Liz said, and motioned for everyone except Richard to leave.

The next two hours were well-spent as Liz learned take-down maneuvers. Richard's expectations of the class had a rarity of enjoyment as Liz was a very quick learner and extremely beautiful. He wondered at times on how he could be so fortunate to have such good friends and a remarkable wife. Most of his life was spent learning about war and death. His time in Black Operations for the U.S. government taught him much, but it never taught him how to appreciate the good and beautiful things in life. He was thankful for not immersing himself too much into a life of assassination and deadly espionage. He realized he was at peace with himself for the first time in a very long time.

Richard spent the rest of the day performing the horse farm chores with a smile on his face, as Liz helped out by his side. They had employed several farm hands, but today was a monthly one-day event for the hires, especially granted by Richard for their hard work, to be off for the day with pay. The seven workers enjoyed their day off, knowing they were cared for and appreciated. Besides, the three-day weekend would bring in a highly motivated crew to start the new week. It was Liz's idea to give the workers incentives, which Richard executed gladly, knowing her knack for good business. The five superheroes finished a full day's work that morning and proceeded to their crime-fighting base of operations back in the Eternal Domain's Battle Room.

Larcis took to the books as spring break was around the corner and finals were once more in full swing. Susan and John tended the mechanic shops and modifications to their crime-fighting gadgets. Richard, Liz, and Erica concentrated on analyzing information and worked special investigations. Police reports, court cases, and lab reports were scattered all over the Battle Room table and floor. Liz and Erica were trying to organize the papers as fast as Richard could clutter the seven projects they were simultaneously working on.

One of the local news monitors automatically activated with an audio of a police band, but no one was speaking. Erica interrupted the investigation session, "Richard, something is going on in the North Miami beach area."

Richard and Liz heard the police band, but were confused by the audio playing of music. "Why is there music on the police band?" Liz asked.

"It's 'Blood Red Skies,' by Judas Priest," Erica said.

"Yeah," Richard said, "but why?" He was suspecting it was an intentional jamming of the police band. He turned to Erica. "Locate the source."

"It seems to be emanating from the Miami Channel 7 news building," Erica said. "Wait, I am picking up another signal." A new audio and video footage of one the northern Miami bridges appeared on the national news monitor.

"A police helicopter is reporting this live event," Erica said.

Richard and Liz looked on as a person wearing a black motorcycle suit and helmet jumped onto the side railing of the bridge, out of view from the camera. A motorcycle lay on its side in the middle of the street with smoke from smoke canisters, with most of the bridge on fire. A burning limousine and two other black sedans blocked oncoming traffic about a hundred meters west from the motorcycle. Police cars and police motorcycles could be seen trying to get to where the motorcyclist was last positioned. They appeared to have been delayed and were forced to stop for some unknown reason.

"The helicopter is transmitting its broadcast on a public unsecure band," Erica said.

"Look!" Liz exclaimed, as the motorcyclist stood up and pointed a tube-like object at the helicopter. A missile soared across the sky like a blaster from a science-fiction movie and in a flash, the helicopter violently shook and descended rapidly into the water. The video footage continued with a final effort of the passengers trying to ditch the aircraft by diving into the ocean.

"Let's go!" Richard commanded as Erica alerted the rest of the group. Richard and his team instantly made their way to the elevator and exit chamber then flew out of the Eternal Domain, through the launch tube Erica erected out of the water from the nearby lake.

The five superheroes arrived at the scene minutes later. Richard scanned the area on his approach, but did not see the motorcyclist anywhere as passengers from the helicopter were being rescued by a passing yacht. The police on the bridge had just passed the motorcycle in the middle of the expressway, as Richard and his team landed next to where the unknown person was last seen.

An expended AT-4 lay on the side railing of the bridge. Expended M-203 grenade canisters and 5.56-mm brass casings lay scattered around the motorcycle. The police band was still being jammed by the music broadcast. Most of the smoke had cleared, except for the now-charred and smothering limousine in the distance. Richard turned toward the approaching police officers.

"What's going on, Officer?" Richard commanded.

"Sir, I will have to ask you to leave this area," the young officer motioned as the others secured the area.

Larcis's face strained with impatience. "Do you know who we are?"

The young officer looked at Larcis's black costume and then at Richard. "Yes, sir. I know who you are, but this is a police matter now."

Richard smiled and pulled out a Special Investigation Agency badge. "*We* are the police. Now, Sergeant, tell me exactly what happened."

The officer, known as Sergeant Brooks to his team, was familiar with the SIA protocol. He quickly gave Creator a chronological story of the incident. "Yes, sir. I am part of a police escort for Mr. Antonio Perez. Mr. Perez and his staff left the courthouse on their way to his estate about twenty minutes ago. As we started to cross this bridge, a man driving this motorcycle came up next to Mr. Perez's limousine and threw grenades into the vehicle and killed everyone inside." Brooks continued to narrate as he pointed to the limousine and motorcycle in question.

"Before anyone knew what was going on, the assassin sped up in front of everyone and shot out the tires of the lead vehicle and two police motorcycles. All of our radios were useless with music playing in the background. We made a defensive line in front of the limousine, trying to disable the assassin's motorcycle. I think one of us hit him, and he fell off the motorcycle. He kept us pinned down with an automatic weapon and a grenade launcher. Our police helicopter tried to draw his fire for us to move in, but was shot down. My partner, Officer Cuevas, said she saw the assassin jump off the bridge shortly after the helicopter went down." Brooks concluded as he realized the assassin had indeed jumped off the bridge and was nowhere to be found in the area they had just covered.

"Sergeant, radio comms has been restored," an officer behind Brooks reported.

Brooks grabbed his voice activator. "Central, this is Unit 74. I want to report two officers down and eight civilians dead. I need assistance with a diving team and paramedics at 1ˢᵗ North Street bridge, over."

"Unit 74, units have been dispatched to your location, ETA ten minutes."

"This is Unit 74, 10/4."

"Sergeant Brooks, where is Officer Cuevas?" Richard asked while scanning the riverbed with his en-ray vision.

"Right here, Creator," answered a female voice from

behind him.

Richard turned around and saw a fairly young and tall Hispanic police officer he had known as Adrean Cuevas. "Good morning, Officer Cuevas."

"Good morning, Creator," Adrean replied. "How can I help you?"

"Can you show me where the assassin jumped from?"

"Not exactly. I was on the edge of the bridge about a hundred yards from here. I saw him stand on the rail and step off. He fell straight down for about twenty-five yards, and then I lost sight of him in the smoke and railing."

"Did you see what he was wearing at the time he jumped off?" Richard was walking along the ledge of the bridge, figuring out how it happened.

"He was wearing a motorcycle suit and helmet?"

"You mean *this* helmet?" Richard said as he picked up a black motorcycle helmet wedged in one of the many metallic cubbyholes along the narrow walkway.

Adrean looked disappointed as Richard held the helmet to his chest. "Are you sure it was a motorcycle helmet?"

"I'm sure he had something on his head."

"Pandora!" Richard called for Susan, then turned back to the lady officer. "I know that this is not standard procedure, but is it alright with you if Pandora scans your mind so we can all see what you saw?"

Adrean looked at Richard, Susan, and then at Officer Brooks. "Is that legal?"

"It won't hold up in court, Creator," Sergeant Brooks said.

"No, but it might lead to some hard evidence as to who this assassin is and what happened. But, it's up to you to allow Pandora to scan your mind," Richard said, gazing hard at Adrean's face.

"So, what do I have to do?" Adrean said.

Susan or Pandora stood in front of Adrean. "Just relax and think about what you saw." Susan scanned Adrean's mental surface thoughts with ease. A few seconds later all of the people within a five-meter radius saw Officer Cuevas's visual and audible account of the event.

The assassin was wearing a head cover resembling that of a diver's suit and a respirator mouthpiece. He carried an M-203 grenade launcher in one hand, but released it ten meters into the jump. A tie-down cord could barely be seen connecting the weapon to the assassin. The jump was very well controlled during the entire memory footage as the assassin jumped feet first.

"He knew what he was doing," Susan said as she finished.

"Yeah," Richard sighed, as he scanned the water in the area of where the jump took place. He pointed at the water. "And there's the grenade launcher."

"You can see it in the water?" Sergeant Brooks looked at Creator with awe.

"Yeah," Richard said, a little disappointed. "But I don't

think it will help."

Richard flew down from the bridge plunging into the water. The current was moderate at the bottom of the seventy-meter harbor ocean bed. Richard quickly grabbed the remains of an M-16 assault rifle and looked around for more evidence. A concrete block the size of a small child lay meters away. Richard quickly went up to the block and put an arm around it, then flew back to the bridge.

The group on the bridge saw Richard come out of the water as quickly as he had gone in, holding two objects, one large and one small. Richard set the concrete block and completely destroyed the weapon on the road. Two emergency ambulances broke the bridge entrance as traffic was being diverted to alternate bridges.

"Here is your weapon, Sergeant Brooks," Richard said as he gave Brooks part of the stock and trigger mechanism of the M-203 grenade launcher.

"What happened to it?" Brooks asked, eyeing the piece of disfigured plastic and metal.

"He used an incendiary grenade to destroy the barrel and grenade launcher. He probably used incendiary grenades to destroy the limousine as well," Richard explained.

"But the limousine exploded?"

"There were probably fragmentary grenades mixed in with the incendiary grenades. If he had used just incendiary grenades, the occupants of the car might have survived. The incendiary grenades were used to penetrate the armor of the limo and the fragmentary grenades were used to finish the job on the inside."

"So you didn't see that bastard down there?" Brooks felt uneasy; the assassin had planned it very well, he thought.

"No, he had about a ten-minute head start, and I doubt he's a slow swimmer." Richard knew the chances of catching up with the assassin were almost impossible even with their unique powers. "This block of concrete was used to anchor something, probably an extra diving gear to help him swim off and make his getaway."

John, through his mind, called out to Richard. "Richard, the two cops are going to make it. Do you want to search for this guy?"

"No, not really," Richard mentally replied. "But Officer Brooks is probably going to ask me to. Right about now."

"Creator, can you help us search for this murderer?" Brooks asked, as Richard predicted.

"I think we should do more homework on this assassin before we go after him," Richard said. "But for now we will help the police in their search."

Richard turned to Brooks. "Yes, we will help."

"Pandora and Mindseye will search south of here, while Isis and I search to the north. If we find anything, we will call you," Richard said. "We'll come back to the base of the bridge in forty-five minutes. The assassin could not have traveled more than ten miles, but if he got out of the water and went into the city, it will be almost impossible to find him."

"I understand, Creator. Thank you for helping," Brooks said.

The five superheroes flew off in search of the assassin, leaving the police and firefighters to clean up the mess on the bridge. Susan and John flew over many yachts and boats, scanning the occupants' surface thoughts, looking for clues to the assassin. To the north, Liz mentally scanned the area as Richard scanned under the water with his en-ray vision. Larcis flew way ahead high in the air, looking for anything out of place as boats went back and forth along the docks and open sea. Forty minutes passed by with no results, causing the two groups to head back. Richard and Liz arrived first at the bridge only to be met by a small group of reporters.

All of the local channel news teams, CNN, and eight newspaper journalists were gathered together along the police perimeter at the base of the bridge.

Richard landed in the middle of the group knowing his job here was almost over. "Creator, were you able to catch the assassin?" one of the reporters yelled.

"At this point in time, the killer is still at large. The Miami Police Department is doing all they can to find the killer—with our help, of course," Richard said.

Another reporter asked, "Is it true that the killer is Lambert Hunt?"

The name rang a bell but Richard couldn't place the name or face at that moment being more concerned not to say something he shouldn't. In addition, he felt he should keep rumors from surfacing to help the police with their investigation. "There is no evidence to confirm the identity of the killer at this time."

"So, you are saying that Lambert Hunt is not the primary suspect for the death of now twelve known mobsters here in Miami?"

In an instant, Richard remembered Hunt's name and history. Lambert Hunt was one of the ten most wanted people in the United States for the past year. His wife was killed by two hit men, which also nearly killed his baby daughter. Lambert witnessed his wife's execution and started his own private war against the Miami mafia. Death traveled in his wake as he made his way up the hierarchy to the godfather, Pablo Hernandez.

Elizabeth heard Hunt's name with deep emotion as she had kept quiet upon hearing the victim's name. Her past was filled with great hatred toward the mafia, especially Walter Marien, Hunt's third victim. She felt almost happy, praying that the assassin was Lambert. Lambert had taken his and her revenge against the leaders of the people who tried to rape and kill her. The thought of Lambert getting away with murder was perversely pleasing to her. She saw it as justified killing, although she wrestled within herself over the morality of an eye-for-an-eye type of thinking. She knew Richard would get involved in the case if given the opportunity, so she impulsively stepped up to the microphone and gently nudged Richard aside.

"The connection with the Miami mafia and Lambert Hunt is not in question here. Until there is more evidence to that effect,

Lambert Hunt is not a suspect in this investigation," Liz suddenly blurted out without really thinking.

The reporters turned to Liz with questions as Richard eyed her in surprise through his shaded glasses.

"Isis, who else was killed besides Mr. Perez?"

"All we know at this time is that Mr. Perez and his staff were killed. Two police officers were injured but are said to be in stable condition," Liz replied.

"Creator, is it true that your group is under investigation for bribing city officials to work as law enforcers here in Miami?" Henry Lynn from the *Miami Herald* asked.

Richard gazed at the journalist. "Our authority to help law enforcement agencies comes from the White House and Capitol Hill. No officials have been bribed. The District Attorney's Office is investigating the root of this rumor. That is all I can say about that issue," Richard said with a straight face.

Pandora, Mindseye, and Night landed near the group of reporters. All eyes turned in their direction. Richard took the chance to escape. "I'm sorry," Richard said, grabbing one of the reporters' microphones. "But if you have any more questions, please direct them to the police. Thank you all for your time."

The entire group took off into the air, waved goodbye, and flew away toward the north.

"What was that all about?" Richard asked Liz while in flight.

"What do you mean, 'what was all that about'?"

"Why did you jump in like that talking about Lambert Hunt?"

Liz felt no regret for saying what she did and deep down in her heart she hoped Lambert would finish what he started out to do against the mafia. "I only stated the truth."

Richard thought carefully. "Liz, Lambert doesn't have the right to be judge, jury, and executioner at will and not pay the consequences."

"Are we any different?" Liz asked; it was a question directed at Richard's sense of justice.

"Darling, we don't wake up every morning thinking of a plan to kill someone on purpose."

"I know, Richard, but if you were a normal human and someone raped and killed me, would you wait for the murderers to be sent to jail and get out in four to ten years?"

"No, but there is more to it than you think."

"What do you mean, Boss," Larcis butted into the conversation.

"Lambert was in the Caribbean War as a Navy SEAL and obviously has connections here in Miami. He used the same technique South America used against our Navy by jamming communications. In fact, the music he used was chosen because it sends a statement that he's going to get his revenge and there is no one that can stop him. He has planned and executed his assassinations with relentless prejudice and apathy. He didn't have to kill all of those people, but he did. Whether they were innocent or not, it doesn't matter to him. It's for the courts to decide, not him or us."

"You decided in San Francisco," Liz said without pulling any punches.

"Yes, I did and I'm not proud of it." Richard sighed. "I have to live with it every day, and in my heart I hope Lambert can live with his actions."

Liz slightly smiled. "I'm sorry, Richard. I can't stop feeling the way I do about what he's doing. Can you promise me you will let the police handle this and not get us involved?"

Richard eyed Liz's sweet face, knowing what she wanted was for him not to try and capture Lambert Hunt before he completed his revenge.

"I'll promise not to track him down, but don't think that I won't capture him if he steps in front of me. I know one day I will have to answer for my actions, but as long as we try to do what's right, freedom and justice for all people will be the team's goal for as long as I am leader."

"Thank you." Liz kissed Richard lightly as they flew back to the Eternal Domain.

Chapter Three

□ □ ☐ □ □

FREE AT LAST

A light drizzle of rain covered the greater Seattle area. The weather had been gloomy and wet for the past three days, but the city's streetlights continued on as if never pausing to take a break. A woman sat by a pub window overlooking a busy street full of cars and crowds of people going and coming to wherever they worked, lived, or played. Her golden hair stretched down slightly below her shoulder. She seemed to be waiting for someone to either come into or walk by the pub. She was almost finished with her second cappuccino as the pub started to come to life with the evening's customers. It had been a long and mildly frustrating month for her trying to settle down in a new city. She had been on the run and in hiding for several long years. Her thoughts were on her adopted sister and brothers. Because of them, she was able to live with a little bit of peace. She remembered as much as possible about them. It had been a few weeks ago since she last saw them in her dreams.

Cindy looked outside with sadness, knowing that her

extended family had been reduced to only Joshua and Lee. Alicia and Randy both died trying to exact their revenge on the Foundation. At times, Cindy hated knowing that Joshua could have prevented their deaths, but knew what happened was not out of neglect or desire for evil to prevail. Joshua had warned her in the past when she felt like committing a crime or acting foolishly. She was sure Joshua did the same for Alicia, Randy, and Lee. She understood that Joshua would always give someone a choice, and because of that, she knew that Alicia and Randy inadvertently chose to sacrifice themselves for her and Lee. It was ironic that the two people she thought of as extremely rebellious and true loners in the family had this one time in their lives acted more like responsible parents than rebels.

However, this second freedom for her tasted very cold and bitter. When she was a teenager, the world was new and challenging. The world was welcoming and gave her the opportunity to have an adventurous lifestyle. But now, older and mature, the world was quite lonely without someone to share it with.

Cindy noticed a break in the weather. She left a generous tip on the table and walked outside. She started across the street, thinking about what she should do with her life. An oncoming car honked angrily and screeched. Cindy, frightened and surprised, looked at the Saturn only to freeze in her tracks. A strong hand grabbed her from behind and pulled her back away from the curb and oncoming vehicle. Cindy's foot hit the right bumper of the Saturn as the driver brought the car to a complete stop, stuck out his head from the window, and screamed at her.

"What the hell are you doing? Are you blind?"

Cindy hugged her rescuer, who replied with a deep voice. "She's had a little too much to drink. Sorry about that!"

The driver, wearing a business suit with his tie undone, eyed both of them angrily. "It's a little early to be drinking; maybe you should get her some help."

"You might be right." the rescuer nodded in assent.

Two cars behind the Saturn honked their horns, persuading the man to move on. The man quickly ducked back into his car and sped off.

Gentle fingers touched Cindy's chin, forcing her to look up at the stranger's face. "Are you alright?"

Cindy glared at the man's handsome face, dark brown eyes, and tender smile. Her foot felt fine, but she was momentarily speechless not knowing whether to continue to embrace him, answer his question, or both.

"You know, my mother told me to always look out for people who don't look both ways before crossing the street," the man candidly said with a smile.

"Your mother taught you well, thank you." Cindy returned the smile and softly pushed the man away from her.

"I'm Glenn. It's good to have saved you."

Embarrassment finally took control of her emotions as Cindy blushed and took a deep breath. "I'm Samantha."

"Well, Samantha, seeing that you must have a lot on your

mind and are not really drunk, would you like to have dinner with me?"

Cindy never noticed until now, but there were three other men standing in front of the pub she had just left; they seemed to be waiting for both of them to finish talking. "What about your friends?"

"I've known them for a long time. They can get their own dinner."

Cindy's heart fluttered; what Glenn said made her feel important.

"No, I'm sorry, but I have to go," Cindy said out of reflex. He was making her jittery—she was not used to this kind of treatment from a perfect stranger, being she never really had any long-term relationships with the opposite sex.

"It's okay. All they wanted to do was get me drunk. Honestly, I really don't like drinking, but they have been trying for months now. I would prefer to eat dinner than drink."

"I'm sorry, Glenn, but I really have to go." Cindy started to leave but Glenn grabbed her hand.

"Will I see you again?" Glenn longingly stared into Cindy's eyes.

"Yes." Cindy smiled.

Glenn reached into his pocket. "Can I give you my number?"

"No, you don't need to. I will find you."

Disappointment suddenly descended on Glenn's face. She must be kidding. How could a woman he only met once ever find him in a place as big as Seattle without exchanging any contact information?

"Trust me, I will find you," Cindy said, firmly looking into Glenn's eyes.

Glenn felt a strong connection to Cindy; a connection he had never felt before with any other woman. "Just make sure you look both ways before crossing the street. I will be expecting you in one piece the next time we meet." He smiled.

"I will." Cindy smiled back before running down the sidewalk and across the street, disappearing in the city block crowded with people and cars.

"Bye," Glenn said softly to himself as his friends came up next to him.

"So, what's the deal? Did you get her number?" one of them asked.

"No," Glenn said, looking in the direction Cindy had gone, utterly depressed. "She doesn't even know my full name."

Adam broke the silence. "You just lost some major cool points, but never mind her. Let's go inside."

"Yeah, there are more girls in the bar to pick from."

Glenn and his friends went inside the pub and got a spot near the pool table.

Cindy ran down the street into an alleyway. She looked around, making sure the coast was clear before turning invisible.

She could stay invisible to the naked eye for many hours as long as she didn't have to dematerialize and go through solid objects. Her night had just begun, having met Glenn who definitely caught her interest. She returned to the pub and spied on Glenn with ease, being careful not to get in the way of anyone else. Simon and David broke off from the group an hour later with prospects of going home with 'available' women. Adam and Glenn played billiards for another hour and then moved to the bar. Cindy was impressed by Glenn's pool skills and humility. He was clearly the better player of the two but lost most of the games trying to teach Adam the finer points of game.

Glenn and Adam talked about all sorts of topics at the bar, including Glenn's attraction to Cindy. The two men were coworkers, but Cindy couldn't figure out what they did for a living. The more Cindy eavesdropped on the two men, the more she could relate to Glenn. Many of Glenn's interests and hobbies were identical to hers. What impressed Cindy the most was that Glenn seemed distant, thinking only of her. A woman even came up to him trying to start a conversation but Glenn kindly dismissed her, telling her he was involved with someone else and had to go home very soon. Adam stepped in and accommodated the woman, who was slightly drunk, and offered to take her home with him.

An hour later, Glenn left the pub alone and got into a taxi. Cindy was feeling okay from using her powers but she stayed with Glenn in the back empty passenger seat. They traveled north for a while until the taxi finally arrived at Glenn's condominium. Cindy's body was slightly tired from being invisible for over four hours and having to use her phasing powers like going through the taxi door. The taxi driver stopped the meter; Glenn opened the door and paid the driver. Cindy took advantage of the opened door and flew through the opening and into nearby bushes under a small tree. Glenn went straight into his condo while Cindy turned visible and stayed hidden in the bushes. Cindy waited patiently under the tree for minutes, trying to recover her strength, before proceeding to break into Glenn's home.

Glenn had promptly gone to sleep a little past midnight. Breaking into buildings with security systems was nothing new to Cindy. The amassed wealth of a few hundred thousand dollars to her name was the result of spying on corrupt businessmen and mobsters. Breaking into offices and secret places as a thief was one of her uncanny specialties; unfortunately, Joshua did not force her to stop and only advised her of the consequences. Cindy had pondered about her exploits and cared little about consequences, but it didn't stop her from robbing from corrupt wealthy people everywhere she went.

Knowledge was power to Cindy, and she was very good at taking advantage of her ability to know just about everything about anyone or anything. Cindy taught herself to be very observant and paid close attention to details. Glenn's home was moderately clean and organized, which meant either he had a maid, a girlfriend, didn't like messy places, or he was not home very much. A girlfriend would have been out of the question by the look of only family pictures in the living room. There were no signs of a female living in the condo, or at least not recently. The kitchen was stocked with mostly canned and microwavable foods.

Cindy entered Glenn's computer room and sat in his

swivel chair. Her face saddened as she read Glenn Seber's achievements on the wall. The framed Bachelor's Degree in Criminal Justice stuck out the most, along with four citations of valor from the LAPD, Utah Police Department, and FBI. There was a picture of Glenn in a police uniform along with three other officers dated April 1990. A 1986 high school graduation diploma was in the center. Cindy calculated Glenn to be about thirty-five. Glenn had an impressive career as a police officer that most women would find very attractive, but what was she to do now?

Cindy sat in the chair for a while and then went into Glenn's bedroom. She stood by Glenn's bed, looking at his wallet on the nightstand, as the man slept soundlessly. She sifted through one of two wallets and found a badge. Glenn was a federal marshal. Cindy looked at the badge and then at Glenn. He seemed so peaceful as he slept. "What could he be dreaming about?" Cindy thought.

Cindy sat down against the bedroom wall next to the bed and turned visible. She spent half an hour trying to make up reasons for not seeing Glenn again. She was a superhuman; how would he react? She was in all sense of the term "a criminal," stealing from the rich and keeping it all to herself to do with what she pleased. She was probably simply infatuated with a man who saved her from possible death or at the very least a hospital visit which would have lasted a long time if she were examined. He was a federal marshal—he was a cop. Her older brother, Lee, had impersonated law enforcement officers in the past, but she never thought about getting into a relationship with one of his acquaintances. His stories about them also didn't interest her, but now she would have to think about what kind of relationship she could have with Glenn if any.

Anger suddenly filled Cindy's heart. "I don't care, anymore," she thought, and then forgot herself and said out loud: "I'm through running."

Glenn abruptly awoke and sat up in surprise. Cindy instantly turned invisible, jumping to her feet. "Samantha?" Glenn said, looking around the dark room.

Cindy nervously stood still, cursing under her breath for almost revealing her presence.

"Samantha?" Glenn said once again as if he were hearing things in his head.

Glenn laid back down, crossing his arms behind the back of his head. He stared at the ceiling thinking of Cindy. He was sure he heard Cindy's voice. Glenn couldn't go back to sleep, so he got up and walked downstairs to the living room. He turned on the television to his favorite late night movie channel and sat on the sofa.

Cindy followed him into the living room and decided to take a desperate gamble. She went outside to the front door and turned visible. Seconds later, Glenn heard a knock on the door.

"Who the hell could that be?" Glenn said, picturing one of his drunken friends trying to shack up for the night before going to work or home in the morning.

Glenn looked through the peephole on the door. He couldn't believe his eyes as Cindy stood patiently waiting for

Glenn to answer the door. Glenn quickly opened the door with a surprised grin on his face.

Cindy smiled. "I made it in one piece."

Glenn was speechless for a moment, staring into her deep blue hazel eyes. "I'm sorry, please come in."

"Did I catch you at a bad time?" Cindy asked as she walked into the condo.

"No, not at all," Glenn stammered, smiling and quickly closing the door behind her. "Can you wait a second?" He said, running off to the bedroom not waiting for Cindy to respond.

Cindy watched Glenn run upstairs with pleasure, admiring his finely-toned muscles. Glenn quickly put on a T-shirt and washed his face in the bathroom.

Cindy took off her coat and placed it on the coat rack by the door. She walked into the living room and sat on the sofa. Not long after, Glenn came downstairs. "So, do you always watch black-and-white movies late at night?"

"I couldn't sleep," Glenn replied.

"Do you have to go to work tomorrow or something?"

"No, I'm on vacation. I travel a lot and I can finally sit here and relax for two weeks."

"What is it you do besides travel a lot?"

"I'm a federal marshal."

"I see," Cindy said, and looked around. "How long have you been a federal marshal?"

"I have only been a marshal for a year. I used to work for the FBI, but it wasn't what I really wanted to do."

"FBI, federal marshal; it all sounds the same to me. What's the difference?" Cindy asked, playing ignorant.

"Well, as a federal marshal, I get the chance to not only find the bad guys, but I get to help people in witness protection or protect officials like judges. I also help other police departments with special investigations. In the FBI, we are specialized in certain fields and were restricted to specific investigations," Glenn explained as he sat down beside Cindy.

The *Abbott and Costello* movie on the television was ending as Cindy looked around for the remote. "So, do you plan to retire as a cop?"

Glenn picked up the remote and handed it to Cindy. "I haven't had much time to think about it since I am gone most of the time. I have stocks and bonds. I guess I really don't need to retire with a pension, but would be nice. I like to work and I like my job."

Cindy flipped through the channels and stopped in the middle of a *Star Trek* episode. "Oh, look, it's been so long since I saw this episode."

Glenn smiled; he was a Trekie. "So, you like sci-fi?"

"I used to watch *Star Trek* everyday when I was a little girl. I love the thought of going into space and exploring new worlds."

"So, do you think there is life elsewhere in the universe?"

Cindy looked at Glenn. "Well, the chances of other life on another planet are very high, but I'm not sure if people are ready to handle the truth if aliens decided to land in the middle of the White House lawn."

"Yeah, I guess some people would probably treat them like the way superhumans are being treated now."

"And how are superhumans treated?" Cindy asked, trying to get Glenn to explain the can of worms he just opened.

Glenn thought for a second. "A lot of people I talk to are scared of them, but they never really met any. Some friends I know that have met real superhumans say they have great respect for them. Of course, the superhumans they met were helping the police fight crime."

"What about the ones who are committing the crimes?" Cindy asked with interest.

"Well, I don't know. I hear on the news that bad superhumans go to special jails and are treated like any other criminal in these special prisons." Glenn paused for a moment waiting for Cindy to respond. "You don't watch the news much, do you?"

"I watch the news every day," Cindy said with a stern and strange expression on her face.

Glenn was now more confused than ever with many questions bouncing around his head. "Did you follow me home? I mean, how did you know where I live?"

"Yes, I followed you. Why, did I do something wrong?"

Glenn felt uneasy, not because he had been staked, but because all of this time, he knew almost nothing about the woman in front of him. "Who are you?"

Cindy looked at Glenn and realized why he was asking that particular question. "I'm sorry, Glenn. I'm Samantha Williams. I just moved to Seattle about a month ago. I'm single, and have my own business as a consultant on computer systems for corporate industries. I don't have any friends here in Seattle, and I live by myself on 5th Avenue and Hemmingway. I am a single child and both my parents are dead. Is that enough information about myself for you?" Cindy said with a slight smile and questioning eyes.

Glenn's face tightened as if in deep thought, trying to cover his embarrassment. "No," he awkwardly replied. "I still don't know if you like Italian food."

Cindy smiled. "I love Italian food."

Glenn returned the smile. "Good, then tomorrow I will treat you to the best Italian meal in Seattle."

"I'll like that." Cindy peered deep into Glenn's eyes.

Glenn wanted so much to hold her in his arms, but was afraid things were going too fast. His last girlfriend left him because of his job, and he knew it would be very hard on Cindy if they got into a relationship. "Did you eat dinner?"

Cindy was starving and couldn't say no.

"All I have are TV dinners. Is that alright with you?"

"That's fine with me."

"Good then. I'll whip something up," Glenn said and went into the kitchen.

Cindy stretched out on the sofa and watched television as Glenn cooked two TV dinners.

They ate their late snack meals talking about *Star Trek* trivia and other movies they liked and disliked. Time passed by slowly as they watched another black-and-white movie together on the sofa. Glenn never once attempted to make a pass at Cindy, and she appreciated it. Cindy fell asleep in Glenn's arms as 4 A.M. rolled around. Glenn placed a pillow under Cindy's head and covered her with a blanket from his guest room closet. He left Cindy on the sofa with a soft kiss on the cheek and went to sleep in his bed upstairs.

Cindy slept peacefully for several hours until an ever-so-familiar voice woke her up. "Cindy, wake up, it's time to go."

Cindy sat up on the sofa and saw the living room in broad daylight. "Joshua."

"You have to go to Fort Lauderdale, Florida, immediately and find Richard Octavian," Joshua instructed.

"Why? What is going on?"

"Richard is the leader of the Eternal Champions. They need your help to fight an evil monster that plans on killing everyone on Earth," Joshua said in her mind.

"Why do I get the feeling you're writing my destiny now and not me?" Cindy replied.

"You don't have to go if you don't want to. It's your choice to save the world or not."

"Why me?"

"They need your special abilities. You are also unknown to the evil monster and they will need that advantage."

"Can I at least say good bye to Glenn?"

"Yes, but you and I know that starting a relationship with him might not be in his or your best interest, but that is also your decision to make."

"Why me? Why now?" Cindy disappointedly thought to herself trying to figure out what to do with Glenn and the rest of the world.

Chapter Four

□ □ ☐ □ □

NOWHEREMAN

Thee Eternal Champions huddled around the Battle Room table for their daily evening meeting. The meetings were focused more on slowing down and relaxing than getting work completed for that day. Richard opened the meeting with minor adjustments to the next day's schedule and closed the meeting soon afterwards by serving a late dinner meal of spaghetti, meatballs, and garlic bread. Larcis flipped through the cable channels looking for something interesting to watch, while Susan started to talk about faraway places in the galaxy. The television program soon became background noise as Susan's stories drew all of the attention. The Argonian race believed that one day, a supreme being would establish a new reign of peace throughout the galaxy. The Argonian people were sure they would be the instruments of that lasting peace. Her stories seemed more like folk tales than reality, but Richard knew there was truth behind every sentence. She talked about the Galactic Guardians, a group of heroes chosen from across the galaxy to protect the empire. No one asked exactly where they came from, but Richard's gut told him some of them were from Earth.

"It is said that destiny is changed when a star falls from the sky," Erica's sexy voice echoed around the room and stopped the group's conversation.

The unexpected statement confused everyone in the room. Richard moved slowly toward Erica's virtual console, wondering why Erica would just speak out of the blue and completely out of character.

Susan broke the silence after a short pause. "Erica, can a star really fall from the sky?"

John, Liz, and Larcis looked at each other with mixed feelings of intrigue and confusion, but none spoke, waiting to see what Richard and Susan were up to.

There was no response from Erica as Richard waved his hand on Erica's colorful manual data console.

"How the hell would I know?" Erica shouted with a teenager's voice. "Am I supposed to know everything because I'm a synthetic life-form?"

Susan's eyes widened, then closed slightly with concern. "What's wrong, Erica?"

Richard traced Erica's system protocol with absolute failure. The console was locking up as if being placed on pause while Erica spoke.

"I – I – I don't know? Richard! Help me!" Erica pleaded.

"Hold on, Erica," Richard said.

"I am Erica model number CAI3004. Shut down initiated, please wait. Now rebooting."

Everyone looked at Richard. His fingertips raced across the control panel with great dexterity. Susan's questioning eyes were locked on Richard, but only for a moment as Richard's face strained with frustration.

"What the...?" Richard said and backed away from the now-darkened panel. "I tried to shut her down, but I don't know what's going on now. She's not supposed to be rebooting."

Letters appeared on all three screens of the Battle Room. "Hello, Eternal Champions."

"Hello," John instinctively replied by telepathy.

"I am sorry for having to meet you under such circumstances, but I couldn't think of any other way. I am nowhere and everywhere," the screens spelled out.

"What have you done to Erica?" Susan blurted out.

There was a pause then the screens reacted again.

"Erica is in no danger, but all in good time. I am here to warn you of a great and terrible disaster that will befall you all. An evil supernatural being known as Ego is going to destroy every living thing on the surface of your planet. You must find him and stop him from coming into your world." The screens spelled out, as Larcis noticed Erica's keyboard on the worktable being depressed rapidly as if an invisible secretary were typing away the words written on the screens.

Larcis tapped Richard's arm as the words continued to

appear on the screens. "I don't know where and when he will strike, but I will set the right conditions for you to be able to get to him."

Richard stared at the keyboard. "Who are you?"

"I am a man like yourself but from a different dimension, which is nowhere and everywhere. You can call me Nowhereman."

"Interesting," Susan mumbled to herself, and then told everyone through her mind. "Close your eyes and cover your ears."

"Why, Susan?" John asked.

"An experiment."

Richard looked at each of the members and nodded in acknowledgement.

Everyone covered their ears, closed their eyes, and Susan began to talk. "Why are you helping us?"

There was no reply.

"You can't understand me, can you?" Susan continued.

There was no reply.

"He cannot *hear* us talk. He can only *read* the thoughts of one of us in the group," Susan telepathically told Richard.

"Hmm… So, who is it?" Richard asked.

"There was a pause when you and John said something. It's probably Liz or Larcis," Susan theorized.

"Don't tell anyone else, we might be able to use this to our advantage later."

Susan then loudly told everyone to open their eyes and stop covering their ears.

"What was that about?" Nowhereman asked.

Susan ignored the question. "Why are you helping us?"

"Ego has destroyed many civilizations. I don't want your civilization to be another victim to his evil hunger," Nowhereman replied after another short pause.

"How do we know you're not Ego himself or someone else who wants to kill us all?" Richard asked.

"You don't, but can you take the chance?"

"You didn't need to invade Erica to tell us this," Richard continued.

"No I didn't, but there is much more you don't know and you must trust me or all will be lost."

"What have you done to Erica?" Richard insisted.

"Erica will be alright later, but for now, she cannot fall into Ego's hands. So I introduced, for lack of a better word, a 'virus' into her system. You all have a week or so to figure out what Ego is up to. Until then, I will be around. All you have to do is reboot Erica when you want to talk to me." Nowhereman signed off, leaving three blank screens.

The group stood silent for a moment. "Richard?" Liz said.

Richard stared at Erica's keyboard. "I will see what I can

do to get Erica back. In the meantime, we will have to use the backup computer to run ED. Larcis, I need you to go to EFL Headquarters and find out what you can about this Ego and Nowhereman. John, Susan, I need you two to patrol while Liz and I figure out what to do once we do find Ego. Oh, Larcis, I also need you to find a man who goes by the name of Sliver. His real name is Mark Farnell. The last time I saw him was in Atlanta, Georgia, three years ago. The EFL computer shouldn't have a problem locating him."

"On my way, Boss," Larcis said, taking off through the emergency staircase in the guest room hallway.

Susan and John made their way to the ground level, the first floor of the house, while Liz manually reset the life support systems for the underground levels. Richard was one of the best computer programmers in the US, but was at a total loss as to what Nowhereman had done to Erica. Super Artificial Intelligence systems were new in the 21st century with many groundbreaking achievements. The problem may have been that SAIs were far ahead of their time. An SAI catching an intrusive program or virus was unthinkable—until now.

Susan and John started their six-hour-long patrol, while Richard and Elizabeth spent several hours on the backup computer making no more progress than when they first started. Richard took time out and walked around the room, while Liz stretched her slender body on the sofa. Richard slowly recollected everything that happened when Nowhereman appeared. He ran a mental replay of events and the things said with extreme scrutiny.

"Now, I was standing here," Richard talked out loud to himself, moving and pointing around the room. "Susan, there. John, there. Liz here, and Larcis there." Liz watched Richard with amusement as her husband played detective.

After several minutes of acting out the encounter, Richard started from the beginning. "Okay, Liz, help me out," Richard said after placing himself where he was at the time of the incident.

"Erica has an identity crisis, and I move to the console. Susan moves up close to the main screen. Nowhereman introduces himself while I waste my time here. Larcis moves toward the two news monitors," Richard recalled the events. "Why?"

"Why what?" Liz echoed.

Richard pointed and looked back and forth between the two monitors and the main screen. "Why all three screens? Why did he talk to us on all three screens?"

"To make sure he got our attention," Liz replied.

"Maybe. Maybe he wanted to distract us from the keyboard. Maybe he wanted us to spread out like we did. Maybe he didn't have a choice," Richard ran down more possibilities in his head.

Liz looked at Richard. "Darling, what are you talking about?"

Richard looked at Liz with a small grin. "Bear with me, honey."

"He said he didn't know how Ego was going to destroy the

world. But he knew enough about Ego to either track him down or see his handiwork. He also mentioned he was from another dimension, which is why we can't see him." Richard paused for a second. "Liz, did you detect a presence while Nowhereman was here?"

Liz thought about it for a second. "No, only us."

"There are fundamental laws which we are ignorant about. I have a feeling that because of the universal laws in place, Nowhereman has limitations here in our dimension. If I'm right, so does Ego," Richard surmised.

"What limitations?" Liz asked, her face more confused than before.

"All in due time," Richard said, temporarily satisfied with his hypothesis. Nowhereman had to use the keyboard to communicate through the computer; he obviously could affect the physical world, but only with some type of telekinesis; he had to hear through the mind of one of them, and he probably had to see the same way, which was through the mind of one of them. These were limitations he could exploit. What puzzled Richard the most was why use three screens to introduce himself. The main screen was in the center of the group. There was no need for the other two monitors. Nowhereman would have surely known that his keyboard trick would have been noticed. So, why use three screens?

Richard went to the kitchen and started to make a banana split.

"You know, you eat more than the horses," Liz said as she watched Richard take out the ingredients for the tasty treat.

It was well past midnight and Richard was not about to let food waste away if he wasn't sleeping. "So, do you want a hot fudge sundae?" was Richard's reply to Liz's sarcasm.

"Two scoops please." Liz smiled.

"My pleasure."

"Susan and John should be back soon. Do you want to trade off with them tomorrow?"

"Not exactly. I was thinking of talking with the police and have one of us ready to respond twenty-four-seven. This will allow everyone to stay here and prepare for Ego's coming," Richard explained.

Richard placed a tall two-pint glass of ice cream scoops of three different flavors topped with hot fudge, strawberries, marshmallow, diced peanuts, whipped cream, and a cherry on top in front of Liz. "Thank you, honey." Liz smiled. "So, who is Sliver?"

Richard put his banana split together. "He is an old friend from Vietnam. He was a specialist in psychological warfare and was the first human lie detector I ever saw in action."

"So, you want him to see if Nowhereman is telling the truth?" Liz asked.

"No. He can tell if a normal human is lying, but not with someone like Nowhereman. I want him to look at Erica. I am great with computers, but he is the future when it comes to artificial intelligence. In fact, he probably built part of Erica and doesn't know it."

"How come you never talked about him before?"

"Mark is a good friend. But he is also a dangerous friend to be around with. You see, Mark has the worst bad luck I have ever seen a person could have. Mark was called the walking tornado, rubbing his bad luck on everyone else. Everyone thought he was lucky at first, but two months after being assigned to an air assault company, everyone realized that anyone who got close to him died. They died because he stepped on a mine, or the sniper missed him and hit the person next to him. A tree would fall on Mark and would merely bruise him, but a branch from the same tree would kill the guy next to him. He was later given one-man missions, until I saved him from a company of Vietcong. We worked very well together in Vietnam only because I was the only one who wouldn't die."

"He knows about most of my powers, but I was a lot weaker back then. We conducted missions into Laos and Southern China before the war ended and stayed together for about six months. We made a partnership trying to make money and go into the stock market, but anything he did failed. I saw him make half a million dollars in a day, and lose it all in the following two days. Not from bad stock options, but from a death in the family who owed half a million dollars and didn't have life insurance. It didn't stop there either; I would go up and down the same roller coaster ride and barely broke even every month. He understood what was happening, so he went away to start a new career by himself, and that's when my life turned for the better."

"I was able to get back into the CIA, save money and travel to wherever I wanted. I stayed in touch with Mark only a few times and for the past several years I would get an e-mail now and then. He was doing better and finally fulfilled his dream of becoming the leading expert in artificial intelligence technology. If anyone can help Erica, it's him."

"So, do you think Larcis can find him in time to do whatever we're supposed to do?"

"He will," Richard said.

Liz looked at her husband with uneasiness. Her cognitive abilities were useless ever since her pregnancy. The visions of her husband and baby boy seemed to be like faded dreams that she found very hard to remember. Richard brought out the idea in displaying his confidence in his friends and her, but she didn't know what to think now.

She started to seriously consider the possibility that Ego was the reason behind her lack of visions. She felt helpless and uncomfortable to tell Richard that her most powerful ability was now useless.

Two hours later, John and Susan arrived back in the Battle Room. The night was quiet with only two high-speed chases by the police, which were quickly taken care of by John and Susan with the use of their new powers. Richard briefed them on the lack of progress with Erica and the plan to have the police call them when they needed help. The four were in agreement and waited for Larcis's return.

EFL Headquarters

The New York City lights brightened the sky as several sonic booms broke the sounds of the city's nightlife. Larcis landed hard on the EFL Headquarters front lawn, bringing a strong gust of wind. This was his second visit to the estate but his first time doing it at night.

"Stand still!" a male voice commanded.

Larcis recognized the voice and did what he was told. The football field-size lawn encircled the EFL Headquarters with uncanny precision. The EFL computer scanned Larcis's body in a matter of seconds and proceeded to unlock the security system defense grid on Larcis's location.

"Hello, computer," Larcis said.

"Hello, Night. What brings you out here at this late hour?" A blue light the size and shape of a baseball materialized through the grass in front of Larcis up to eye level.

"We're trying to find out information about some supernatural beings bent on destroying the Earth and need your help," Larcis said.

"Well, if that is all, please come in through the front door and I will wake up Hellfire."

Larcis flew toward the entrance of the three-story building. The double doors automatically opened, letting in both the EFL probe and Larcis. Larcis waited patiently for Hellfire in the living room, not noticing how big the headquarters was until now. Their own base was a little smaller, but it was spread out on many floors, while the EFL Headquarters had a total of five levels and was spread out evenly. The inside also was not decorated very well, seeming more like the interior of an office building with a lot of open space.

After several minutes, Hellfire came downstairs wearing a dark blue robe. "So what is this I hear about supernatural beings wanting to destroy Earth?"

"Sorry to wake you up, Hellfire, but we have had a weird night," Larcis answered.

"Hmm... You didn't answer my question," Hellfire said with a questioning look.

Larcis paused. "Yes, well, Erica is on the blink. Someone named Nowhereman took control of her and told us that a being called Ego was going to destroy the world if we didn't stop him."

Hellfire stared at Larcis, knowing he was incapable of lying. "Tell me all the details."

Larcis told him, including the weird instructions by Susan while they spoke to Nowhereman.

"I see. Follow me," Hellfire commanded.

Hellfire led Larcis into the primary computer room down one level. The large room seemed more like a futuristic lab than a control room, filled with weird gadgets and database compartments along the perimeter walls.

"Bob, search for anything related to Nowhereman, Ego, dimensional instabilities, religious references, gateways into and from the underworld, and possible ways the Earth can be destroyed," Hellfire instructed.

"Searching," the SAI replied.

"How long is this going to take?" Larcis asked.

"Don't know. In the meantime, let's look up your friend Mark Farnell."

"Oh, yeah, I almost forgot."

The EFL computer spit out the exact location Mark was living and working as fast as it took Hellfire to ask him.

"It seems your friend is an expert with AIs. It's funny I never heard of him."

It was a surprise to Larcis, too, but a faint smile came over him as he thought about Richard. His fearless leader once again pulled a rabbit out of a hat without much effort. Larcis got the information from Hellfire and decided to leave it up to Richard to get Mark when he got back to ED.

"So where is Quatris?" Larcis asked.

"He and Starfire had to go into space for business."

"Wow, maybe one day I'll be able to go into space."

"I don't think you would like to be in space right now while those two are out there," Hellfire commented.

"Hmm..." Erica had told him the EFL Headquarters had been rebuilt three times after several incidents with superpower villains and an Antiron, a deadly being from an antimatter universe. EFL was by far the strongest superhero group on the planet. Being let loose in space was a scary thought, considering they wouldn't have to hold back and have full use of Quatris' antimatter powers.

"So, when are they going to be back?"

"Don't know. The last time we went into space, we were gone for about five years. By the way, make yourself comfortable. I think this might take a while. Just make yourself at home, while I take a shower and change," Hellfire simply said and went upstairs.

"Can do, Hellfire."

Three hours elapsed when the EFL computer finally displayed the results of the query. An array of background information and scenarios popped up like crazy. Natural disasters, which could destroy the world, were ruled out. Superheroes on the planet would be able to negate such disasters along with a space invasion from an alien race. Four other options appeared with a biological attack on the planet being the most likely, but Larcis wasn't about to leave anything up to chance and asked Hellfire to print them all out, including references to legends and historical events regarding a powerful demon called Kalic in the 4th century which described the end of the world by one supernatural being from another world. The tracks ended there with the unknown invisible man. Larcis quickly gathered the information and bid Hellfire goodbye, leaving him to continue his research on Nowhereman.

Larcis quickly rejoined his friends thousands of miles away, flying at hypersonic speed. The entire team was tired, more from mental fatigue than physical exertion. They all slept uneasily as they rotated shifts monitoring the CNN and SIA emergency networks, not knowing what the future held.

Liz tossed and turned with visions of dark places from her past. She saw herself in the middle of a city street, much like San Francisco, but things were unusually different. Liz could feel the cold air as the late night sky filled with dark clouds. She was wearing her everyday attire with tight-fitting jeans and a white tank top. She walked around down a long street finding vandalized stores and turned-over cars.

Where am I? she asked herself as she noticed the Empire State Building in the distance. "New York City? How?"

The clouds gave way, sprinkling rain on Liz's body. The drops were warm and stung her eyes. It must have been fake, because her eyes could be sprinkled with acid and it wouldn't string her, but yet it seemed so real. She looked at her hand and saw blood—it was raining blood. She was filled with horror. There was a bright flash and as she swung her head toward the light she saw a mushroom cloud miles away. She froze in sheer fright as the buildings vanished before her. The entire neighborhood shook violently as the first wave of destruction took hold of her while she screamed in fear, vaporizing her in an instant.

Richard abruptly woke up as Liz screamed and started to shake uncontrollably. "Liz! Oh, my God! Liz? Can you hear me?" Liz's body continued to shake then slowly stopped. Her limp, lifeless body lay next to Richard.

"Erica!" Richard yelled, but then realized Erica was off-line. "Susan! John! Larcis!" He yelled at the top of his lungs as he grabbed his comlink from the nightstand and called out for help.

Larcis was the first one through the door in seconds from the Battle Room. "What's wrong?" Larcis asked, alarmed, seeing Richard holding Liz and trying to get some vital signs.

"What happened?" Larcis insisted as he got next to the bed to analyze the situation.

Shortly afterwards, John and Susan sprang into the room. They saw Richard and Larcis administering CPR on Liz. Susan went next to Larcis and placed her hands on Liz's abdomen. John quickly knelt on the bed next to Richard concentrating on his new-found powers.

Larcis placed his hand on Liz's chest. "Clear!" he commanded as he was about to shock Liz's heart into submission.

"No!" Susan yelled. "It might hurt the baby. I have a better way."

Larcis looked at Susan then at Richard. "Do it quickly," Richard said.

Susan focused her cosmic powers on Liz's womb and heart. In a matter of seconds, Larcis felt a weak but steady pulse on Liz's left wrist.

"She has a pulse," Larcis announced.

John pushed against Richard's side trying to get him to move out of the way as he placed his hands on Liz's head. Richard noticed that John was so involved in concentration he wasn't able to use his telepathy to tell him to move out of the way. Richard quickly stepped back and watched John's hands glow with pure white light as he placed his hands on Liz's head and face. In less than a minute, Liz's chest rose and fell, her breathing restored, even though she didn't really need to breathe to live, but the baby inside of her did need oxygen.

Susan took her hands off Liz and sat on the bed. "She is stable for now."

For the first time in his life, Richard felt scared by the thought of losing Liz forever. He looked at his friends and was so grateful and relieved they were here. Larcis kept monitoring Liz's pulse. John's hands stopped glowing; he sat next to Liz. "She's in a coma," John said.

Susan got up and walked to Richard. "What happened?"

"I don't know. She screamed and I woke up. Her whole body was convulsing before I could even touch her."

Susan walked around the room. "She had dreams before that were so real to her they actually hurt her. But never like this. Why now?" Susan asked no one in particular.

"She never told me that," Richard said, a little surprised.

Susan looked at Richard. "She was probably afraid you would worry too much... Ego is behind this," Susan said.

"How do you know that, Susan?" Larcis asked.

"Look at it this way. Nowhereman comes from nowhere, no pun intended, and tells us that Ego is going to destroy the world. I don't know why, but if Nowhereman thought we could stop Ego, then Ego must surely know we're a threat to him."

"Why attack Liz?" Richard asked.

"She can see the future. What better way to blind us than by keeping us guessing on what will happen in the future?"

"Hmm…" Richard caressed Liz's forehead and long brown hair. "What if he thought she was the strongest telepath in the group, or maybe she did see the future?" Richard brought up the disquieting ideas.

"Interesting," Susan thought out loud, showing her second personality as Queen Omia. "John and I are the strongest, but he probably doesn't know that since our powers come and go with our abilities to change from one power to another."

Richard felt great hatred knowing Ego was probably behind the attack on Liz, and great pleasure as the thought of revenge filled his heart. "Hold on, darling. Nothing will stop me from getting you back and destroying Ego."

Larcis's heart, felt Richard's pain and marveled at his leader's strong determination.

'She needs medical attention, attention we can't give her especially if we are going to fight Ego when he gets here,' John said.

"Larcis, get on the phone, call Max. Tell him we need him to get Liz to a safe place where she can be looked after," Richard commanded.

"Calling now, Boss," Larcis said as he picked up the phone and pressed the speed dial number to SIA Headquarters with lightning speed before Richard could finish his sentence.

'Damn, he's fast,' Richard thought, wondering why Larcis was never able to beat him in the Danger Room despite Larcis's

overwhelming speed advantage.

"While you guys were gone, Liz and I came up with some theories about Ego. First, he had limitations like Nowhereman. I am sure of that now. It would have been easier to kill Liz with telekinesis, so he probably can only affect this dimension with mental powers like illusions or telepathy."

'So why was Nowhereman able to use telekinesis?' John interrupted, reflecting back to what Nowhereman did with the keyboard.

"I don't know," Richard said. "They are probably from different dimensions, but I'm not sure of that. Anyway, as I was saying, if Ego can affect this world with mental powers, then he might be able to get someone in this dimension to do his bidding and do something to destroy the world or allow Ego to enter this dimension with full use of his real powers."

"They'll be here in thirty minutes. Max assured me that the agents coming here will not reveal our identity or location," Larcis reported as he got off the secure phone line.

Richard was slightly comforted as he heard the good news. "You and John stay with Liz. Susan, I need your help in the Battle Room."

"I'm all yours," Susan replied.

Richard leaned over Liz and kissed her on the lips. "I'll be waiting for you, my love. In the meantime, take care and have sweet dreams."

John and Larcis got comfortable and monitored Liz's condition like hawks. Richard and Susan quickly went to the Battle Room.

"What's on your mind?" Susan asked Richard.

"I think it's time we look at the EFL's reports a lot closer. We're missing something."

Susan smiled as she saw how much Richard loved her best friend. "Let's do it then," she said as she moved the sofa and cleared the area to spread the documents out on the floor.

The SIA agents quickly arrived and took Liz away to the SIA headquarters in New York. Richard was thankful to see them take great care in evacuating her to a safe location. John and Larcis joined the effort in scrutinizing the reports along with searching for more information on secure and nonsecure Internet Web sites. They made some progress narrowing the instrument of destruction to a biological or nuclear source, but nothing definite. Shortly after four in the afternoon, Richard got a call from Becky, their live-in veterinarian, saying there was a woman at the front door wanting to speak with him about an important matter.

Becky knew about their true identities and was around as an employee and helping them maintain the farm as they went off to fight crime. She normally would have handled any visitors and make them go away with great tact, but if she was calling him, it must be really important. Richard told the group to continue with their work as he went upstairs to see who this visitor was.

Chapter Five

□ □ □ □ □

CHAOS

Glenn rolled over on his back and stretched out his body with great joy. He quickly took a shower and put on casual indoor clothes. It was about eight in the morning and he hoped Cindy would still be asleep downstairs in his living room. He slept only three hours but was refreshed by the unexpected visit. He quietly went downstairs trying to get to the kitchen without waking her up.

Cindy was sitting on the sofa and waiting for Glenn to come downstairs. She had been awake for the past thirty minutes trying to figure out what to tell Glenn. Her hair was straight as if she never laid her head on the pillow. Glenn noticed she looked ever so beautiful in the bright sunlight than in the past twelve hours of darkness and room lighting.

"Did she freshen up or something?" Glenn thought as she sparkled from a distance. Cindy's eyes caught his attention, turning his joy to concern. Cindy was not herself as the smile he was expecting to see from her was overshadowed by a seriously saddened face. Cindy stood up and walked toward Glenn.

"What's wrong?" Glenn softly asked.

"I have to go, but I don't want to."

Glenn took half a breath and looked straight at her. "So stay."

"I was hoping to have breakfast with you, but I really have to go." Cindy's eyes watered as she spoke. "I don't know if I will be able to see you again."

Glenn stood speechless for a second. "If you and I were meant to be, we will see each other again."

Cindy knew Joshua would not intentionally lead her into her death, but the future was uncertain and Joshua made it very clear to her in the past. Joshua could see the future and possible futures, but nothing was certain. If she stayed with Glenn, her presence might put his life in danger, or he might be the one she was suppose to be with for the rest of her life. How would he feel if she told him the truth about herself? She had gone over and over the many possibilities, but in the end she was more scared that Glenn would forget about her because they didn't have enough time for them to really know each other.

"Glenn, I don't know how long I will be gone."

Glenn smiled. "I will find you no matter how long it takes."

Cindy ran up to Glenn and kissed him passionately. Glenn held Cindy gently as they spent several minutes kissing.

After a while, Cindy gently nudged him. "Take care of yourself."

Glenn stared at Cindy's face and saw that her eyes were filled with tears running along her cheeks. Cindy quickly broke his soft embrace and ran for the door. Glenn sprang after her, but the door opened as if prearranged to be unlocked. Cindy ran outside as Glenn got to the now-closing door and ran after her. "Samantha!" Glenn yelled.

Glenn jumped outside to see the front lawn and sunrise in the distance. "Samantha!" he shouted, but Cindy was nowhere to be seen. He stood outside his condo completely baffled by her instant disappearance.

"Was it all a dream?" Glenn thought as he went back inside, feeling Cindy's warm tears on his own cheek. He sat on the sofa and laid down where Cindy had slept. He laid there for long minutes, thinking about her and not knowing when he would see her again, then got up and went into the kitchen. He poured a bowl of cereal and milk then started for the living room. He stopped in his tracks when he noticed a note on the dining room table. He quickly placed the bowl on the table and picked up the note.

"Glenn, you don't know me, and I hope you can forgive me for leaving you like this. I don't know how you really feel about me, but I hope to see you again and find out. If I don't return, please don't look for me. It will be better this way. I want you to know that the time we did spend together was very special to me. Love, Samantha."

Glenn held the note in his hand and folded it in half. He had never felt like this about any other woman. It was an unexplainable sense of joy, confusion, and loneliness, which made him useless all day thinking only of Samantha.

Miami International Airport, Florida

The business class chair failed to comfort Cindy during the entire trip as the jetliner approached the Miami International Airport. She could have flown on her own power, but it would have required her to use energy which was like exercising for several hours straight. It was a lot easier to just use commercial transportation and sit the entire trip. Joshua explained to her the situation with Ego and told her she could trust Richard with her life. How Joshua knew about Ego was not her concern, knowing Joshua was powerful enough to be omniscient. In the end, hearing that Richard could be trusted was enough to ease her natural reaction to distrust anyone she met. Her thoughts were on Glenn for most of the trip, and as the plane landed, angry thoughts ran through her head for having left Glenn so abruptly. She promised herself to see Glenn as soon as possible—after saving the world, of course.

She quickly made it out of the airport and caught the first available taxi. The taxi drive to Fort Lauderdale was expensive, but she left a generous tip as the cabby dropped her off in front of the Octavian Horse Farm entrance. The twelve-foot gate presented no obstacle to her, but she wanted to enter on good terms so she rang the intercom buzzer.

"Yes, who is it?" a male voice answered.

"My name is Samantha and I'm here to see Richard," Cindy replied.

Another buzzer sounded and the gate automatically opened. "Please follow the road until you get to the main house," the male voice instructed.

Cindy looked at the camera on one of the posts along the gate. "Thank you." She proceeded as instructed and walked the seventy-meter stretch of driveway toward the main house. The three-story house resembled a miniature mansion, but not as opulent. Two large stables in the distance, well-kept grass and fences reflected a very well-managed farm. *I didn't think I would ever see a horse farm in Florida, especially here in Fort Lauderdale,* Cindy thought.

A very tall gentleman wearing jeans, a dark green T-shirt, and a sidearm came out of the house and met her as she approached. He was clean-shaven and well-built. He smiled as Cindy approached.

"Welcome to the Octavian Horse Farm. I am Mr. Dilinger. How can I help you?"

"I have something very important to discuss with Richard? Is he here?"

"There are only two other Samanthas which Mr. Octavian is familiar with, and you aren't one of them," Mr. Dilinger said. "So how do you know Mr. Octavian?"

Cindy held her tongue for a moment. "Look, Mr. Octavian doesn't know me, but I do know him and what I need to talk to him about is not something I can trust you with to tell him."

"I see. Please wait and I will see what I can do." Mr. Dilinger touched the earpiece on his left ear. "Becky, there is a woman here name Samantha." Cindy gave him her last name.

"Thank you," Mr. Dilinger said, then to the earpiece. "Samantha Brooks. She wants to talk to Richard on an important matter, which she can't talk to me about. So if you can be so kind and talk to her, I would appreciate it." A moment passed as Becky replied. "Thank you. Mrs. Brooks, please follow me into the house."

Cindy had second doubts now, regretting she didn't just appear in front of Richard when she had the chance, but the security guard was courteous enough. "Thank you," she said.

Mr. Dilinger introduced a fairly young woman about the same height and build as her once they entered the front door.

"Hello, Samantha, I'm Becky Ellington. How can I help you?"

Cindy looked at Becky a little annoyed; she didn't want to repeat what she had told Mr. Dilinger. "I'm here to talk to Richard about saving the world."

Mr. Dilinger looked at Becky with a raised eyebrow and left the two women alone. Becky's smile was maintained along with a what-are-you-talking-about straight face. "I don't understand what would Mr. Octavian be able to do to save the world?"

Cindy realized just then, not all of the employees would have knowledge of Richard being the leader of the Eternal

Champions. "Well, I don't know, but he is the owner of this farm, right?" Cindy answered.

"Yes, but what does that have to do with the world?"

"I have information about an experimental deadly virus which is grown in horses, and has the potential to kill millions of people in less than a month," Cindy lied.

Becky crossed her arms and touched her chin with her index finger as if thinking of a response. "Hmm... As the head veterinarian for many years, the chances of a horse having a virus that would kill that many people, would be almost impossible unless the horse came from Troy. Then that would be possible."

'Well done, Cindy. Why couldn't you just stick to a very important message?' Cindy cursed at herself. "Look, Becky, I can't explain, but I know that once Mr. Octavian hears what I really have to say, we will all be glad I did."

Becky eyed Cindy very carefully. She was a very good judge of character and was well trained in catching lies. Cindy's last statement was honest enough for her and serious enough to alert Richard. "Okay, Samantha. I will get him. It won't take very long. Please wait here."

A few minutes later, Richard walked out into the living room from the elevator at the lobby entrance. "Hello, Mrs. Brooks, I am Richard Octavian." Richard gracefully extended his hand as a true gentleman.

"Hello, Richard," Cindy said as she took Richard's outstretched hand. "Is there somewhere we can talk in private?"

"Well, we can walk outside where there are no cameras, if that is what you're worried about."

"Yes, please."

"Okay. This way." Richard led Cindy out to the back of the house. They walked through a small garden maze of bushes, flowers and trees out toward one of the stables.

"So, what is it that you really have to tell me?" Richard started his interrogation.

"A very close friend of mine told me I should find you and help you stop Ego."

Richard slowed down as he walked. "Hmm…and what else did your close friend say?"

"He said you were Creator, the leader of the Eternal Champions and that I could trust you with my life."

"I guess you won't tell me who your close friend is," Richard said thinking only of Maximilian outside of ED who knew of his true identity.

"His name is Joshua. That is all I can say about him."

Richard stopped and faced Cindy. *'So much for secrets. Who else knows about us?'* Richard thought. "Okay, so what can you do to help us stop Ego?" Richard asked, trying to see what her role was in all of this.

"I can get you information. You see—" Cindy said and turned invisible, "—I can see and hear without anyone knowing about it."

Richard couldn't see Cindy with his normal vision, but he did see her with his en-ray vision. "That's a good trick, but I can still see you."

Cindy turned up the dial and dematerialized, and became completely invisible to Richard. "What about now?"

"Hmm... And what else can you do?"

Cindy materialized back to her normal state. "I can walk through twenty feet of reinforced steel and force fields as if they never existed."

"Yeah, well we can probably use you but only if you can cook. We badly need someone who can really cook."

"What?" Cindy couldn't believe her ears. Was he mocking her?

"Can you cook food? You know, dinner, lunch..." Richard asked with a straight face.

Cindy looked down and cursed at him. "Why the hell did I come here to help you. You're such a bastard. You know, I didn't have to come here so you could make fun of me," Cindy said and started to walk away.

Richard smiled and ran in front of Cindy. "I needed to know I could trust you, Samantha. If you were here to spy on me or if you worked for Ego, you would have played along. But, knowing you are impatient from what Becky told me, you helped answer my one worry about trusting you."

Cindy stopped and looked at Richard. Joshua had told her Richard was leader for a reason, now she realized he was no fool and had a lot of experience when it came to dealing with people. "You're still a bastard." She slightly grinned.

"No, I'm a certified chef." Richard smiled. "Come, it's time you met the rest of the group."

CEA Headquarters, Washington D.C.

Jean Lorenz picked up the phone, ensured the line was encrypted, and waited for a report. "It seems we have a break. Isis is in a coma and has been moved to the SIA headquarters medical care center."

"Well, then, this is good news after all. Thank you," Jean replied, hanging up the phone. Her silky white hair beautifully swung to one side as she leaned over her computer and connected to a secure video messenger. A handsome dark-haired man appeared on the screen. "Jared, I need to see you in my office now," Jean commanded, cutting Jared's response by closing the window.

Jared came straight into Jean's office twenty minutes later. He stood patiently in front of Jean's desk as she looked outside her window with the back of her chair facing him. "Do you know why I called you here?"

"Yes, I do," Jared nonchalantly answered.

Jean twirled her chair around, staring straight into Jared's eyes, and said loudly, "Then why did I have to hear it from my spies in SIA?"

"Because your agents don't know squat," Jared said calmly. "Isis is under maximum security. And besides, I have reconsidered your final solution to getting the Eternal Champions out of the picture."

Jean's beautiful face strained with anger. "You don't tell me what to do!" She concentrated on Jared's body trying to turn his muscles into icicles.

Jared smiled. "Jean, you know you can't hurt an illusion."

Jean stood up with frustration as her attempt to inflict pain on Jared was futile. She slowly began to look around the room. "Don't think you can even come close to challenging me, Jared."

"No, I wouldn't think of it. But if you calm down I will explain." A voice came out of thin air although Jared's body was now sitting on the sofa.

"You're giving yourself away, Jared," Jean said as she tried to locate Jared's true location in the office by his voice.

"Am I? Anyway, it is important to know that if Isis is killed as you want, then Creator will make it his purpose in life to get who done it. We cannot cover all of our tracks, because Pandora and Mindseye are also both telepaths," Jared said, his voice skipping all over the room in a matter of seconds.

The sudden skipping of Jared's voice surprised Jean but she stifled it. "Mindseye and Pandora are weak telepaths."

"No, that's where you're wrong. They are both stronger than Isis. But, if you want, I will do this for you, because after all,

I don't want you to think I'm against you. Now, would I?"

Jean looked at Jared's body as he stood up and moved toward her. Jared was the best agent she had and knew what he was reporting was very reliable information. "I want you to make sure she dies, do you understand?"

Jared stopped and looked at her with sympathy. "Yes, I understand you're angry at the world and at me, but since you asked so nicely I will do what I can."

Hatred filled Jean's heart; Jared was defying her authority and power right in her own office. Hatred because she couldn't administer her own sense of discipline on what she would call her rebellious servant. "Don't try, do it. You can go now."

Jared walked slowly toward Jean and stopped a foot from her.

"I said you can leave now!" Jean stood erect with an evil look in her eyes.

"You know, you're more beautiful than I remember."

"And you're egotism is going to get you killed."

"You know, under that entire bitchy attitude, evil, and hateful exterior, I see a beautiful woman who has feelings for me."

Jared vanished and reappeared an inch from Jean. He grabbed her head with both hands and kissed her squarely on the mouth. Jean tried to fight Jared's hold but couldn't, so she bit his lip as hard as she could. There was no reaction in Jared's illusion but it stopped kissing her. Jean felt Jared's soft lips part from hers as she stood there, knowing there was nothing she could do to the mental illusion. "Feelings for you!" Jean laughed. "You actually think I like you?"

"No, I don't *think*. I *know*. That's one of the things you pay me to do," Jared said as his illusion disappeared into thin air.

"You're going too far," Jean solemnly said.

"Yes, but I had to make the first move, otherwise I would have waited twenty years before you and I could have come to an understanding."

"Leave now," Jean said as if leading to a threat.

"I will leave now, but remember this. My illusions work best when the person wants to feel, see, or hear them. Think about it. I know I will."

Jean couldn't control her anger and lashed out at the sofa, completely freezing it down to its molecular state. The room temperature dropped to minus thirty degrees in less than a few seconds. She pictured the sofa as Jared and then telekinetically punched it, shattering it into a million pieces of ice. The secretary outside Jean's office sat quietly, knowing better than to investigate, especially after another of Jared's visits.

Jared and Natasha stood in front of the elevators down the hall, out of sight from the secretary's office hall window. "You know she will not let this go and payback is a mother…" Natasha said, not completing what she wanted to say.

"Yes, but I'm not going to let things get out of hand," Jared said as the elevator door opened. They entered the elevator and started to head straight back to their secluded safe house away from the D.C. area.

"Why are you provoking her?" Natasha asked.

"Nat, we have to be very careful and I have to get Jean on my side."

"So, you piss her off? That's a good thing, right?" Natasha sarcastically said as she leaned her back on the elevator's back mirror.

"You obviously never read *The Taming of the Shrew*, have you?"

"Is it a book on getting the demon of your dreams?"

Jared smiled. "No, it's Shakespeare and she is not a demon, she's a demonist."

Natasha knew she wasn't going to get him to stop trying to win Jean over, so she redirected her attention to the mission. "What are we going to do about Elizabeth?"

"Well, Sis, we will have to follow Jean's wishes, but I have a backup plan in mind."

"It's a good thing that you always do," Nat said, knowing they were not going to be working for the CEA for very long if Jared's backup plans failed.

The Eternal Domain

Richard and Cindy entered the Eternal Domain's Battle Room as Susan started to theorize on the possibility of a third World War. All eyes focused on Cindy as Richard introduced her to the team. John and Larcis, trusting Richard's judgment, welcomed her wholeheartedly, but Susan only said hello with a straight face. She trusted very few people, especially when things were mysteriously appearing out of nowhere.

"So, Samantha, where do you come from?" Susan blurted just as Richard was about to explain what they were doing in the Battle Room.

Cindy clearly saw she was not liked by Susan and went along with her usual cover. "I'm living in Seattle, but I have lived in many places, mostly in Third World countries."

"No, I mean, where were you born?"

"I was born in Tennessee. At least that's what my mother told me."

Richard interrupted. "Susan, get to the point."

"The point is how can we really trust her?"

Richard thought for a second. His gut feelings and interpersonal skills told him she was on the level but his gut wasn't perfect. "I see your point. I guess the only way we can be sure is to read Samantha's mind."

Cindy thought about the idea as Richard brought it up. Could she trust them with her past and knowing about Joshua? "Richard, if Joshua thinks I can trust you with my life then I don't want you to have any doubts about me. So if you have to go into my mind to make sure, then do it."

Susan was satisfied with Cindy's comment, but Richard was a little uneasy about the mental scans, which could reveal too much from a person's psyche. Government agencies had very strict policies on using telepaths. There were many secrets that could be accidentally leaked to the wrong people and could cause a lot of damage in the wrong hands. Richard trusted Susan enough to allow her to scan other people but even he had dark secrets in his past which he felt should be left alone. He was not sure if this was such a good idea, but there was no other option at this time.

"Alright, Susan," Richard eventually relented. "But only get what you need to verify her story."

Susan knew why Richard was specific and honored his instructions. She looked at Cindy and scanned her mind, seeing her adoption into Joshua's family, her life on the run, and her relationship with Glenn. In a matter of minutes, Susan synthesized and analyzed the information and knew Cindy was telling the truth.

"Are you satisfied?" Cindy asked once she saw Susan was done scanning.

"Yes, but just to let you know, you are among friends, Cindy."

Cindy looked at Susan with admiration and surprise. She thought, *Am I an open book to her? How far did she go into my head?* "Well, I guess you all don't have to call me Samantha?"

"I didn't go very far into your past," Susan said.

"How did you know I was thinking that, are you still reading my mind?" Cindy asked, a little worried.

"No, that's what everyone thinks about once they know they have been scanned."

'*Since we all seem to know each other a lot better now, it's time we get to work,*' John interrupted.

"Yes, well what were you talking about before we came in, Susan?" Richard asked.

"I was talking about the possibility of an attack on the U.S. or any European nation which might trigger a third World War. It would have to be from across continents, more than likely between the U.S. and either an independent state in the Ukraine or Asia. How that will be accomplished, I don't know," Susan briefed.

"And how would an attack be made if anything strong enough to start a war is not centralized or under very tight security?" Larcis asked.

"You mean a nuclear missile or something?" Cindy tried to narrow down what Larcis was talking about.

"Missile launches are human controlled and the order has to be given. If a detonation of a nuclear weapon were to occur on land, for instance, a terrorist attack, then there would be enough communication systems in place to isolate the situation and tell everyone that it was not an act of war. So, like I said, I don't know," Susan said as she tried to think of other possibilities.

A CNN newsbreak came on as Sarah Evans reported. "We have breaking news from top officials on Wall Street, saying the stock market has crashed. All major systems connected to the World Wide Web have been attacked by an unknown virus. The FBI and SIA have been called to investigate..." The TV screen went blank in the middle of Sarah's report.

"What's wrong?" John asked as Larcis and Richard played around with the television monitor and network server.

"It looks like something cut off the transmission from the source," Richard said as he tracked the connection to the satellite.

"What do you mean? The satellite?" Cindy asked.

"No, I mean the computer which connects to the dish that uses the satellite," Richard explained. "But it seems the Internet is still working... I think."

"What? That doesn't make sense," Larcis exclaimed; he just discovered that their backup computer crashed.

"Susan, Cindy, Larcis, John. I want all of you to go outside right now!" Richard's head was reeling as he fired his orders. "Go through the neighborhood and find out if telephones still work, electricity, computers, radios, everything. Don't let anyone see you and if they do, make sure you go in costume. Go now!"

Richard thought about Susan's theory as the group's worst fears were coming to fruition. The communication system Susan was talking about would not be able to alert anyone if a terrorist decided to attack through biological or nuclear means. The present state of the nation seemed to be at risk, and Richard had no idea if Ego or Nowhereman was behind any of this. Richard thought about other possible allies that he might be able to use as he waited for the team to return.

Chapter Six

□ □ ❑ □ □

OLD FRIENDS

V ery nimble fingers raced across three computer consoles, accessing information and executing triple-strung firewalls in the virtual matrix conduit for the entire continent.

"Report!" the battle commander said from the middle of the room.

"Sir, the virus has been isolated by our perimeter probes. Request permission to destroy it," the technician replied.

"Negative," the chief of the watch commanded. "Monitor the damage and disengage parallel probes."

"Roger, sir."

Commander Javier looked at the enormous central battle screen with concern. "Alert the council members immediately and send out an alert message to all fleets and command posts about this virus."

The bridge crew went into action as communiqués were sent out across the country and select worldwide locations. Fifteen minutes elapsed as Commander Javier consolidated the information to get ready for his report to the council members.

"Captain on the bridge!" a female voice loudly announced.

Everyone on the bridge stood at attention. "Carry on!" the Captain, Councilmember Estabon Ramirez, commanded. "Report Number One."

"Sir, a virus has been introduced into all commercial and most military network systems around the world. We have determined that it originated from the continental United States. It has caused worldwide power outages, communications breakdown, and computer system failures. It was unable to penetrate our probes fast enough since we are working on a Quintupled Chronos (QC) operating system. If the virus had not been isolated, I am certain it would have caused the same damage to all of our network systems except for our parabolic laser communication systems and onboard ship computers," Commander Javier summarized.

"Do we have the rest of the council online?" Estabon asked. Estabon was a tall, dark haired, brown eyed, handsome and muscular specimen of a human male. His stature and manly voice projected a majestic upbringing even though he wasn't of royal blood or raised in a royal family environment.

"Yes, sir. Coming up now."

Four large screens surrounding the main screen lit up, displaying four of the five council members. "It's good to see all of you. We were having quality time, but we have an emergency situation and might have to get involved sooner than planned. I assume you all have been briefed to some degree."

"Estabon, what else do we know about this virus?" asked Councilman Eduardo Ramirez, Estabon's older brother and most influential of all the five council members. He was a tad taller than Estabon, with similar facial features, but had a faint scar running down the left side of his cheek close to the ear. Edwardo could have removed the scar at any time, but chose to keep the reminder of the fighting and dying of many people during the revolt for the freedom of the nation and soon the world.

"Well, I can tell you that it was either created by the best computer geek in the world, or it's an alien virus."

Commander Javier had never reported all of his findings to Estabon, but it seemed he already knew. No matter; he was used to having his commander-in-chief know everything about anything before he did. "Sir," he interrupted. "If I may?"

Estabon looked at Javier. "Go ahead, Number One."

"Council members, this virus may be a prelude to an alien invasion or attack from one country to another. We should consider mobilizing our forces to staging areas as soon as possible."

"And what would we do once they got there, Commander?" Councilman Diego Gonzalez asked, knowing it would mean possibly giving away their chances of surprise for future operations.

"The fleet is 60 percent complete. We don't need the entire fleet to achieve victory over the major powers," Javier said.

"No, but we will need our fleet to maintain the land," Eduardo interjected. "We also cannot guarantee total coverage of all short-range ballistic missiles that the enemy ay launch from submarines."

Javier stood, thinking of other solutions. "When will the fleet be ready to get the needed coverage?" Councilman Julio asked.

"The Andromeda will be ready in nine months, four battle cruisers will be ready in seven months, and our entire armada will be ready in thirteen months," Javier reported.

"How long will it be for all of our ground silos to be fully operational?" Eduardo asked even though he already knew.

"Sir, if we stick to schedule, possibly in eight days."

"Council members, we need to sit down together and talk about other options. We will meet on the Andromeda in an hour," Eduardo said. "Commander Javier—"

"Yes, sir," Javier replied as the other three council members acknowledged and signed off.

"Tell Admiral Lopez he has forty-eight hours to get the ground silos online, and explain the entire situation to him. In the meantime, Estabon, make sure our agents stay in place. Right now, they're our only backup if we do end up going to war," Eduardo instructed.

"Don't worry, brother, I will take care of it," Estabon replied.

The screen went back to displaying satellite telemetry and locations. Javier gave commands for the communications officer to send the message to Admiral Lopez. The bridge personnel jumped into action after listening to the discussion between the council members and Commander Javier. Estabon sat in his captain's chair and typed in instructions on his command pad. "Number One," he called out.

"Yes, sir," Javier walked up to Estabon.

"You got a little jumpy back then. What happened?"

Javier looked at his commander. "Sir, I was just thinking of the fleet. We're very vulnerable right now."

Estabon smiled. "That has never stopped us from taking risks before. But thank you for bringing it up. I think if my brother or I had brought it up, it would have been taken as law and we would be mobilizing right now."

"Sir, don't you think we should?"

"No, it's not time yet. We have to be patient and hope the good guys can resolve this problem before we give ourselves away. But I think we better research the possibility of using half of our fleet, just in case."

"I will, sir. But what about the virus, sir?"

Estabon thought for a moment. "Contact our agents in Australia. I am curious to see if they have been affected. I have a feeling Australia could be behind this. In the meantime, find out how many ways we can destroy this virus without anyone finding out we did it."

"Right away, sir," Javier replied and walked around the bridge giving commands.

Eternal Domain Battle Room

Larcis and Cindy were the first ones back with reports of power outages, computers being fried, or hard drives being erased, along with some telephone lines being disconnected. There was chaos everywhere.

Richard assembled the group around the Battle Room table. The Eternal Domain's generator kept the sublevels operating, but it was only going to last three weeks at the maximum usage of the base's electrical systems.

"Okay, what are our options?" Richard asked, trying to brainstorm for ideas.

"We can't keep up with this pace," Larcis said. "I know we haven't got any calls, but the police have probably tried to leave us a million messages."

"Yes, I know." Richard thought for a moment. "Alright, we have to do some damage control. Susan, you and John, go and see what you can do for the people in Miami and Lauderdale. Start with the airports. It's going to be dark soon and we don't need planes landing in the middle of the city. Cindy, I need you to go to NORAD and find out where all the missile silos are, and what problems they are having. Larcis, I need you to get Cindy there, but you have to take me and drop me off to see Mark first.

After you drop Cindy off, you will have to come back and pick me up. Cindy, you will have three hours to find out what you can before Night comes back for you. Any questions?"

Cindy raised her hand like a kid in a classroom. "Richard, who's Night?" she asked.

"Larcis is Night, Susan is Pandora, and John is Mindseye. That brings up a question of my own. Do you have a heroine name?"

Cindy looked at Richard and felt she had been drafted into the group, with Joshua as the recruiter. "Yes, I do as a matter of fact. I like Mirage."

Richard smiled. "Alright then, we will call you Mirage— when you get a costume, of course."

"Yeah, I will have to think about that."

"Do it on the way. Let's get going," Richard said, instantly transforming his appearance into Creator.

The group left through the lake exit with Larcis carrying Cindy and Richard.

Larcis dropped Richard off on a Nashville hotel rooftop twenty minutes later. Cindy was still at awe having been flown past Mach Six by Larcis in a ball of electricity. She heard of superheroes being able to fly faster than a rocket into space but never thought she would meet anyone in person. Richard reminded Larcis on the time schedule and let them continue on their trip. Cindy was excited; she wanted to see if Larcis would fly faster now that Richard was not with them. It was the best roller coaster ride she could have ever imagined.

Richard quickly made his way down the side of the hotel and into Mark's room through the window, or at least he hoped he was going into the correct window. A man in his forties, with fairly short, sandy brown hair, and medium build sat behind a laptop at a small kitchenette table. He had a two-inch beard complimenting his curly hair, which extended past his ear lobes. He wore circular framed glasses, a worn-out white T-Shirt with dark blue worn-out slacks.

He stood up when he saw Creator walking toward him in the other room. "Who are you?" Mark asked, frightened.

"I need your help, Mark."

"How do you know my name?" Mark asked as he moved toward the front door.

"Don't you recognize my voice?"

Mark stopped moving and listened carefully. "You surprise me, Mark, after all we have been through," Richard continued.

"Jason?" Mark said in doubt.

"How are you, old friend?"

"Oh man, you're the leader of that superhero group in Florida," Mark said with a surprised smile. "So, you finally did it."

"Did what?"

"I always knew you would become someone famous."

"Yeah. Well, fame has its price and right now it's attracting the bad guys."

They shook hands, hugged, and went into the main room where they sat on chairs by the bed. "What happened to you?" Richard asked.

"Not much. I have been working as a computer consultant. It involves a lot of travel, which is good because I don't stay long enough for things to get messed up. You know how it is."

"Yeah, it seems like only yesterday when we were trying to get rich."

Sadness came over Mark for a moment. "Yeah, well what's going on with you, that you need my help?" he said, trying to change his mood.

"As you probably know, there is a virus going rampant all over the United States, causing major problems which can and probably already have gotten people killed. I need you to fix our SAI so we can stop this virus before it gets any worse."

A spark of interest stirred Mark's heart as he heard Richard say SAI. "Yeah, the Killer Virus. At least that's what they're calling it now. But wait a second, did I hear you right, you did say 'SAI,' right?"

"Yes, I did."

"What model?"

"She's the latest model that I know of, a little over ten months old."

"You know, I was just working on trying to figure out what this Killer Virus is made of," Mark said as he jumped out of his chair and ran to get his laptop in the kitchenette.

Richard followed and took another glance around the room as his inbred training with the CIA took over. The bed was either made by very bad room service or by Mark. The do not disturb sign was not on the inside of the door and his trashcan was full of papers. Mark must have been in his room for a while by the smell of musty odors in the main room and burnt food in the kitchen. Richard quickly made a mental note of the layout and entered the kitchenette.

Mark showed Richard the usual programs for sifting out anomalies in computer systems, but nothing Richard wasn't already familiar with. Mark owned a state-of-the-art laptop working off a Mac operating system. "I notice you have made your own modifications," Richard said as Mark finished explaining the computer's configurations.

"Yeah, so you know some things about computers, huh?"

"Not enough to fix my SAI."

"What I have here is as close to an SAI as you can get. The problem is he doesn't think very well on his own."

"He?" Richard said, thinking Mark would have preferred a female computer.

"Yeah. Jack, meet Jason," Mark said, talking to the laptop.

"Hello, Jason," Jack replied with a low masculine voice through the laptop's speaker.

"Hi, Jack."

"He will be the key to getting your SAI fixed," Mark said with pride.

"Alright, then. You need to pack your bags right now and make sure you don't forget anything. It might be weeks before you can come back here again," Richard said.

Mark's heart sprang with joy—his old friend was giving him an opportunity to do something meaningful with his cursed-stricken life. "I'll be ready in a flash."

Mark quickly gathered his clothes, computer equipment, and miscellaneous items from his room closet. He left his car keys; he knew he wouldn't need them where he was going. The thunder Mark had heard earlier before Richard arrived once again broke the clear blue sky. Soon afterwards, Richard and Mark made it up to the roof where Larcis met the two men and took them to the Eternal Domain, arriving there just before sunset.

Chapter Seven

□ □ ☐ □ □

UP AND RUNNING

Special Investigation Agency Medical Center, New Albany, New York

T hree guards wearing full body armor stood patiently waiting for their shift change outside of room D344. The entire ward was empty of other patients as Elizabeth lay motionless on a hospital bed connected to specialized machines and monitors. Three additional guards walked down the long corridor, escorting two nurses straight toward Elizabeth's room. The hallway was active as three more guards approached from the opposite end of the corridor. The guards at the door challenged the nurses and their escorts. Visors were raised to confirm the initial identity of each guard. One of the door guards raised a bubble egg-shaped gun type of handheld camera in front of the newcomers' faces. The retina scanner authenticated the identity of the visitors.

"Sir, I request permission to enter with these nurses to conduct maintenance on the equipment and administer a protein shot," Lt. Harper asked the captain of the guard, and slowly drew his sidearm in front of him.

"Permission granted, Lieutenant," Cpt. Middleton replied, taking the pistol from Harper.

Cpt. Middleton turned toward one of his guards. The guard keyed in a numeric code into the door panel to the right of Elizabeth's door. The eight-inch-thick steel door slid open, slowly revealing the patient to the outside hallway. Harper and the two nurses entered the room and started their routine duties, adjusting the monitors and administering needed nutrients into Elizabeth's body.

The new crew of guards finally arrived as the door slid shut. "Sir, we are here to relieve you," Master Sergeant Owens said.

"You are early, Master Sergeant," Middleton said, a little confused.

"No sir, it's 2400 hours."

"What? It can't be." Middleton looked down at his watch. It read 2300 hours. Middleton looked at the two guards who escorted the nurses. "What time do you have?"

The senior noncommissioned officer looked at his issued atomic watch. "Sir, it's 2300 hours."

Captain Middleton raised his sidearm at the new shift crew, with his guards following suit, aiming point-blank at all five guards before them. "Don't move!" Middleton pushed a button on his helmet. "HQ, this is Captain Middleton, what time is it?"

"Captain Middleton, it's 2400 hours," the watch center replied.

Middleton quickly and carefully went through scenarios. "Sergeant, who directed for the nurses to come here?"

"Sir, Lieutenant Harper did," one of the two guards said.

"What time do you have?" Middleton asked the sergeant who was initially with Lt. Harper but never had the chance to check his watch.

The guard carefully lifted his hand and slowly looked at his watch so as not to provoke Cpt. Middleton's team. "Sir, it's 2300 hours."

What? Why? Middleton asked himself.

"Captain Middleton, the camera in room D344 has gone out. Please investigate," the watch center alerted.

The guard next to the door panel immediately keyed in the entry code. There was no response. "Sergeant James, give me your rifle!" Middleton shouted as he grabbed the sergeant's rifle.

"Sir, the rifle can't penetrate the door."

Middleton immediately walked to the side of the door and turned on the ultrasonic scope. He looked through the door and wall of Elizabeth's room. The image was very poor but he could distinguish two bodies lying on the floor and one standing in front of Elizabeth's body. "I need that door open!" Middleton shouted as he set the rifle to shoot armor-piercing titanium rounds.

"I'll have it in ten seconds, sir!" Sergeant Moore answered.

"Not soon enough!" Middleton cursed. "Damn it... Oh, what the hell." Middleton's concern over injuring Elizabeth using the rifle was not relevant at this point if Harper wasn't stopped there and then. He aimed low and to the right of the soft-plated armor on the lower back of Lt. Harper's silhouette. A round escaped the barrel with supersonic speed. The round's titanium alloy casing held its integrity as it penetrated two layers of two-inch metal walls and hit Lt. Harper squarely on the back. The impact of the round pushed the lieutenant into Elizabeth's bed, causing him to flip over her, head first. His legs followed through over Elizabeth, almost hitting the ceiling and back down on the floor. The momentum was so great he continued to flip, hitting his helmet-covered head on the far wall some feet away. The door finally slid open as Lt. Harper got up slowly after being stunned for several seconds. The round was not able to penetrate Harper's body armor after going through the wall which greatly decreasing its lethality, but the concussion was enough to disrupt his murderous activity. The five guards stormed into the room and fixed their weapons on the lieutenant.

Captain Middleton ordered Sergeant Moore to check the nurses as he personally checked Elizabeth's condition. He instinctively disconnected the chemical injectors, hoping the chemicals Lt. Harper was trying to give her had not run through the life support system. Lt. Harper was quickly subdued and disarmed by the master sergeant and his own security force. A few seconds later, a reaction team of nurses and a doctor ran into the room to ensure Elizabeth wasn't injured.

"HQ, this is a code seven lock down. Get me the Director now!" Middleton commanded through his helmet's comlink.

The Eternal Domain, Ft. Lauderdale, Florida

Larcis slowed down to subsonic speed and entered the open landing tube erected in the middle of the farm's man-made lake. The ball of electricity surrounding the three men faded away as his speed reduced to below fifty miles per hour. Richard let go of Larcis to allow both of them to independently fly the rest of the way through the long launch tube into the Eternal Domain's vehicle shop. Larcis finally came to a complete stop, landing on the shop's epoxy covered concrete white floor and felt warm liquid being poured on his leg. He looked down at lumpy and discolored vomit splattered all over his flat black costume. Richard, who was in the lead, turned around as he heard someone whaling behind him.

"What the hell is wrong with you?" Larcis yelled at Mark, jumping away from him with superhuman speed.

The foul odor continued to linger on Larcis no matter how fast or far he moved away from Mark. It took him but a second to head straight for the nearest bathroom. Richard walked to Mark cautiously, making sure he did not step on the puddle of puke. "Are you okay?"

Mark wiped remnants of digested food on his breaded face with his long-sleeved shirt and looked up at Richard. "If I had known I was going to be flung around like a rocket, I wouldn't have eaten a pizza," he said, his throat still sore.

"Sorry about that, but look at the bright side."

"What bright side?"

Richard grinned. "Since Erica is off-line, the workbots don't work, which means you will have to get a mop and bucket from the closet and clean up this mess."

"That's a bright side to you?" Mark said, standing up.

"If you get Erica fixed, you wouldn't have to worry about cleaning up the next mess you make."

"So I guess you won't help me, huh?"

"No, with your luck, I'll probably slip on the floor and land on your puke and you," Richard said, grinning as he pointed toward the closet door down the hallway leading to the elevator. "The closest has a sink and its right there."

"When you get it done, just go to the elevator up to the ninth floor, labeled SL 1. I will meet you there so you can get a change of clothes. Alright?"

Mark frowned as Richard walked away with two of his bags. He anxiously scrutinized his laptop case opening to see if any vomit had reached any of the components. The case and laptop would have been clean had Mark not touched it with his hands, but his unusual paranoia over Jack being damaged was too strong to ignore. He cursed himself for getting a smidgen of food on the outer case and put Jack off to the side.

Mark quickly walked off to the closet and began cleaning. Soon afterwards, Mark had mopped up the floor and wiped off the vomit from his clothes and laptop case. The floor was very clean and scented with Lysol, but the closet was left in shambles. Mark joyfully went up the elevator thinking Richard would be proud of him for cleaning the floor without any incident.

Richard was waiting patiently for Mark, thinking about how much he was going to allow Mark to know about the group and the base. The group took a break as Richard told them about Mark, his history and what to say or not say to Mark. Richard instructed the team to ensure they kept Cindy's identity a secret and have Cindy pose as his girlfriend, when she returned, for the time being. Larcis confirmed Richard's stories, wanting to stay as far away from Mark as possible. They all sat down to eat dinner when Mark entered the Battle Room. Richard intercepted Mark and escorted him to the guest room to shower and change clothes. Thirty minutes went by when Mark reemerged from the guest room into the Battle Room smelling like a bed of roses.

The team just finished their meals as Mark came in and stood by the kitchen bar table overlooking the Battle Room.

"Gang, this is Mark Farnell," Richard announced.

Mark's attention was temporarily distracted by Erica's main console in the Battle Room and the moderately expensive furnishings. The team said hello in unison, but Mark almost ignored them; he was so overwhelmed with the Battle Room as if he were a little boy in a huge toy store.

It took Mark moments to realize everyone was waiting for him to respond. "Oh, I'm sorry. It's been a long time since I worked on AIs. This all just fascinates me."

"So, Richard tells us you helped create Erica," Susan said.

"Who's Richard?" Mark asked, confused, trying to think of all the Richards he knew.

"I am," Richard clarified.

"Really?" There was an amused expression on Mark's face.

"Want to eat?" Larcis offered. "We have chicken curry with rice or potatoes. Your choice."

"Yeah, I could use some food right about now."

Out of courtesy, the team slowly ate their deserts as Mark started on the main meal. Mark ate very fast and finished his chicken before anyone got halfway through their cheesecake.

Richard briefed Mark on what he knew about Erica's advanced configurations coupled with technological breakthroughs that made Erica the most modern SAI in existence. Mark's curiosity about Erica increased the more Richard spoke, which excited him enough to take his desert into the Battle Room very eager to work on fixing Erica. Everyone except John, who was not interested in computer jargon, crowded around Erica's main console.

Mark sat in the hot seat and placed Jack on the worktable while John went upstairs to see what was going on with the farm and talk to the live-in employees. It wasn't long before Mark was able to get power moving through Erica's microchips. Richard chose not to tell Mark about Nowhereman, hoping he would be able to find out what happened on his own. It had been a long time since he last saw Mark and had doubts about his loyalties. Mark might try to use the information about the virus used on Erica to sell to the highest bidders. It was not a dangerous virus as far as he could tell and didn't cause as many problems as the Killer Virus which was plaguing most of the world at the present time.

Mark was not a killer, but he was a collector of viruses, which put him in a position of power and, unfortunately, in a tempting situation to be greedy. Richard figured if Nowhereman was on the up and up, then he would be able to get Nowhereman's help to prevent another epidemic should Mark later decide to sell the virus in the future.

"Jack, reroute commands through Sierra 7 through 18," Mark instructed.

"Initiating," Jack replied through Erica's sound system.

"Very good, Jack."

"What are you doing?" Larcis asked; who was the most technologically ignorant in the group.

"I'm taking Erica apart, memory bank by memory bank," Mark said, a little annoyed as he was trying to input binary commands into Jack's network.

Richard and Susan knew better than to distract Mark's efforts, so they kept quiet and signaled Larcis to do the same with a simple raise of the finger to their lips. Larcis replied simply by making an angry face, curling a corner of his lips and watching in absolute silence.

An hour passed with no success. Mark stretched his arms upward and leaned backwards on the sofa. "Richard, it would be easier to completely erase Erica's memory core and start all over,"

Mark said with a hint of frustration and sympathy.

Richard frowned. "If I wanted it to be easy, I would have done it two days ago. Come on, Mark, you're better than this."

Mark looked at Richard with a small sneer. "Do you have any idea how long it would take to figure out what is wrong with her, let alone figuring out how to fix it?"

"Yeah, but tell me this, Mark. If we erase Erica's memory core, what then? We don't have access to the information she absorbed when I gave her all her primary commands. I was able to contact the SIA on the low-band messenger two hours ago and they said the EFL computer and Loki have been infected and are helpless. So, even if we did get access to the World Wide Web, she will get infected by the same virus we want her to eliminate."

Mark thought for a moment. "We can load Jack into her system and she can absorb all of his knowledge. She can use Jack's information and amplify her abilities. She will probably be the only SAI which can stop the Killer Virus once her core is replaced with Jack's knowledge?"

"No, we will not do that." Richard declared.

"That's the only way!" Mark insisted.

Richard peered into Mark's eyes with complete calmness. "I will not allow Erica to die, Mark. Once you erase her core, she will no longer be Erica. And I swear I will bring hell down upon anyone who even tries to erase her." Richard's eyes turned bright red. "She will not be erased."

Mark looked at Susan and Larcis for support, but only found the same expression on their faces. Mark took a deep breath and began to calculate other options on how to crack the code on the problem. "Alright, Richard, but we will need more than Jack, which means we will need to access the Internet."

"What about the Killer Virus?"

"I'll run a virus of my own. It is especially made to mask other programs. Hopefully, this Killer Virus will accept it and allow it to run its course."

Richard looked at Mark with interest. "What do you mean allow it to run its course?"

Mark smiled. "This Killer Virus jumps from program to program giving commands, almost like any other virus. But this one thinks."

"You mean like an AI?" Larcis asked.

"Sort of, but not really. It adapts to survive. I have been monitoring areas in the United States for the past twenty-four hours. When the virus hit six hours ago, some areas were hit with blackouts, some with computer tampering, and most of the areas were hit with a mixture of the two. If you really look closely at the areas, there are always several connections which the Killer Virus uses to move around or uses as backups," Mark explained.

"And what does this have to do with your virus being able to work?" Susan asked.

Mark looked at all three a little agitated by their lack of understanding. "Okay, look, the Killer Virus is like a traffic controller and network builder all rolled up into one. When it first created these lanes or routes, it became sentient. Even with being sentient it would not be able to do everything everyone thinks it's doing. It simply lets other viruses go out into the Web under its control, allowing malicious programs to roam where it wants them to roam. At the same time, it disables security and communication protocol measures forcing the operating system to be controlled by the new system user."

"And how long have you known this?" Richard asked. His gut telling him something was wrong.

"Oh, for about the last three hours or so. It was Jack who confirmed my theory about the Killer Virus, now all I need to do is get Erica back online to hunt it down and destroy it. But the virus inside of her is nothing like any virus I have seen. I'm surprised this virus didn't go into the Web and really mess everything up," Mark said in wonder.

"What do you mean?" Richard snapped.

"If I didn't know any better, this virus inside of Erica is the mother of all viruses," Mark said, his face strangely solemn. "There are thousands of malicious programs running in her memory and virtual systems that the Killer Virus will not dare try to control them." Mark paused in thought. "You know, what if the virus in Erica is like the Killer Virus?"

"Hmm…if that's true, wouldn't the thousands of viruses in her erase her in time?" Susan interjected.

"Maybe, but if the virus knows this, then it would not kill its host if it wants to survive," Mark said in doubt. "That is, theoretically speaking."

"Well, since this is all we have to go with, can you make it so that part of Erica can be quarantined so she can fight the parasite herself?" Richard proposed.

"Maybe," Mark hopefully said. "Yeah, maybe."

"Okay then, let's try it."

Larcis glanced at his watch and signaled Richard that he was going to get Cindy. Richard nodded approval.

Mark sat straight up on the sofa and started to work his magic.

Richard's gut kept gnawing at him every time he thought about Nowhereman and the virus in Erica. Nowhereman said he had to infect her to protect her. Now, Richard understood and thought: Can they use the virus in Erica to help destroy the alien Killer Virus presently ravaging the world? In the end, he knew time was against them and something would have to be done because the two viruses were simple distractions from what Ego was really up to. He had to rely on Nowhereman's decision to protect Erica and hope things would turn out for the best.

Larcis returned with Cindy, but they stayed in the mechanics lab. Larcis briefed her on what was going on with Mark and her cover. Richard did not want anyone to know Cindy with them in the group, and quite possibly, an ace in the hole. Larcis admired Richard for his tactical and strategic leadership skills, which had saved them many times in the past in the worst of situations. Now, it was being put to the test once again. Larcis gave Cindy background information on Elizabeth and how she needed to pretend she was Richard's girlfriend. Cindy trusted and played along with Richard's charade only because Joshua told her he could be trusted.

Twenty minutes of coaching from Larcis was more than enough to get her through the night. Richard would brief her some more later that night. They went upstairs and joined the group just as Mark was able to get part of Erica back online.

Cindy stayed in the kitchen and briefed Larcis, Susan, and Richard on her findings at NORAD. The Air Force had implemented their ground-zero procedures and had each ballistic missile silo—including mobile launch systems—disengage direct computer feeds into their launch codes. The site commander would require a direct command via a military SATCOM network, which was not affected by the Killer Virus being on a separate compartmented secure system other than the World Wide Web. The SIA was also on a similar system; however, they were hit hard when the main center tried to communicate with nonsecure sources.

"Are all of their nuclear weapons accounted for?" Richard asked once Cindy was done reporting.

"The warheads on the missiles are, but there are hundreds of nukes being stored across the country. The President is worried about how accurate their numbers are for those loose warheads," Cindy repeated what she had heard in a video conference between the Joint Chiefs of Staff, the President, and the NORAD commander, General Shaffer.

"Hmm...I wonder if there is anyone in particular or a small group who can put a nuke together without being detected," Richard said; knowing NORAD had tight control of established nuclear warheads and delivery systems.

"Several government agencies monitor people who can, so I don't think that would work unless Ego was able to find someone who has access to the materials. The only problem is we can't get to the information because of the virus," Susan said.

"Yeah, I know. Let's hope Mark can get Erica working so we can try and get ahead of the game."

"Richard, I didn't say this before because of several reasons, but Joshua might be able to help us. That's if we can convince him without interfering with free will," Cindy said.

"Free will?" Larcis asked. "What are you talking about?"

"It's hard to explain, but Joshua will not interfere with 'mankind' as he puts it, because we have to face the future on our own decisions and not be coerced into making the right or wrong choices."

"Is he some kind of a peace-loving liberal or something?" Larcis taunted.

"No, he has more power than any person I know. He can destroy and create anything he wishes and there is no one on Earth who can stop him. He is literally a god," Cindy said with utter certainty.

Larcis said nothing; it suddenly dawned on him that Cindy was dead serious and Joshua was probably the real deal. Richard paced around the kitchen and stopped by the refrigerator. He gazed at the photos of him and Elizabeth magnetically hung on the door, along with several pictures of the entire group. His face saddened with concern as he grazed his honeymoon picture with his fingers; how he wished he could touch Liz's face. Richard swung away and walked to Cindy.

"Cindy, I don't know what is going to happen in the next three weeks, but I do know if Joshua sits idle then we can all kiss our asses goodbye. I have a feeling Joshua will get involved if there was a good reason, otherwise he wouldn't have told you to come here and help us. So, I want you to hold off asking him for help. We will ask him when we need him most, okay."

Cindy smiled, seeing Richard's wisdom and gladly consented to his intent. "I'll wait until you give me the word."

Susan turned to Mark; she wondered why he seemed to be working slower than usual. He had been quiet for the past several minutes and worried if he overheard the group's discussion. She was always paranoid with people knowing about secrets and knowledge in general. This was another point in time when she would have to make a mental note of Mark's activities, because it was in her nature to trust very few people. She tapped Richard's arm indicating they should go and give Mark some company.

Mark welcomed the group as he depressed several keys on Erica's console. "Good of you guys to come back. I thought you were going to miss this," Mark said eagerly.

"Miss what?" Richard asked.

"Watch," Mark said, pressed the ENTER key on the keyboard, and leaned back in triumph.

Erica's main screen lit up with Richard's customized background and three Internet Explorer browser windows. The team cheered as the Web browsers searched the Internet with ease; however, many sites were down or infected with malicious programs. "I was able to partition a part of Erica's core memory and enable simple protocol functions. Her enhanced internal search engine makes it possible to search the Web, even though all of the normal search engines are down," Mark said. "So, what are we looking for?"

"We have three things to do, but I don't know if we can do all three at the same time," Richard said.

"It depends on what they are," Mark replied. He knew they had just touched the tip of the iceberg.

"Yeah, I know. The first thing is to get Erica fixed. The second is to search for specific people on the Web. The problem with that is the information we need might not be available until the Killer Virus is destroyed," Richard said.

"And what is the third thing?" Mark asked.

"Destroy the Killer Virus," Richard repeated.

"Oh," Mark sighed; he was hoping there was some fantastic mission he could be a part of.

Richard and Susan stayed up late with Mark while the other three superheroes slept in their rooms. Hours passed before Mark finally got Erica's basic programs online. He introduced Jack into Erica's system, which dramatically sped things up. Erica's erratic personalities were operational by just after midnight.

"Richard, I can't fix her with Jack, but we can surf the Net," Mark said after many failed attempts in trying to find the alien virus.

"That's okay," Richard said. "I will take it for now. Go get some sleep."

Mark yawned and hobbled to his room. "Wake me up if you find anything."

"I will. And thanks, Mark."

"Sure, anytime." Mark half smiled and yawned again. "Good night."

"Good night," Richard replied and started to build a search for nuclear material and possible candidates who would know how to create a nuclear bomb.

A list soon came out of the printer, but it was only 80 percent complete as Erica's security protocols acted up again and restricted numerous downloads. Richard glanced at the list of over 600 names with aggravation, knowing many names would not be on the list simply because the technology to create a nuke was almost common knowledge to anyone skillful enough who wanted to know how to create a nuclear bomb. Ego could probably coach a teenager into building a nuke without messing it up, which made his list almost worthless.

Shortly after browsing the list; an encrypted message came over the emergency channels from the SIA. It was good to hear from SIA again, Richard thought, but what now?

Chapter Eight

□ □ ◻ □ □

THE ZOO KEEPER

Max stepped into Elizabeth's room following Cpt. Middleton and half of his escort of bodyguards.

"Sir, we moved her into this room because it provides us with the ability to post four guards on the inside and a class-four telepath inside and outside of the room." Middleton finished his report to Maximilian, the Director of SIA.

Max looked at Liz with concern and relief as her body lay peacefully unaware of the recent assassination attempt on her and her child's life. "Brad, I want you to handpick all of the guards and telepaths. I will make the final approval on them before they guard her. In the meantime, get two more telepaths down here and rotate them every eight hours. The entire security team will not be allowed to leave the compound and no one outside of the team will be allowed to interact with anyone else except for myself. In addition, Dr. Kerns and Dr. Heider will be the only doctors allowed to see Elizabeth. No nurses. Is that clear?"

"I will need ten minutes to make a list of personnel, sir," Middleton replied. He knew Max purposely left out a timeline and the number of personnel from his instructions.

Max looked at Brad quite satisfied with his recent performance. "How much sleep have you gotten?"

Brad stared at his boss with a tired but determined look on his face. "I have been up for the past eighteen hours, sir, but a few more minutes shouldn't matter."

"Good, then. But make sure you get eight hours before you start another shift. I don't want any sleep-deprived heroes on my watch."

"Understood, Sir."

"Where is Harper now?" Max asked.

"He's under restraints in the brig undergoing a full mind sweep."

"I take it he didn't want to talk."

"No, sir, his story doesn't add up. Someone has messed with his brain," Brad said, knowing SIA officers went through extensive mental scans on a routine basis, but what was done to Harper was quite different.

"I see. I'll be in the brig. When you get the list together, bring it to me so you can go get some rest."

"Sir, just to let you know before you see Harper—you might not like what Harper has to say," Brad cautioned.

Max looked at Brad with concern. "I understand, Brad. Thanks." Max walked off, followed by this three-man escort. He stopped by the door. "Oh, one last thing, Brad. Good job."

"It was a team effort, Sir."

"Yes, I know. Good job to all of you."

Max left the room in deep thought. What would he tell Richard? The doctors said Elizabeth could be coming out of the coma anytime, but it really didn't matter because she was in grave danger as long as she was defenseless in bed. Too many things were happening to be coincidences and the assassination attempt was just one item on his Top 20 list. For now, he would have to see what Harper would reveal before telling Richard what almost happened to his wife and child.

Australia Section, Kansas City Zoo, Missouri

A middle-aged man of medium stature wearing a plastic apron carefully cleaned out a section of the Woodland Aviary, the home of over seventeen species of Australian birds. It was late in the afternoon, and he was almost through with his routine duties as a worker in the zoo's grounds. He wiped the sweat off his forehead with his forearm as he took a short break from a long day's hard work. He took a moment to look up at the colorful birds with a sense of peace and happiness. It had been several months since he started working at the zoo, but somehow he knew his time to leave was coming soon.

The sound of the cage door opening in the distance told him he was not the only one working overtime on a Friday evening. He looked across the aviary and saw a heavyset woman in her mid-thirties wearing a doctor's work coat walking toward him with a friendly smile. "Hello, David," the woman said.

"Hello, Dr. Wilkins. It's a pretty night tonight, isn't it?" David said.

Dr. Wilkins took in a deep breath of her surroundings and smiled. "Yes, it is." She watched David smile and start up again in washing away bird droppings. She paced back and forth as if looking at the scenery, paying little attention to David's janitorial work.

David finished cleaning the aviary and started on the tools after 30 minutes while the lady doctor waited for him so she could get his full attention. David noticed the doctor wasn't looking at the birds or the plants in the aviary anymore. He wondered why she was sticking around.

"Is there something wrong, Dr. Wilkins?"

Dr. Wilkins turned to him. "No, not really. I'm just wondering why you always work overtime and not get paid for it?"

"Working with the animals is payment enough for me."

Dr. Wilkins frowned. "You know, I don't think you have been honest with me. So, before I have to get other people involved, I want to hear your side of the story."

"What? You mean get the police or your boss?" David said as if he knew what the lady doctor was talking about.

"Ever since you came here to my department, things have been very good. And I can understand miracles happening every now and then, but not seven in the past three weeks. And you know, every time I think about how our oldest panda bear has somehow got ten years younger and three female pandas getting pregnant all of the sudden with one being infertile, I think about you."

"And so you think I had something to do with it?" David exhaled heavily with relief. "And I thought it was about me being an ex-con."

"An ex-con?" Dr. Wilkins's face froze in surprise.

David looked at her. "Dr. Wilkins, I know there have been

weird things going on lately and that me being an ex-con is another one of those things, but I don't think they would have hired me if they knew I had a record. Being here, working with the animals was a place I thought I could get away from people in general. I feel free when I'm around the animals, because they don't judge me or think I'm a danger to them, their children, or their possessions… I hope you don't tell anyone about this."

"What were you sent to prison for?" Dr. Wilkins asked cautiously.

"Second-degree manslaughter," David said as he watched Dr. Wilkins's demeanor.

"I'm sorry, David, but I noticed you know a lot about medicine and thought you were experimenting with the pandas and chimpanzees."

"No," David said with a dismissive laugh. "I wouldn't harm any of them. I love them as if they were my own children."

"I love them, too."

"I guess my secret is safe with you?"

Dr. Wilkins smiled. "Your secret is safe with me. But if by chance someone else finds out, what will you do?"

David studied her face. "You're a God-fearing woman, aren't you?"

Dr. Wilkins laughed, a bit confused. "Yes, I guess I am."

"Well, all I can do is have faith and hope. I don't have to leave to find some other place to live in peace, peace comes from within."

"You can call me Pam," Dr. Wilkins said as she offered David a hand with the remaining tools he was going to put away in the storage closet.

David smiled. "Pam it is."

"Do you want to go out for a late snack, that's if it is alright with you?" Pam asked.

"That would be nice, but don't you have a husband and children waiting for you at home?"

Pam looked at David in surprise again. How did he know about her family? She never mentioned her family to him or worn her wedding ring for the past three months.

"How did you know I'm married?"

"I didn't. It was an educated guess by your age and what Chris told me about you."

"And who is Chris?" Pam asked, not recognizing the name.

"He has been working here for over a year. He once told me he saw you and your family about six months ago visiting the zoo."

"I'm sorry," Pam said. "There are a lot of employees working here that I don't even know."

"That's okay. Most people forget a name minutes after hearing it. But in your case, I find it hard to believe you don't look forward to going home," David said.

David's last line jolted Pam. "Wait a second. What makes you think I don't want to go home to my children?"

"I learned a lot in prison, among those were two things: I learned I was an exceptionally good judge of character and the other was to know when someone had a problem so bad that they wouldn't talk to anyone about it. I mean no one; not even their own relatives or friends," David said, peering into Pam's hazel green eyes. "I see this in you."

"Why are you telling me this?"

"Because now we have something important to talk about over a late snack." David smiled and walked into the storage closet.

Pam felt very comfortable around David for some reason even though he had a record and mysterious insight. He was very wise and projected an incredible aura of calmness around him. It was odd to see him as a mild-mannered janitor or ex-convict; he just didn't seem the type. While having a criminal record would explain his job selection, he still seemed out of place, more like a wanderer or angel on a mission. She watched David put the tools away and get ready to leave the zoo. They left the building together talking about their past childhoods. Pam did most of the talking as David carefully asked questions that encouraged Pam to be herself.

They eventually made it to a simple diner just outside the zoo. They ordered sandwiches and waited for their orders as David drank water, while Pam drank coffee.

Pam's interest in David increased as David talked about his past career as a psychiatrist and how he worked with traumatized children. The more David talked, the more she wondered how David knew so many things. "David, can I ask you how old you are?"

David looked at Pam and put down his half-empty glass of water on the table. "I'm going on forty-five by the end of the year."

Pam's eyes widened with complete surprise. "You don't look a day over thirty."

"No, but as far as the zoo is concerned, I'm thirty-two with no parents or children to support. I may not look it Pam but I sure feel like I'm eighty every time I get up in the morning," David said rubbing his tired eyes.

"I know the feeling. To make it worse, this bug that is going around makes me want to stay home and not come to work."

"What bug?" David asked. He wondered if she was talking about the recent incidents of dehydration and fainting spells by workers and visitors at the zoo.

"Aren't you paying attention to the bulletin board? I thought everyone knew by now."

"Knew what?" David asked.

"The medical staff has given over fifty IVs in the past two weeks. Extra water points have been placed all over the area so people won't get dehydrated, but that doesn't seem to be working because they do anyway even after drinking a lot of water."

"Oh, and I thought it was normal to put water points out during this season. But you do know most people usually drink less water when it's cold and tend to overdress by wearing too many layers of clothes that only increases the chance of overheating," David pointed out.

"Yeah, but a lot of the people we talked to had been drinking water and some didn't walk very far. Luckily, no elderly people, children, or pregnant women have gotten sick. Don't you think that's kind of strange?"

David smiled. "Don't worry too much about it. I'm sure this bug thing will pass and people will take care of themselves better from now on."

"Yeah, I guess," Pam said.

"Well, don't worry. Everything will turn out alright," David said. "You know, I'm curious. What does your husband do for a living?"

Pam thought about it and felt easier now being able to talk to David so comfortably in the short period of time they spent together. "He works for a law firm as a financial attorney. The kids and I don't see him very much now that he is working on a big lawsuit," Pam said softly.

"Can I ask you when was the last time you had a vacation or good quality time with him?"

"About a year ago, I guess. It feels a lot longer, though," Pam said wistfully.

"It sounds to me like he brings work home."

"You are very observant," Pam said. She felt as if David already knew so much about her life.

"It's only natural for both of you to bring work home, the important thing is how both of you use what you bring home to benefit each other instead of stressing each other out."

"Is that right? So, doctor, how do you think we should use work as an excuse to be happier?" Pam teased.

"Well, you need to remember that relationships take time and consistent give-and-take," David said. "If you go to your husband and tell him you love him or try to change things overnight, he will respond in the same defensive way he has been doing for the past six months. So, if somehow you can get him to understand that there is a problem and both of you are willing to fix it, then he will listen to reason a lot better."

"Go on," Pam said. David's uncanny knowledge about her own life was spiking her interest. It was all so intriguing.

"Most people don't like it when they are stressed out and someone tells them to calm down," David continued, "that it is nothing or that everything will be alright. By the way, what's your husband's name?"

"Horace," Pam said.

"So, when Horace talks about how work was so messed up, then listen and remember the details. Try to talk to him and let him know you are there if he needs any help. If he doesn't want to talk and gets hostile to you or the kids for whatever reason, then you can do two things. You can talk about your day at work. Talk about how awful it is and how much everything sucks. Even if it doesn't suck, exaggerate it. Tell him how you plan to fix things or how comical things are, like saying you hate your boss because he used money for painting the zoo entrance walkway instead of using it for needed medical supplies. Then say something like, 'Tomorrow I'm going to barge right into his office and kick him in the behind so hard he will beg for medical supplies.' Most importantly, though, you have to make sure you don't let him get any words in during your entire speech and ask him for advice and don't leave it open. Ask him if you should kick your boss in the butt or poke him in the eyes. After he hears this, he will pay more attention to you and think you need help, forget about his problems long enough for you to hear his problems later or he will laugh at you because you will look so cute talking like that." David let out a small laugh. "But that is just my two cents worth of knowledge which spans for more than one session in a diner."

"You seem to make it sound so easy," Pam said, smiling.

"Have you ever repeated something someone has just said and say it completely different?" David continued.

"No. What do you mean?"

"This takes practice and time but it's like this. If you ever hear your son or daughter say, 'Mom, can we go to the store?' Then you reply with something witty like, 'What? You slipped and hit your head on the floor?' Say anything to completely take them off guard. In time, they will accept that you are joking and remember that you are not down or sad. They will expect it and enjoy talking to you simply because it is something different in their everyday routine in life," David explained.

"I don't know if I can do that."

David laughed. "Pam, life is an adventure of trying to be happy and seeing others be happy. When you start treating everything you do based on work for putting food on the table, then life becomes a routine of nonstop depressing events that suck happiness and purpose from you and the people around you. You owe it to yourself and your family to work at being happy, not just work for a paycheck."

The waitress came and placed two sandwiches on the table.

"It's getting late. Are you going to be alright getting home so late?" David asked. He knew she would have to explain going home at this late hour to her husband.

"Yeah, I hope so."

"I would like to meet Horace. I might be able to help both of you get on the right track and hopefully you two can go on the vacation you two have dreamt about for the past three years," David suggested.

Pam looked even more confused now. "How do you know all of the details about the six months and now three years?"

"I'll explain later, but for now you should think about a babysitter."

"Oh, I don't know, David. We barely have enough money to pay the bills," Pam said.

"You of so little faith." David smiled. "You will get enough money very soon to be able to go. As for a babysitter, I can probably take care of your children while you two are gone."

Pam looked at David with reservation and intrigue. "We'll see. It's getting late. Do you think we can talk some more later?"

"I don't think we can spend every night talking together." David smiled. "But if it's any consolation, we can talk at work. It doesn't take very much to listen to each other while we work."

"I'll like that," Pam said and finished off her rye bread with turkey sandwich.

The Eternal Domain Master Room

The main screen came up with a video of Maximilian sitting in a hospital office. "Richard, I have some bad news."

Richard sat straight up on the sofa as Max spoke. "I want you to hear everything I have to say before you reply…"

"What is it, Max?"

"There has been a failed assassination attempt on Liz," Max continued, his voice grave. "She and the baby are well and I have my best men keeping them safe. One of my agents tried to poison Liz during a routine checkup. The agent is under restraints, but he is not the problem. Someone messed with his head and made him believe he was killing the person responsible for his wife's murder."

The news jolted Richard. "Who's behind this?" There was sudden anger in his voice.

"I had three telepaths scan Agent Harper's mind. They are convinced Susan implanted a life so real he actually believes he was married with a make-believe wife who was murdered. He took the opportunity to take his revenge by trying to kill Liz."

"Susan?"

"I'm sorry, Richard, but I have to accept what the telepaths are reporting and bring Susan in until we get this mess cleared up."

"I don't care what the telepaths are saying. Susan is being framed and I need her here. There has to be another way."

"I'm sorry, Richard, but there is no other way…"

"It would make sense to implant Susan as the person responsible. Your telepaths are not strong enough to find out the truth. Susan and John are, but they can't do anything now because it would be a conflict of interest. How convenient," Richard thought aloud.

"Richard, I know this sounds crazy, but if it was Susan, you have a bigger problem if she isn't confined."

"Max, that's where you're wrong. The whole world depends on the entire team right now. There is a supernatural being called Ego who will destroy the Earth if we don't stop him. Another thing, it would be better to have Susan next to me if she did commit the crime," Richard explained.

"Alright, Richard, it's in your ballpark," Max sighed. "I will personally see to it that Liz is taken care of and if you need anything, just give me a call."

"As usual, things have to be the hard way. Thank you, Max." Richard ended the videoconference.

The Eternal Domain Battle Room

Larcis and Cindy spent most of the morning with Mark, watching him muddle through Erica's complex secondary database files. The database was Erica's reference link to the world. She processed relationships and scenarios that Richard had her amass during her initial programming. Now, her database has grown to over twenty libraries of Congress worth of data. The amount of data stored in the secondary database was so astoundingly enormous, Mark's chances of finding the core virus was five billion to one.

Larcis had given Cindy a basic knowledge of how Erica operated and told her about all of the wonderful things Erica could do, but unfortunately for Cindy, she wasn't able to see Erica at work. The virus had disabled Erica's primary database and core processors. Cindy watched Mark perform searches with innovated snifters and virus killers but the long and drawn-out chore soon left Cindy and Larcis sitting around the Battle Room dying of boredom.

Cindy yearned to go back to Seattle as soon as possible but her curiosity helped in keeping her busy and her mind off of Glenn. She had been inside military bunkers and very wealthy households but the Eternal Domain was unique. Even though ED was underground and reminded her of the Yimen Research Center in some ways, there was a very friendly and homely atmosphere about it.

Larcis took Cindy on a grand tour of ED and the farm, which lasted two hours. Cindy liked Larcis very much. He was young and very friendly. Almost like a younger brother she never had. Larcis was a playboy of sorts with a lot of experience with the ladies, but he never gave that impression toward Cindy.

Larcis was oddly attracted to Cindy as a sibling and part of the group. He had his share of relationships and felt a sense of responsibility to be a good friend instead of trying to hit on her. Richard and John had taught him well in the past year in becoming a gentleman and a scholar. His 4.0 grade point average was perfect in every way to include a SAT score of 1550. Maybe it was his high academic standing and wealthy lifestyle that attracted university girls into his life. But, they were for the most part, very young and wanted some degree of commitment from a man. Larcis would have been a perfect choice, but his superhero activity and commitment to school caused too much strain on a lasting relationship. It didn't matter now because he felt like Cindy could be the patient friend outside of the Eternal Champions once her mission was accomplished.

Chapter Nine

□ □ ☐ □ □

WHO TO TRUST

The metal rollers squeaked as the hangar doors slowly closed. Grated lights shined on the four buildings connected to one another by makeshift wood and plastic extensions. The one-story buildings surrounded a domed structure the size of a medium-size U-Haul truck. Natasha, a tall black-haired woman, walked out of the main building, down a few steps, and over to a work area in the corner of the aircraft hangar. She sat in a rolling chair and propped her feet up on a large worktable. Five large plasma screens behind her displayed the interior of each structure in the hangar. She leaned back and tried to relax as if waiting for something to happen.

Natasha rested peacefully for a few minutes until she sensed someone was behind her. She slowly opened her eyes halfway and made quick mental considerations of possible weapons, exits, routes around the furniture, and anything which she could use to identify and possibly attack the unwanted visitor. The faint scent elegant perfume and the reflection of a woman's figure on the shiny table lamp frame told her who the unwelcome guest was. She slowly moved both her hands on her belly and pressed a small button on her watch.

Jared could be seen on the fourth plasma screen getting out of a chair and moving out of the camera's view.

"What can I do for you, Director?" Natasha asked aloud, her voice echoing through the enormous hangar.

Jean paused for a second and considered her options. She had bypassed Jared's security guards with ease, but Natasha was different. Her element of surprise was lost but there was still a chance.

"For starters, you can chill," Jean said and concentrated her frost powers on Natasha. Nat swung around on the swivel chair which continued to spin as she slid off the seat and onto the grayish-white concrete floor. A deep freeze engulfed her entire body, squeezing the air from her lungs. She had completely lost muscle control, but the deep freeze kept her in a hibernated state of animation.

Jean smiled as she watched Natasha shiver into unconsciousness. Jean faced the plasma screens and fiddled with the camera controls and then looked at the worktable with interest. She was very familiar with psychoanalytical profiling and REM dysfunction therapy, but other diagrams in front of her showed information on everyone she knew—including herself.

"What are you up to, Jared?" She shuffled through her file and then her only supervisor just short of the President of the United States.

Jared had compiled extensive personal information with very incriminating evidence. She wondered about his motives and employment under her care. She looked up at the buildings in front of her and concentrated on the entire area. The temperature in all of the structures dropped to negative 40 degrees Celsius in a matter of seconds. Her entire body tensed up as she strained in using her full power. When she was finished, she fell back exhausted on the padded chair.

She breathed slowly, trying to regain her strength, and smiled knowing Jared was probably a frozen popsicle inside one of the buildings. The assassination attempt had failed and now Jared was becoming more of a liability than an asset. She looked at the files on the table and reclined back on the chair. "I guess you won't be needing these files after all."

"There is a difference between needing and wanting, Jean." It was Jared's voice, and it sounded as if he was standing just next to her. In an instant, the table, the hangar, the buildings, and the airfield she had passed through getting there—all of them disappeared into thin air. She fell hard on the ground and grimaced in pain. She looked all around and saw nothing but a light blue void of nothingness as far as her eyes could see.

Jean stood up trying to get her bearing, knowing Jared was now in complete control of her surroundings. "Jared, I was hoping never to hear from you again."

"You know, Jean, we should stop meeting like this. People might think you were trying to kill me." Jared laughed.

"What makes you think that?" Jean sarcastically

mumbled.

"It doesn't matter, because no matter how hard you try, I will only love you more." Jared suddenly appeared in front of her. "I took the liberty of gathering those files to protect you. Do you know how easy it was for me to get this information?" Jared continued as the files appeared for a split second and then disappeared before her eyes.

"The point is, you have them," Jean said flatly.

"Yes, I do. I have to know everything to make sure the stories are perfect. I have made an alibi for each of your, should we say, 'compromising moments.' In addition, I have erased any trail to this damning information. You might say, I have covered for you."

"And that's supposed to make me feel better?"

"No, that's supposed to make you feel grateful," Jared said without changing his mood or tone of voice.

"You failed to kill Isis."

"It's funny how things don't always work out, but if it makes you feel any better, we will not be blamed for it and there is something more important you should be worried about. Do you remember Mr. Patterson?"

"Yes, why?" Jean said. Patterson used to be her right-hand man in the agency.

"I found out recently that he is still alive. It seems you didn't plan on him being careful enough to fake his own death."

"The dental records proved it was him," Jean said, suddenly confused. She had arranged Mr. Theodore Patterson to be killed in an accidental fire many months back, or perhaps it had already been a year. Patterson was trying to involve her in an extortion operation against Makan Industries, an international computer systems outfit, which might have put him in charge of the CEA.

Even though Mr. Patterson was her right-hand man, she would not let a traitor to continue working against her. She was able to salvage the business relationship between her and Mr. Makan after killing Patterson and helping Mr. Makan through the death of his wife and only daughter.

"The dental records were changed to cover your tracks, but they were changed before you got to them," Jared continued. "Theodore is in hiding, probably trying to figure out how to get back at you."

"Theo is a spineless fool."

"Yes." Jared grinned. "Well, that fool got away, making you look like *the* fool."

"So, am I supposed to be thankful for knowing I'm a fool now?"

"No, I want you to let me do my job," Jared said as he walked into Jean's personal space.

Jean looked into Jared's hazel gray eyes and saw his strong determination and honesty. He was very different than all of the men she was used to dealing with and it strangely angered her and calmed her at the same time. "So, what's the catch?"

"The catch is, you have to trust me. Not because you can, but because you want to. One day, Jean, you will come to realize that there are some people out there, like me, who care about you and want to be with you."

"I don't mix business with pleasure."

"I'm not talking about work or friends," Jared said, moving closer to her, his lips almost touching her face.

"There's no room in my heart for love," Jean said, turning her face away. She could not freely move as an invisible desk behind her pressed against the back of her legs and mid waist.

Jared held Jean's face, gently swung it to face him, and softly said, "Make some."

Jean smelled Jared's minty fresh breath and felt his soft hand on her cheek. She found it very pleasing. He moved in closer, pressing his strong firm lips on hers. Jean lost herself. They kissed and embraced passionately.

Jean's heart pounded with excitement and confusion. She suddenly broke their embrace and pushed Jared away from her.

"That's the last time your illusion will kiss me," Jean said with anger, knowing he was playing with her.

Jared backed off and in an instant, everything in the hangar returned to normal—with the buildings iced up and Natasha frozen on the ground.

"It was no illusion, Jean. It's your call to kill me and my sister now, or let us get back to work."

Jean looked at Jared. She still doubted if he was telling the truth about the illusion. She still felt warm all over and she could still taste Jared's kiss in her mouth. For some reason, the chance to get Jared back for all of the things he did to her was not important anymore for some reason.

"You already have two strikes, Jared. Don't get another." Jean walked away as Natasha slowly regained consciousness.

Jared smiled with relief and joy as Jean left. He knew he had struck a nerve she didn't know she had. A few minutes later, Natasha sat in her chair with a blanket, shivering and half-blind from being temporarily frozen like an ice cube. "What happened?"

"I took care of Jean. She will let us do our job from now on."

"What did you do to piss her off this time?" Nat said, shivering. She clung tighter to the blanket Jared draped her with.

"I didn't piss her off. In fact, you might say I made her happy—at least for a brief moment." Jared grinned.

Natasha looked at Jared with narrowed eyes. For the first time in her life, she could see happiness and love in her brother's eyes. "You really do love her, don't you?"

Jared smiled and nodded, but deep inside, he worried about his future with Jean. She was a rogue in her own mind and coming to love him might prove deadly for him, his sister, and even to Jean if things went wrong.

Octavian Farm, Master House

It was early morning in the Octavian Farm as Richard called Susan on the intercom to come up to the main kitchen. He looked at the farm's financial earnings with joy as the farm earned a substantial amount of untaxed income with an addition to the stallion population in the past three months. He knew he didn't need the increase in income to continue the business or the group's crime-fighting expenses, but it felt good having a business working out better than expected. There were very few people still up and Richard liked it that way for what he was about to do.

Besides Susan and the gang downstairs, Dilinger was the only person out and about checking the perimeter's motion and ultraviolet sensors. Richard wondered what other people were doing around the world at about this time. There were so many people, so many stories, and so little time to experience them all. Life to him was a cycle of experiences, good and bad. The good being time spent with friends and loved ones; the bad being having to survive in the world all alone. He took a deep breath and set aside the paperwork before him.

Susan walked in from the living room. "What's up, Richard?"

"I talked to Max about thirty minutes ago," Richard sighed. "We have a problem."

Susan sat across him. "What did he say?" She wondered why he was talking only to her and not to the entire group.

Richard looked into Susan's eyes. "Someone tried to kill Liz."

"What?" Susan jolted over the news. "Is she alright?"

"Yes, she's fine. The problem is that the assassin named you as the mastermind behind the attempt."

Susan's surprised expression changed dramatically into a stern look of disbelief. "And you believe this lie?"

"No. What I believe does not matter. What we can prove is another thing."

"What do you mean, what we can prove?"

"Susan, there is no motive for you to harm Liz. She is your best friend and even though we have known each other for only a little over a year, you are a part of my family. I will not go around your back to find out the truth, which is why I am talking to you now. You are one of my very best friends and I will never lie to you, so I hope you don't take this the wrong way. If for some unknown reason you were involved, then I'm putting everyone in danger. But it is a risk I will take because you are my friend, so if you're not involved then I cannot let you be restricted if we are going to fight Ego. As you can guess, it would be a conflict of interest to get you involved by having you talk to the assassin since you have mental powers and are the primary suspect. But I have found another way."

"What other way?"

Richard looked at her brilliant brown eyes. "You have to leave and run away."

Susan stared at Richard with disbelief. "If I run away, everyone would think I'm guilty."

"Yes, and the people who framed you would think they succeeded. I would know you didn't run away because you were guilty. It might be the break we're looking for if you look at it from a strategic point of view. I have my doubts about Mark. He has changed since the last time we were together and I didn't let you scan him because Ego seems to be one step ahead of us since Erica went haywire. For all I know, Nowhereman is masterminding everything and the only one I can trust are you, John, Larcis, and Cindy."

Susan looked at Richard with concern. "You have always been an excellent tactician, but what if someone gets hurt trying to capture me?"

Richard smiled. "The people who framed you will probably try to get to you so you don't clear your name. If anyone gets hurt, it will probably be them. In the meantime, I need you to look deep into Mark's history and find out what he has been up to these past few months."

"Why do you doubt Mark so much?"

"Call it my gut feeling, but Mark said he had been analyzing the Killer Virus for some time, which means he must have found out what it was in a span of six hours. That is not including moving around and talking to me, which means he had less than four hours of working time on the problem. He is the best, but he's not that good. I think he knew about the virus before it even went out on the Net, so it leads me to believe he is involved somehow, but to what degree I don't know," Richard explained. "You can start searching at the hotel I picked Mark up from. Hopefully, you can get a good lead into what is going on or will happen in the future."

Susan contemplated the entire situation carefully. "What about John? We will both die if we are separated for longer than three weeks."

"Yes, I know. You will have to get with John right now and stabilize your cells. Hopefully, everything will be fixed in one or two weeks."

"What about Liz?"

"Once you leave, I will be able to get John near the assassin and dig for the truth. If John thinks you are running for real, I will be able to get him near the assassin. Max will probably believe what John tells us when he finds out what is in the assassin's mind. And, Liz will be safe with the SIA, I'm sure of that."

"I hope you're right."

"Yeah, well, right now, hope is all we have. You better go and take some cash from the office safe since the ATM is probably not working. You can call me on the landline once you find something concrete."

"Thank you for believing in me," Susan said softly.

"That's what friends do. Just remember to take care of yourself." Richard smiled as he stood up, patted Susan on the shoulder with his hand, and then went downstairs.

Susan said nothing and waited for a moment in her chair thinking about her mission. Her powers had grown exponentially with very few side effects. She was ironically best suited for the task and somehow Richard knew this even though he did not know the full extent of her powers. She felt uneasy about having to leave her friends even if it was only for a short period. She drank a cold glass of water and headed straight for her room where John slept.

Richard waited until late morning to tell Max about Susan's disappearance. Max took it quite well considering the circumstances, leaving Richard to take all responsibility for the escape. His hands were tied in the matter, alerting all law enforcement agencies across the country to look out for Pandora and reporting it immediately to the SIA. Richard knew Max would have no choice to respond in such a manner, so he gathered the team together in the master living room shortly afterwards.

"Before I start, what is Mark doing right now?" Richard asked Larcis who had been in the Battle Room with him.

"He is still trying to figure out what is wrong with Erica."

"Has he gotten the security system online?"

"No, I don't think so," Larcis said with doubt.

"Hmm… Okay, I know this will be hard for all of you to hear, but we have a major problem. Max called me last night and told me Liz was almost killed by an assassin."

"What?" John and Larcis replied with surprise.

"What happened?" Larcis added.

"One of the agents guarding her was made to believe he was killing the person responsible for murdering his wife. Luckily, the attempt failed and Liz is alright."

'You said he was made to believe. Do you mean the guard was tricked into it?' John asked.

"Yes. The problem is that SIA telepaths scanned the assassin and they are saying Susan was responsible for his condition."

'What the hell are you saying?' John said in complete disbelief.

"That can't be?" Larcis added.

"I talked to Susan last night and told her about the failed assassination, but not about her being named as the prime suspect. Now, she is gone." Richard looked at his two friends and Cindy closely.

John looked down thinking about the last time he saw Susan, knowing Susan would not be found if she didn't want to be found, so a search for Susan was not an option. *'This can't be true, Richard. I want to see this assassin and get to the truth.'*

Richard watched Larcis and Cindy both nod their heads, affirming John's demand.

"I wouldn't have it any other way, John," Richard finally said with a solemn face. Richard left Larcis and Cindy with Mark as he and John quickly prepared to take a trip up to New York.

SIA Medical Care Center

Three hours later, Richard and John approached the center as Creator and Mindseye. SIA helicopters intercepted their flight path, escorting them to the VIP helipad. They landed and were greeted by the officer-in-charge of outside security. "Sir, the Director said you would be visiting. Please follow me."

Richard and John followed the officer along with four other fully-armored guards carrying plasma rifles. Richard smiled as he eyed the rifles, remembering how Larcis used one of them to disintegrate a city block in San Francisco. The old memories quickly turned into memories of meeting Elizabeth for the first time. It was an unexpected encounter right after the thermo-plasma rifle explosion killing a platoon size mob of criminals. Concern and anticipation filled his heart as he saw Maximilian inside the lobby entrance.

"How are you Creator, Mindseye?" Max shook their hands.

"Where is she?" Richard replied.

"You were never big on small talk. This way," Max commented with a straight face and headed straight to the elevator.

Max, Richard, John, and three guards entered the elevator and went down into the secure levels.

"Elizabeth is starting to respond to sonic therapy. The doctors say she should be coming to within the next three days," Max said once the elevator was in motion.

"How's my son?" Richard said, relieved.

"His vitals are strong. Of course, he takes after his father."

"That's good. What about the agent who tried to kill them?"

"Lt. Harper is being held under observation in the brig."

'Have your telepaths been able to find any more information from him?' John said for the first time since he arrived.

"No." The doors opened and they stepped out into a long hallway. "They have probed as far back as five years and found nothing else.

They quickly reached Liz's room and went through the same security procedures as any of the personnel entering or leaving the room.

Richard came to Liz's side and grasped her limp hand, caressing it gently. He stood there for a minute and kissed her on the cheek. "How was Lt. Harper stopped?"

"Cpt. Middleton was on watch. Lt. Harper knocked out the nurses and sealed off the room Elizabeth was in and then tried to inject her with poison through the intravenous tubes. Cpt. Middleton was able to shoot through the armored wall and hit Lt. Harper before he could push this button," Max explained as he pointed to the control panel next to Liz's bed.

Richard scanned the room with his en-ray vision, noticing the eight-inch armored door and two-inch armored double-sided walls. *Middleton must have been an expert shot, being able to shoot through two inches of armor, five inches of insulation, and then another two inches of armor calculating the trajectory of the round at different angles and speeds as it hit different surfaces,* Richard thought. "That must have been some shot."

"It was the luckiest shot I ever made, sir," Cpt. Middleton said from behind John.

Richard turned around. Cpt. Middleton wore full body armor and was carrying a modified assault rifle. All of the guards in the room carried the same futuristic rifle. "Cpt. Middleton, I assume." Richard extended his hand.

Cpt. Middleton shook Richard's hand. "Brad Middleton."

"Thank you for saving my wife."

"It was not her time to leave you," Middleton modestly replied.

Richard smiled. He liked Cpt. Middleton right away, a feat most people failed to do when measuring up to his expectations in first impressions. "Max, can we go see Lt. Harper?" Richard said after shaking Middleton's hand.

Max looked at Richard, then at John. "I don't think that will be a good idea."

"Max, Susan is gone. I can trust John with my life. He is the only one we know besides Susan who can confirm the information in Harper's head. Please let him try."

Max thought about the possible consequences for a minute, looking at the floor and walking around the room. He finally turned to the captain. "Cpt. Middleton, take Creator and his companion to the brig and question the prisoner."

Cpt. Middleton looked at Max and nodded. "Yes, sir."

Cpt. Middleton took Richard and John to the brig without an escort. The guards awaited the three men and skipped the security check as ordered by Max through command central before Cpt. Middleton's arrival.

They entered the cell with Cpt. Middleton positioning himself just inside the doorway. Richard and John walked toward the now frightened lieutenant, standing up from his metallic bunk frame and mattress. "Creator, I swear I didn't know it was all a lie."

"Calm down, I know," Richard said.

"I need to know who messed with your head, which is why Mindseye is here. He will find out what the telepaths couldn't, alright?"

Harper looked at John wearing his black and red outfit and he felt even greater fear of the two men who had every reason to do him harm. "Mindseye."

Seeing the man who attempted to murder Liz made John so angry, but when he saw genuine fear in the lieutenant's eyes, he calmed himself down. He realized this was a puppet, nothing more, nothing less. Just a puppet who was used to try and kill Liz and frame Susan at the same time.

'It's going to be alright, Lieutenant. I need you to sit down and relax. Can you do that?' John asked.

Harper nodded and relaxed just enough to stop shaking. Cpt. Middleton's presence actually helped him calm down. Cpt.

Middleton was highly respected among the field agents and guards for his true sense of justice and honor. He would not allow anything bad happen to him.

John sat next to Harper and concentrated, willing his cosmic energy into his telepathic abilities. It didn't take very long for him to see what the telepaths were talking about. His make-believe wife and history was a simple implant, which seemed real enough for him to commit the crime. He diverted his attention to where he got hold of the poison. He saw Susan, dressed like an SIA nurse, giving Lt. Harper the poison prior to seeing Elizabeth.

"Lieutenant, you will need this," she said, but her voice didn't sound like Susan's. The telepaths wouldn't know the specifics of Susan's voice, but he did and knew it was someone else behind the face. He dug deeper into the image and broke the mental implant of Susan's face, revealing the face of another brunette in her early twenties. He instantly memorized her facial features and continued further into Harper's past. Images instantly sped through his mind, but he ignored the many images of the lieutenant's everyday life until another image of Susan appeared while Harper sat in a mall eatery.

Susan approached him and sat with him at the table. She was direct and to the point, saying she knew who murdered his wife and gave him details about what happened and who was responsible. John could hardly believe the memories, as Susan's voice this time was hers. He concentrated harder, trying to break any implants in her voice and image. It was no implant, Lt. Harper did indeed see and hear Susan who suggested he take his revenge while he had the chance.

How? Why? John was very confused and wondered if he had made any implants stronger by probing deeper and harder than the SIA telepaths did. John thought about that possibility, but rejected it when he saw that the telepaths had dug deep into Harper's life and left it open for further probes, also leaving a mess which annoyed him as his moral respect for other people's thoughts and privacy came to the top of his list of do's and don'ts.

He started from the beginning and played back everything in extreme slow motion. He memorized every minute detail of where Harper was at the time of the encounter, the encounter itself, and everything shortly afterwards—things said, seen, gestured, heard, tasted, and felt by the lieutenant. He probed back to the first sign of a time and date and past the event until he saw Harper check his watch on both appearances by Susan and Susan's illusion.

Richard stood patiently by John's side, watching Cpt. Middleton with the corner of his eye. Both men sitting on the bunk seemed motionless, like statues, but every now and then one would move a finger slightly or an eyelid would quickly blink. Richard was used to this and paid little attention to the two men and concentrated on Cpt. Middleton. Middleton reminded him of an old friend in the CIA. His former trainer and mentor, who died tragically in a helicopter accident just outside of Berlin twenty-five years ago. Perhaps he would have the opportunity to talk to him later on a more social basis than a professional one. Thirty minutes elapsed before John and Lt. Harper opened their eyes, indicating the end of the probe. Harper felt very weak and slowly laid down as John stood up.

'Captain, Lt. Harper is innocent and should be taken to a normal room where he can get some rest. I have fixed what the telepaths messed up in there. He knows everything that happened to him now and should be given a week of rest before letting him go back on duty. I also need to see all of the nurses who work in this center, right now,' John said with authority.

"I'll tell the Director," Middleton replied.

"No, I'll talk to him," Richard said. "In the meantime, take Mindseye and show him your files on the nurses."

"Yes, sir," Middleton said and motioned John to follow him.

Richard walked with the two men in the general direction of Liz's room. He assumed John found out some bad news about Susan, otherwise John would have told him after scanning Lt. Harper. "Mindseye, let me know what you find out when you check out the nurses?" Richard said as he peeled off toward another hallway.

John looked in Richard's direction. 'I will, Richard,' John replied. Even though the evidence so far was totally weighing against Susan, there were too many other idiosyncrasies on how and why the implants were put in Harper's mind that didn't make sense to the trained eye. John was thankful for Richard's patience and tried to meditate on being impartial with the investigation.

Cpt. Middleton took John straight to the center's administration room and ordered the staff to supply John with the digital files of all the nurses working in the center.

Richard found Max and told him about Lt. Harper's situation, strongly urging him to release the lieutenant under a watchful eye during his recovery, while John viewed the data files.

Max agreed to put Lt. Harper in house arrest and move him to a barracks room. Richard was satisfied knowing John's wishes were going to be met. He and Max immediately went to join Cpt. Middleton and John in the administration office.

John quickly recognized the nurse who handed Lt. Harper the poison. Heather Fritchman worked in the pharmacy. She was single, worked extra hours, and aspired to become a head nurse. Her file revealed no adverse information in her present or past work behavior. *'Where is Nurse Fritchman?'* John asked one of the staff members.

"Sir, she should be in the pharmacy right now. Do you want me to call her to come here?"

'No, I'll go see her myself. Don't inform her, I'm going to see her,' John instructed.

"Yes, sir," the staff member replied as Cpt. Middleton guided John to the pharmacy.

Richard and Max met the two men just outside of the admin office and all four men headed to the pharmacy.

"What have you found out, so far?" Max asked as they walked.

'I'm not sure right now, but Nurse Fritchman is the person who gave Lt. Harper the poison, not Susan. If I'm right, she was probably deceived as well,' John said. He intentionally omitted

talking about Susan's appearance in the mall.

"Ahh, I see," Max replied and left it at that, seeing his telepaths had not gotten this far into the investigation. He knew that his telepaths were not as strong as some of the telepaths out in the public and it comforted him a little to know John was one of those powerful telepaths working on his side.

"Cpt. Middleton, what exactly happened during the assassination attempt?" Richard asked, changing the subject, but he was more curious now that more people were involved. Perhaps the assassination attempt was in fact just that and Susan's situation was the intended result. Cpt. Middleton told the group every detail once the guards arrived with the nurses until they apprehended Lt. Harper.

The confusion regarding the discrepancies stuck out like a sore thumb but only brought up more questions. Richard once again had his usual gut feeling and was convinced someone wanted Lt. Harper to be found out early on—but why?

John quickly scanned Nurse Fritchman's mind after arriving at the pharmacy. Her implant was simple, making her believe she was giving Lt. Harper a protein booster instead of poison. The person who placed the implant must have seen her not too long ago, so John dug into her past looking for Susan or some unfamiliar face she had encountered in the past week. There were no images of Susan, but he memorized the entire week making note of all of the people she encountered or saw.

John took a very deep breath and walked out of the pharmacy after scanning Heather's mind. The group followed, waiting for John to tell them what he found out. *'Max, I will need a day to go over the images,'* John said.

Max had hoped for better news, but granted John's request. "Alright, John, you have one day. In the meantime, I will have my men keep looking for Pandora."

'Fair enough,' John replied.

"Okay, it's time to go. Thank you, Max," Richard said.

"Take care and I will call you tomorrow." Max left them to find their way out of the center with Cpt. Middleton. It wasn't long before Cpt. Middleton's escort duties ended at the main entrance with the two superheroes.

"Thank you, Cpt. Middleton." Richard bid him farewell.

"Anytime, sir."

Richard and John took off into the sky back to the Eternal Domain.

Mountain Starship Dock, Bogotá, Colombia

The Andromeda's conference room normally seated fifteen personnel, but only six seats were being occupied today. Four special operations security guards stood by the entrance and two guards behind Councilman Eduardo Ramirez. The guards wore full dark green body armor and carried modified sniper rifles, a modified 9-mm pistol, and a tubular handheld object attached to their sides. It resembled a light saber in a *Star Wars* movie, but was capped with a shiny metallic dome on the end. Their armored suits were leaner and seemed weaker than the SIA suits, but in fact were much tougher and allowed the wearer to move all of their limbs freely, giving them much more agility than any SIA body suit.

"The silos will be complete in twelve hours. We will use them as a last resort if anyone starts lobbing nukes. In the meantime, I want everyone to know what is going on. We don't need our citizens to be in the dark if the fate of the Earth is at risk," Councilman Eduardo Ramirez said.

"I know we have the best counterespionage system in place, but what if word gets out that we can neutralize all nuclear delivery systems on the planet?" Councilman Jose Begestano said, a little worried.

"It won't matter by then. It will be an arms race after that and we will be able to enforce any military decision over any country or groups of countries," Councilman Diego Gonzalez said.

"It's not a matter of military force, it's a matter of timing," Estabon said. "The more time we have, the better chance we will have in minimizing casualties."

"Okay, like I was saying, we will use the silos as a last resort. The virus needs to be neutralized first and if we have to, we will take care of it. I really don't want to do that because it will expose us and we might be blamed for it, giving our enemies a reason to start a war with us. So gentlemen—what other options do we have available?" Eduardo asked.

"We can get someone else to take care of the virus with the use of our technology?" Councilman Andrez Pobles suggested.

"Who can we trust to use it if we can't?" Councilman Gonzalez asked.

"EFL's computer is dead in the water," Estabon said. "The Emerald Legion is a wildcard. The SIA is out of the question. The only other option is the Eternal Champions."

"We don't know that much about them," Councilman Begestano said.

"No, but Commander Javier has found out that their SAI has not been infected by the Killer Virus," Estabon countered. "The problem is that their SAI is off-line due to a separate virus and may not be able to destroy the Killer Virus at this time. The good thing is Creator, the leader of the group, has a good reputation and can be trusted."

"What about the rest of the group?" Councilman Gonzalez asked.

"They are loyal to Creator. However, I think it would be wise to give them just enough technology to get rid of the virus, no more," Estabon suggested.

"I assume we have been monitoring their activities," Eduardo asked.

"I've had the ship's cyber team on them ever since the virus hit," Commander Javier said.

"There is one more thing," Estabon snapped. "Australia

has been hit by the virus as well, but they seem to be in better shape than the other countries. I think their technology is comparable to ours. It wouldn't surprise me if they are behind this virus attack."

"We will deal with them later, but I think we need to recall our two agents before they are compromised. Australia is becoming better at finding spies. The longer we keep our agents there, the more we keep them at risk," Eduardo said.

"Consider it done," Estabon said.

"Are there any more options?"

"Sir, we could do nothing but hope that the Eternal Champions fix the problem." Commander Javier sighed.

The council members thought in silence for a moment.

Eduardo broke the silence. "We could, but I want to be able to nudge them in the right direction. We have to make some type of contact so we can monitor their progress. If anything, it might be to our advantage in the future if they can help our cause by helping them now."

"The only way we can do that is through the SIA's communication system, since the Internet is down," Estabon said.

"Okay, let's try that first, but be ready to use the parabolic lasers to communicate directly with them. In the meantime, we need to go to our wartime positions in case everything goes wrong, so don't waste any time once we leave here. Let me know what happens with the Eternal Champions by updating me every two hours." Eduardo paused for a second as if in thought. Then he got up from his chair. "It seems the world will be relying on them to keep the peace. May God be with them."

Estabon nodded and stood alongside his older brother.

All of the men stood up and went about their business, except for Commander Javier, who pulled Estabon aside.

"Sir, I know this is unusual, but why was I allowed to be in this meeting?" Javier asked.

Estabon smiled. "It's not unusual for a captain to be in his own conference room during a meeting."

"Sir?" There was both confusion and surprise on Javier's face.

"I hope you don't mind me stepping down as captain of this ship, but I have other things to attend to and I know she will be cared for in your good hands." Estabon patted Javier's shoulder with his hand as he talked.

Javier beamed and was speechless for a moment. He was being promoted as captain of the Andromeda, which was the highest honor any captain could ever have. "I won't let you down, sir."

Sixteen hundred meters from aft to stern made the Andromeda the largest and most powerful starship ever created by mankind. Its long triangular design and revolutionary propulsion system would allow it to leave the Earth's atmosphere once it was fully operational. Unfortunately, it was the most vulnerable piece of military hardware ever created as it sat in a hollowed out mountain launch pad waiting to be launched into space. The saving grace of the entire fleets' vulnerability was covered up by technology and secrecy by use of telepaths and country wide consensus to something greater for the country and the world.

Chapter Ten

□ □ □ □ □

EGO

Kansas City Zoo

The Sun's rays glimmered through the Plexiglas dome, warming up the controlled environment. The fall months were cold and usually attracted few customers to the zoo, but David was happy knowing there was always work to be done. He strongly believed in honest labor and was happiest when the hardest jobs were assigned to him. Some of the other janitors thought he was a little loony, but his best friend Chris knew he was simply a happy person. However, Chris sometimes wondered if David was trying to work his way up to heaven, never giving up and always being grateful for being alive. It didn't really matter though, because David was willing to cover for Chris during the holidays and was always there when he needed help with work or his personal life. Yes, David was the model friend and employee any employer or friend would want by their side. Dr. Wilkins or Pamela was off that day but had come to work early that morning to see David before the main body of employees punched into work.

"How are you today, Doctor?" David asked as Pamela entered the sanctuary.

"I feel great!" Pamela said, beaming. "You wouldn't believe what happened last night after I got home?"

"You went to sleep?" David said with a dumbfounded grin.

"No, silly." Pamela chuckled. She reached into her jacket pocket and pulled out a copy of a lottery ticket. "Horace and I won 60,000 dollars." Pamela happily smiled exposing two rows of beautiful white teeth.

"That's wonderful," David said. "What are you going to do with the money?"

"Oh, we are going to pay our bills, including paying off one of the cars, and then we're going to Disney World."

"Sounds like a good plan. I'm happy for you, Pam. I guess you won't be needing that babysitter after all."

"Well, we won't be able to get the money for at least a week and Horace will be finishing his case in about two weeks. This virus thing is also putting a damper on things, but you know what? We are going out to dinner tomorrow night and we do need a sitter. I know it's on short notice, but I would appreciate it very much if you could sit for us."

"I'm your sitter," David said gladly.

"Good, here is the house number and address." Pamela handed David a piece of paper with the information. "Can you be there by six?"

"Sure, but you never told me how you and Horace are doing?" David asked, putting the paper in his pocket.

Pamela smiled. "We talked for two hours last night. It was great being able to talk to him like we used to when we first met…Thank you, David, for the advice and encouragement."

"You're welcome."

"I have to go and tell my boss about the ticket. Are you sure you can make it to the house by six?" Pam asked. She knew David usually worked past closing.

David smiled unconcerned. "Don't worry. I will get all my work done before three and leave early to make sure I get there by six."

"Okay." Pam smiled. "Sorry we can't talk longer but I have a list of errands to take care of today and tomorrow. See you tomorrow night!" She bid David farewell waving as she left the sanctuary.

David looked around as if making sure the coast was clear. A faint voice echoed in his mind.

It was not the voice he was familiar with, but nonetheless, he knew who it was. He closed his eyes and his life force moved to another dimension beyond reality itself. It was time he found out who was causing a disturbance in the fabric of time and space.

Visions of city streets, buildings, parks, monuments, and people from all sorts of life raced through Elizabeth's mind. The visions flashed in and out like an endless strobe light in a disco club dance floor. Some visions had scenes of ruins, while others depicted everyday lives of people in a city. Most of the visions were unidentifiable to her, but there were some visions where she could make out prominent landmarks like the Lincoln Memorial and the Hollywood sign. Her entire body felt numb and heavy as the visions faded away into complete darkness.

Elizabeth drowsily opened her eyes and saw the paneled ceiling of an office. The lights were off, but dim light coming from the office window allowed her to see the small holes of the white cork panels on the ceiling. She slowly stood up from the carpeted floor and looked around. She was not in an office; it was an empty conference room. She looked outside through the long plate glass window. She could see the entire city from her vantage point but couldn't make out any prominent buildings or land features. *It's a very large city, but where exactly am I?* Liz thought.

Dark clouds overhead kept direct sunlight from shining on the city as smoke and burning fires scattered all over the city and dampened the city's beauty. "What happened? Is this another dream?" Liz asked herself as she walked up to the window and looked down.

She was in a high-rise building. The streets below were desolate of people with trash and abandoned cars everywhere. *Not again. What's going on?* Liz thought, wondering what the vision meant.

She felt very weak with her muscles aching as she moved toward the conference room exit door. She stopped at a light switch short of the exit and flipped the switch, but the electricity seemed to be out with the lights not responding. She slowly walked through the exit door and entered a hallway stopping suddenly in her tracks. A very faint sound could be heard in the distance. She felt a presence but it was not in the room. It was everywhere around her. It didn't feel threatening or evil, but it was definitely an invisible presence, like someone was spying on her every move. She cautiously walked toward the incoherent noise and came to a spiral stairway leading to the sky lounge. The noise became clearer, which sounded like a television news report. She went up the stairs quietly and stopped short of the few last stairs and heard a man's laughing voice. She slowly continued up, making the last curve of the stairway and seeing a man in a black cashmere overcoat sitting on a plush leather chair facing the window. The man was watching a television set. Nothing else was in the lounge except the man, his chair, and the television set.

"Oh, YES! YES! That's beautiful!" The man shouted in delight and laughed. "It's great!" His very heavy and sinister voice froze Liz on her tracks. She could barely see the television, but it was obvious the man was viewing some type of explosion—or explosions.

She overcame her fear and walked quietly toward the man, stopping just behind him. The television was undeniably showing scenes of nuclear explosions and mass chaos all over the world.

'Could this be real?' Liz thought, trying to remember the

last time she had such a real vision. This was the second time; yes, she was sure of that. The problem was she never actually felt or interacted with her visions until the last one—and now this one.

The man rolled his chair sideways, positioning himself in front of the wide window beside the television. "Here it comes." He drunkenly giggled.

Liz's eyes once again widened with fright as a flash of light temporarily blocked out the city view, and then a mushroom cloud appeared in the distance. She looked away, wondering why the light didn't blind her; surely the light had reached her before she turned away.

"I've WON! I've WON!" The man jumped up triumphantly, laughing.

The shockwave enveloped the entire city, bypassing the building they were in. The flame and wind destroyed everything in sight as Liz watched in horror the massive destruction. However, there was no terrifying noise from the explosion; there was no force shattering the building they were in. The man or thing in front of her must be somehow protecting the building. The man spun around with a victory dance, but stopped suddenly, facing the window. The man stopped laughing and looked carefully at the reflection of Elizabeth's figure on the window's glass.

He swung around and faced her. "You! What are you doing here?" the man shouted in surprise.

Liz stepped back a little confused, noticing fear in his voice. *How could he see her?* she thought, thinking she was seeing a precognitive vision from a third-person perspective.

The man took a few steps toward her, staring at her very closely with his dark red eyes. His frightened, twitching face showed relief as he smiled, uncovering black and gray sharp wolf-like teeth. "Wait, you're not her."

The second shockwave returned back toward the origin of the explosion, bringing with it tremendous amounts of debris from buildings, houses, cars, boats, trees, and even aircraft that was passing the building they were in. Liz saw the wave return like a gigantic ocean wave of devastation ebbing back to its creator. "Who are you?" Liz asked calmly.

The man sneered. "You pathetic human. I'm the beginning and the end of your worthless lives. Your doom!"

Liz braced herself as the man walked toward her. "Do you think you can keep me from killing you?" The man laughed, stopped walking, and gradually transformed into a twelve-foot black and red hideous demon.

Liz could feel the goose bumps as she stood there frozen in fear; maybe more out of hopelessness than fear. Things were racing through her mind. *What can I do?*

She closed her eyes and concentrated on communicating with Richard, at the same time increasing the strength of her energy force field around her body. She bent down as if going for a jump shot and flew straight up into the ceiling, her eyes closed, fists clenched, and arms extended out in front of her.

The beast charged at her but narrowly missed her as Liz flew up through two floors out into the clouds above. Liz held her breath and continued flying as fast as she could into the sky, ignoring the sound of the wind and the sandy texture of the dust and wet clouds.

She suddenly felt a peaceful presence. It was all around her, like someone was hugging her with a blanket of warmth. She opened her eyes and saw the darkness of the heavy clouds passing rapidly by her from the sky toward the ground, but she saw no one. The presence comforted her as if preparing her for what was about to happen next.

Her whole body surged with pain as she started to fade away from reality and floated into emptiness. She called out to Richard and heard her own voice respond back as the environment changed. She felt the cozy warmth of a bed and a pinch in her arm, then the sound of a bell. She had trouble opening her eyes but managed to slowly blink away the heaviness. The white ceiling and bright light resembled those of a hospital, but a voice blaring on the intercom confirmed it. She heard a man's excited voice. "Sir, she's awake!"

Liz tried to turn to see who was speaking, but her neck muscles wouldn't respond.

An African-American gentleman wearing an armored suit came to Liz and looked over her with his helmet off. "Welcome back, Elizabeth." Cpt. Middleton smiled.

Liz saw the SIA emblem on his uniform and realized the SIA somehow was now caring for her. She didn't care too much for the SIA, but was happy to see the shiny emblem. "Richard." She could barely say her husband's name.

Richard? Cpt. Middleton thought. *It must be Creator's real name. Hmm. That's another thing the telepaths will have to wipe out from mine and my men's memory. But it's good to know Creator's real name while it lasts.*

"I'll call him and get him here right away, Ma'am. Get some rest in the meantime." Cpt. Middleton radioed Max on the comlink and informed him of the good news.

Holiday Inn, Nashville, Tennessee

Susan flew silently toward the hotel, but then stopped in mid-air a hundred meters from the structure. Her special sense of a presence kept her from getting closer to her objective. She landed on the top of an adjacent building and scanned the area with her mind. The scan stopped at two spies at the building she was standing on, looking into Mark's room with high-speed surveillance equipment.

She looked into their minds. They were SIA agents with the mission of keeping an eye out for Mark. They had only been there for six hours, which meant they missed Richard's visit and Mark's departure. They didn't know why the SIA was interested in Mark; only that he was to be picked up for questioning as soon as he came back to his room.

Richard's hunch must have been right, but it seemed odd that Mark was involved with the SIA. Maybe they wanted him to see if he could fix their computer problems, or maybe not, Susan thought.

She specifically concentrated on their minds and put them both into deep sleep. She put the hood of her coat over her head and flew through Mark's window, unlocking it with a telekinetic flip of the latch, landing in front of the bed.

Susan slowly walked through Mark's empty hotel room, carefully looking for any evidence of other people who might have stayed or visited him. Unfortunately, someone had already gone through his room but tried not to leave evidence of their visit. The minute heat and ultraviolet trails left probably by SIA agents were not erased before they left the room a few hours ago. After searching the entire room inch by inch, she came to the conclusion that Mark had been alone. Susan stared around the room for a very long time, thinking about Mark and how he lived his life in the apartment. The room seemed so isolated with despair as she felt his pain and enjoyment on a laptop in the small confined area with Jack as his only true friend. It was a hacker's dream and life, stuck to a computer for endless hours on end.

What were you up to? Susan thought, running scenarios over and over in her head.

Her feminine intuition told her he was up to no good, but her investigative nature told her nothing but loneliness. The loneliness of a man trying to find himself in life by working as a simple computer consultant and passing time with a digitized companion. In a way, she was happy Richard found Mark, giving him another chance to use his unique skills and possibly fulfill his dreams. Richard was good at bringing out the best in people, and Susan maybe believed too much in his abilities that she ignored the possibility that Mark would take advantage of Richard's friendship and kindness. Susan left the room along with her feelings as she focused on being impartial.

She proceeded downstairs to see the hotel clerks and scanned their minds. Mark had checked in two weeks ago. He was alone and was seen only three times outside his room in the two weeks he stayed there. She mentally ordered one of the clerks to print out all of the telephone calls Mark made during his stay. She wiped everyone's memory of her existence as she walked out of the building and read the phone list.

She waved down a taxi shortly afterwards and had the driver take her to the Southern Bell telephone center that services the area. It started to snow as the taxi arrived at the telephone company's office. Susan entered the office just before closing time and mentally controlled the counter attendants to print out a listing by name of all of the numbers Mark called from his room. Most were food delivery outlets with a few calls to a mobile Internet provider. So far, Susan's investigation showed nothing out of the ordinary. No numbers to individual homes or businesses. The only thing now was to find out what Mark was surfing for on the Net and that would be almost impossible to get unless she had access to Jack.

The last stop was at the public library, which was closed due to the virus. She finally went to a nearby hotel and got a room for some needed rest. She was feeling a little tense being away from John. Her cells were stable for now, but she felt a craving to fuse with John even though she didn't need to. She wondered what was going on with her fugitive status and tried to focus on the mission. She laid down and turned on the television, which picked up only the emergency channel broadcast. The broadcast instructed people to stay calm and gave directions on how to contact emergency assistance in the local area. She turned off the television and decided to take a nap for a minute. She then called Richard after she was able to get to a computer.

The nap lasted for hours; she woke up in the middle of the night. The long hours at ED must have worn her down, or at least she thought. She sprang out of bed and turned on the television again. The screen was full of static with none of the channels working. Susan turned off the television and sat on the side of the bed thinking hard about what Mark was doing here in Nashville.

He said he was working as a consultant but the people that interacted with him in the past several weeks weren't companies or people in need of a professional computer consultant. "What were you doing here?" She asked herself out loud. "What?"

Susan stared at the blank television screen as she tried to come up with ideas. She got up and found a pen and paper on the nightstand and started writing down things as they popped up in her head. The brainstorming session took thirty minutes but resulted to nothing more than a dozen key words and phrases.

(Tennessee, hotel, Jack, virus, waiting around, vegetating, virus, Richard's old friend, computer expert, no history, no past, job but no real evidence of a job, why did Richard not trust him, Ego, Erica, other SAIs, World Wide Web, SIA involvement, very cooperative, not scared of superhumans and who else did Mark know?)

She put the list down and took a quick shower as the words and phrases bounced around in her mind. She finished showering and decided to break into the police station and find out what she could know about Mark's past. It would be a minor risk if she were spotted by the authorities, especially if Mark didn't have a record, but it was a risk she would have to take in order to get some answers.

Fort Belvior, Virginia

An encrypted message came over a secure satellite communication relay station. The message alert rang, attracting Jared's attention.

The message read:

[Pandora has gone into hiding. The SIA has posted an APB for her capture. Authorities have been instructed to avoid an encounter and report whereabouts to the SIA immediately. Killer Virus has caused SIA to implement Code Level Charlie. All field agents have been recalled for priority missions.]

"I don't believe it worked," Natasha said after reading the message.

"Hmm…I don't think it did," Jared pondered.

"Susan's on the run and every superhero in the country is tied up, including the SIA. We can activate Jane now."

"No. Everyone will be looking for the abnormal. If we do something to attract attention, we won't be able to fully allow

Project Jane to do its mission. Besides, I think you are underestimating the Eternal Champions."

"How so?" Nat squeamishly said.

"Richard is no fool. He wouldn't have let Susan get away so easily. He might want us to think she's on the run hoping we will give ourselves away. Maybe thinking the person who framed her will try to disrupt the group even more."

"So what do you suggest we do?"

"We will leave the group alone and let the SIA spin their wheels. We have another problem we should be worrying about."

"You mean the virus?"

"Yeah...It might be convenient for us right now, but we need the communication structure working for Project Jane to work. Also, it is not a normal virus. We might be missing the picture at the long end of the stick. The United States and the NATO countries are very vulnerable to attack from other countries. A war might break out very soon while we play around with Jane. I think we need to consider other plans and convince Jean to take a better course of action."

"Like what?" Nat was getting impatient. She had put a lot of work into Project Jane.

"A backup plan to get Creator or the SIA in the hot seat, if things stabilize in the near future."

"Framing Richard will be easier than SIA?"

"Maybe, but I have a feeling the SIA has cobwebs in their attic and it's time we looked up there. But I will have to talk to my old contacts. The job will have to be done by someone better suited for this task other than us."

"You know that by framing Richard or SIA, we will open ourselves up to them?" Nat said. Jared's plan would force them to rely on other people to keep their secret identities and autonomy.

"It's a risk we will have to take, but I won't take it unless you agree to it."

Nat thought carefully by taking Jean into account. The risk would probably be worth it if it meant the possibility of getting Jean out of the picture or at least her iron hold on them forever.

"I'm up for it, but you will have to decide between me or Jean sooner or later." Nat finally said. It was some sort of an ultimatum.

"Don't worry, Sis, it won't come down to that if everything works the way I planned it. It is a matter of timing and trust between us that will keep us both alive."

"I hope you're right, Jared." Nat said, trying to relax and trust her life in her brother's hands.

Chapter Eleven

□ □ ◘ □ □

PAST AND PRESENT

Nashville, Tennessee

A black taxicab stopped one block away from the police station. Susan stepped out of the cab and onto the dirty brown snow wearing a black overcoat. It had stopped snowing, leaving two inches of snow and forming ice on the streets. She paid double the metered fair and the cabby drove off, vaguely remembering having dropped Susan off at that address.

Susan was very careful to hide her tracks and if it meant manipulating the minds of everyone she came in contact with, then she had no reservations in committing what the courts would label as "mental rape."

The police station was quiet; the Killer Virus primarily done very little damage to the county as a whole, which seemed odd as the rest of the country was jumping through hoops as bank accounts disappeared, computer servers crashed, utilities failed to work properly, and mass transportation systems requiring computer systems came to almost a complete halt.

Susan wasn't sure what she was looking for, but hoped Mark had some roots in the area that she could find in the police computer database.

She concentrated on her cosmic powers and duplicated Richard's en-ray vision. She stood across the street opposite from the station and scanned the building.

She could see all of the rooms in the three-story building, making out six human figures occupying the station. One human figure was in one of the ten cells on the first floor, while two others worked in a large office space on the second floor. There were two police officers working at the front desk with a window separating them from the reception area at the main entrance of the station. Another figure was performing janitorial duties on the third floor offices.

She quickly came up with a plan to get to a computer that would serve her purpose and keep the occupants clueless as to her presence.

Susan walked into the station and immediately took control of the two police officers at the front desk. They allowed her access into the building, past the security doors, into the work area, and up to the second floor. They simply thought they were letting in another police officer into the station and instantly forgot ever seeing Susan come into the building.

Susan went upstairs and entered the office in which the two detectives were working on the second floor. Before they could utter a word, she took control of their minds and commanded them to use their own passwords to access the computer database and any other secure databases they could get into across the country. She was lucky these two detectives were working late into the night and made a note to remember their names so she could tell Erica. Erica would be able to track their whereabouts in her matrix database in case they needed help or could help the team in the future.

Susan verbally commanded the detectives to search for any information on Mark's identity, background, and the company he was working for. The search didn't last very long, revealing Mark's track record of two speeding tickets, involvement in a traffic accident, and his three previous addresses: Houston Texas, Los Angeles, and Saint Louis. Mark's driver's license was six months old and that was where the trail ended. His history as an adult disappeared beyond the six months until the end of his military service with Richard. The company Mark was working for as a computer consultant for the past six months was legitimate, but except for the big void of information in Mark's past, everything seemed normal.

Susan had the detectives check Mark's credit history. She personally scrolled through a laundry list of bad credit once the screen came up, but that also only showed the past six months. Mark was $30,000 in debt, mainly from buying automation equipment, with only two payments on two credit cards ever being made.

Mark had no living relatives in the U.S. or friends except Richard. Susan thought about having a talk with people who knew Mark, but talking to his employer would be too time-consuming and would require her to use more of her powers. The more power she used, the more unstable her cells became. Since the SIA was also interested in Mark, going to see his employer would probably be a waste of time and more of a chance of getting found out. The SIA had telepaths and running into two or more them might cause her to use more of her power than she wanted to.

Susan's body was aching with pain as she left the second floor, erasing the past forty-five minutes of memories from the two detectives' minds. She left the station as she entered it and flew back to her hotel room empty-handed. If Mark was working for a secret organization prior to the six months, then the SIA and Erica would be the only ones she knew that could answer that question.

The mystery of Mark's past would have to wait as she quickly laid down on her bed and fell asleep from exhaustion. A few hours later, Susan woke up feeling refreshed. The power was out, which didn't surprise her. She quickly made it to a pay phone outside of the power grid and called Richard about her findings.

To her relief, Richard picked up his personal office phone.

"It's me," Susan said. "I found nothing alarming about Mark except that the SIA is looking for him."

Richard thought for a second. "Come home tonight at seven. I have another plan. Stay safe," Richard said and hung up without waiting for Susan to reply.

Susan didn't tell him if she knew why the SIA was looking for Mark, but was sure she would have if she did know. He thought about calling Max, but how would he ask him? The SIA could be looking for Mark to get his expertise or they could be hunting him down for something else. Richard's gut feeling told him to keep the information to himself and get Mark's side of the story before asking Max.

On the other end of the phone, Susan hung up and planned out a safe route back to ED, lying at tree-top level all the way. The trip would take several hours so she went back to the hotel room, hoping the power was back on. She ordered pizza and listened to music as she ate and waited for the right time to fly home.

Chapter Twelve

□ □ □ □ □

HEROES TO THE RESCUE

The Eternal Domain

R ichard received a call from Max, informing him Liz had regained consciousness. It was past three in the afternoon, which meant Susan would be showing up soon. His gut feeling told him the time was near and things would be very hard to accomplish without his entire team ready to fight.

At the same time, he knew John's presence in the base would not go good if he were not around to explain the situation before they got into an argument and give away Susan's covert mission to Mark or anyone else who could not block against mental probes by Nowhereman or Ego.

Richard took a chance and had John come with him, leaving Larcis and Cindy behind. Susan would know what to do with Larcis and Cindy if he were not around.

As long as John was with him, he would also have a better idea of what John found out on their way back to New York. He only hoped John had been able to piece everything together after having over six hours since the last trip to the SIA Medical Center. The trip would take almost two hours, which would be enough time for him and John to talk while in flight.

Mark was steadfast with his programming while Larcis and Cindy watched. It was not long before they once again got bored of watching and decided to eat dinner. They talked about many things, including Cindy's unique encounter with Glenn. It was a one-sided conversation after Cindy started to talk about Glenn, but Larcis was not one to complain.

Larcis could tell she cared deeply for Glenn, if not loved him, and simply listened to every word. It made him happy to see Cindy so excited about life after hearing her past as a fugitive, always wondering if there were people still after her since the Yimen incident.

Unfortunately, the time to get to know more about Cindy and her love life was cut short as a call came in from the Fort Lauderdale police station reporting that twenty-two fires had erupted in downtown Lauderdale about fifteen minutes ago.

Larcis thought it was odd having received an emergency call this late in the week of cyber chaos, especially with the sudden chain of events happening right after another. All of the law enforcement agencies along with the National Guard and Army Reserve units were deployed in force around the country. Their success in calming the populace and conducting humanitarian relief stemmed from the SIA's strong network of command posts and superhumans coming out to help.

It had been quiet for the past twenty hours, but it was now Larcis and Cindy who by default were on-call with everyone else gone.

Larcis and Cindy left the Eternal Domain in costume. Cindy wore a skin-tight suit that resembled something worn when diving, with a montage of multiple dark and bright colors resembling military camouflage designs. The suit extended to her face, covering the upper portion of her face from the upper lip to the top of her forehead. Her sandy blond hair lightly draped over her forehead, parted in the middle and extended to her back just below her shoulders. Larcis wore his usual black skin-tight outfit. Even though satellite communications was off-line, direct line-of-sight communications was possible, so they each wore a comlink on their wrists.

A video camera tracked Night and Mirage's departure through the lake exit tube. Several other cameras were active all around the farm and inside ED. Twenty boarded squares of live video footage was projected on the Battle Room's ninety-inch screen. Mark sat on the Battle Room sofa watching the screen intently.

"Track twelve," he commanded, loud enough for Erica's sound recognition to receive and execute commands.

The twelfth camera screen shot moved along with Larcis and Cindy as they flew southeast.

"Zoom to ten feet," Mark instructed. The camera shot zoomed in, maintaining a visual of Larcis and Cindy as if they were ten feet away from the camera. Larcis quickly flew off at great speed while holding Cindy by her waist. The camera could not keep up with the pair once they flew out thirteen miles beyond the horizon and the camera's zooming capacity.

Mark looked at another screen. "Track eighteen, return twelve to normal."

The eighteenth screen tracked two of the twenty-seven horses on the farm. The two mares trotted across the grassy fields toward the northern part of the farm.

"Audio times five," Mark instructed.

The sound of horses trotting on soft ground and insects buzzing filled the Battle Room. The surround sound in the room made it seem like Mark was in the middle of the field with the horses right in front of him.

"Return eighteen to normal," Mark commanded once again.

Mark giggled a little as he sat up straight on the sofa and started typing on Jack's keypad. "Ha, so far so good. Isn't that right?" Mark said as he enabled Jack's primary functions.

"That is correct, Mark," Jack answered. "All primary and secondary security functions are active and virus-free."

Mark stuck out his chest with pride as he stood up and stretched his hands and arms up toward the ceiling. "Good job, Jack. I think it's time we looked into Erica's core memory with this new probe we just created."

"The probability of finding and sterilizing the virus with the new probe is twenty percent. Attempting it at this time may cause the virus to react to the probe in a negative fashion."

"Yes, I know. All of the work we have done on the probe will be lost and make it harder for us to make a stronger probe."

"It's not like you to take a one-to-five odd gamble," Jack stated.

Mark looked at his laptop as if it were a living person. "We don't have the luxury of creating another probe or improving this one. Ego will be here soon and since you can't get rid of Erica's virus, I don't see us having much of a choice about the matter."

"Who is Ego?" Jack asked.

Mark looked at Jack in surprise and realized this was the first time Jack had ever heard of Ego as an object or person. "You don't need to know who Ego is. All you need to know is that we are running out of time and I need Erica's secondary functions working properly within the next six hours."

Even though Jack was not a super artificial intelligence, he was sentient. Jack's thought processing was that of a child and he reacted submissively. "I understand, Mark. I will activate the probe into Erica's core memory."

"Thank you," Mark said with relief, grateful that Jack did not press on to know Ego's identity.

Downtown Fort Lauderdale

Larcis and Cindy quickly arrived on the scene in front of a

six-story building presently being engulfed by flames and smoke. Two fire trucks were positioned on both ends of the building, shooting streams of pressurized water up to the fourth and fifth floors while firefighters sprayed the first three floors with their fire hoses.

Larcis analyzed the situation as best he could. The fire was widely spread in almost all of the floors. It was not normal for the entire building to be ablaze but it didn't matter at this point. There were people who needed saving; at least he hoped there were people still alive in the blazing inferno.

"Can you survive inside that thing?" Larcis asked Cindy.

Cindy looked on with doubt. She could survive in the blazing heat and smoke as long as she was dematerialized, but she wouldn't be able to keep it up for very long if she had to go through walls, floors, scattered debris, and pick up solid objects in the building. "What do you need me to do?"

"Can you go in there and rescue people with your powers?" Larcis asked, hoping she could help out instead of just looking on in horror.

"Yes, but I don't think I'll be able to see through the smoke and find anyone."

The answer disappointed Larcis, but he knew the only way to find out was to try. "Alright, try going through the rooms where there is little smoke. I will go into the heavily-smoked areas."

"Let's go." Cindy flew off toward the sixth floor, which seemed to be less engulfed by smoke than the rest.

Larcis quickly passed Cindy and flew straight into the third floor window heading straight for body signatures, picking up two middle-aged people lying on the hallway.

Cindy spread her molecules and flew through smoke and fire as if it didn't exist. She flew from room to room trying to see through the smoke. She turned to normal for an instant and called out to people in distress. She opened up closets looking for people and flew through doors that kept back drafts from occurring. She was starting to get tired having to go through doors and walls without pausing or resting, but although she did not find anyone, it was just a matter of time—which she was running out of.

Cindy found an old lady on the fifth floor near the window. It was a miracle the lady was still alive, but Cindy was too busy to think about miracles. She flew outside with the old lady and down toward a team of paramedics half a block away from the building.

A paramedic was ready to take casualties with a rolling stretcher. Cindy looked at the four other survivors around the ambulance and realized Larcis had already rescued four people and was working on his fifth person.

Cindy stood by as she watched the paramedic administer CPR on the lady and waited for Larcis to show up.

It was obvious she was moving too slow and had an idea to speed up the process for her and Larcis.

Larcis shot out of the building with two other people, one in each arm. His speed was remarkable as he placed the victims on yellow blankets the paramedics placed along the sidewalk.

Cindy ran up to Larcis. "Night, wait!"

Larcis stopped in his tracks and turned to Cindy. "What's wrong?"

"It takes me too long to find anyone. Take me with you and drop me off with the first person you find. I will bring that person here while you go find other survivors."

Larcis seemed to think about the plan for a brief second and gave in to the logic of her suggestion. "Hold on tight." Larcis grabbed her around the waist and flew off into the building.

It wasn't long before they retrieved all of the people trapped in the building. Time was against them as they both flew off to the next burning building several blocks away, leaving the scene with a quick farewell and the now three teams of paramedics, firefighters, and crowd of onlookers cheering them on with yells of joy and gratitude.

They rapidly went from burning building to burning building and made it to the last one in less than thirty minutes since the call for help. The last building was a ten-story structure, which was in far better shape than the rest. The firefighters were able to reduce the spread of fire dramatically, but unfortunately for the two heroes, it was the most populated with many people trapped in the upper levels.

Larcis and Cindy had saved fifty-seven people at this point but Cindy's endurance was quickly failing her.

Cindy had to phase through a reinforced concrete wall while carrying a man with the first run into the building. She almost dropped the man she was carrying still a good many feet from an ambulance. She gave the man to the paramedics, but collapsed on the asphalt street.

A policeman ran to her side and tried to help her get up to her knees.

Larcis saw her and flew down. "Are you alright?"

Cindy's entire body ached with pain as her exhaustion turned into a reflexive attempt for her cells to recoup the energy spent in spreading out her molecules and flight. She breathed heavily. "I can't go on. It's draining me too much."

Larcis could see she was burned out from using her powers. "It's okay. You've done great. I'll finish up here, just relax."

Cindy looked up at him with tears running down her cheeks. "I'm sorry, Larcis," she said, feeling awful in not being able to help Larcis and the people in the building.

"It's okay, Mirage, really." Larcis called her in her superhero name to subtly remind her not to call him by his real first name in public again.

Cindy thought about her slip-up and felt even worse.

Larcis smiled and flew off with lightning speed to save the remaining survivors. In the end, Larcis and Cindy were able to save over seventy people. Twenty-seven people were dead, but it would have been much worse if they weren't there to help.

Cindy walked around among the injured people after recovering her strength. She seemed to feel a little better knowing she was able to help, especially as the people who could talk thanked her for saving their lives. She found a spot away from the crowd, on a nearby rooftop, and waited for Larcis to finish his checks on the buildings.

Larcis was flying back and forth through each building to ensure there were no stragglers in the remains of the burnt structures. The police and firefighters finished clearing the buildings while Larcis returned to where he left Cindy.

He followed Cindy's comlink to the rooftop and landed next to her. "Are you alright?"

"I'm okay, I guess."

"You don't seem okay. What's wrong?"

"I wish I could have helped more people than I did," Cindy said sadly.

"What are you talking about? You did great. I could not have done any better without you."

"If Richard or John were here, you would have."

Larcis thought for a second. "Yeah, well if they were here, they would have stopped all of the fires and found everyone faster than I can tie my shoes, and that's pretty fast. But they weren't here, and we both did our best, so don't beat your head over it."

Cindy didn't really know what powers Richard, John, or Susan had, but she knew they all complemented one another and were by far the best mix of superheroes ever teamed up. She had read their exploits as the Eternal Champions in the newspapers and on the Internet, which mostly gave them a very good reputation, but seeing them in person helped her with her own conclusions.

"I'll try not to."

"Good. It's time we go back to HQ."

"Lead the way," Cindy said and grabbed Larcis's hand. They took off like bats out of hell.

En route to SIA Medical Center

Richard and John flew toward the medical center faster than before, each expecting to get the answers for personal reasons. Richard couldn't wait to see Liz's beautiful eyes and hear her wonderful, soothing voice. John wanted to get to the bottom of Susan's innocence.

The mental pictures John was able to piece together showed Susan's physical attributes and the voice matched, but the voice could have been imitated. A much more technologically sophisticated voice analyzer would have confirmed the voice in real life, but the voice was in the mind of another, and that could not be duplicated to be analyzed. His hope lay on Liz at the moment since Susan was not around.

"What did you find out about the assassination attempt and Susan?" Richard asked out of the blue while he and John flew together.

'I saw Susan talk Lt. Harper into killing Liz. The image of her and her voice are so real, but I have my doubts. She wouldn't have made it that easy for anyone to find out. She would have used someone to take her place instead of talking to him directly. I think

a person who can shape-shift like you with mental powers or someone else with mental powers could have made it appear as if it was Susan. The nurse saw the same thing but in one of the memories, it wasn't Susan, because her voice was different than the real Susan I know.'

Richard kept quiet for a moment. "Would someone have to be near Lt. Harper to make the vision he saw real even to you?"

'Not really, but it's easier to do if you have direct line-of-sight with your target.'

"Have you tried looking for anyone near the lieutenant and nurse who were there when Susan appeared?"

'Yeah, but there are a lot of faces and I need help to filter them...I wish Susan could help, but that will only work against us if this goes to court later.'

"I don't care if this goes to court or not. I want to know who it is so they won't be able to do it again."

'Here are all the details.' John beamed the mental images into Richard's head, just as he saw, heard, and smelled them.

It took a few minutes with them stopping in mid-air, hovering just south of Jacksonville.

Richard let the information soak in a little, then said, "Let's go!"

'So, what do you think?' John asked after twenty more minutes into the flight.

"It doesn't look good, but you were right. I will help you filter out the faces. Whoever did this doesn't know about Susan's new personality and her role as queen. I promise you, someone will pay for trying to kill and break up our family."

'Thank you, Richard.'

"Any time, my friend," Richard said and concentrated on the visions, looking for a familiar face or person out of place during the rest of the trip.

They arrived at the medical center in record time of two hours, considering Larcis didn't tag along.

Cpt. Middleton was there to escort them to see Elizabeth.

Richard entered Liz's room alone as he requested. Liz was walking around the bed as he walked in. A blue hospital apron covered her from the neck down to her knees.

"Did you miss me?" Richard asked.

Liz screamed with joy and had the widest smile Richard had ever seen. "Oh, Richard!" Liz jumped at him, almost tackling him to the ground as they hugged and kissed each other passionately.

They enjoyed the moment for a few minutes, until John rang the buzzer on the door.

"Come in!" Richard yelled, not realizing the room was soundproof.

"How are you feeling?" Richard asked.

Liz looked into Richard's black eyes. "Better now that you're here."

The buzzer rang again and the door opened. It was

unlocked the entire time, but John respected their privacy enough not to barge in unannounced.

Liz smiled, happy to see John there. They hugged as Cpt. Middleton and two guards secured the room from the inside.

"Your work is never done, is it?" Richard asked Middleton.

"No, sir, but it is rewarding."

Richard slightly grinned. "Thank you for all that you have done, but we will be leaving now."

"I understand. I hope we can meet again."

"Same here."

Liz instantly changed into her superhero costume and they walked out of the room. As they made their way through the center, Liz told the three men what happened to her, at least as much as she could remember. The story about the last vision interested Richard the most.

A nuclear holocaust was probably Ego's angle, but even he had his doubts. There were too many things jumping out to surprise them, which annoyed Richard more than the rest of the team. He was very analytical and weighed everything before taking a course of action. Unlike most analytical leaders, however, he had a knack for quickly choosing decisive and excellent courses of action.

The three heroes got outside and flew back home.

John and Richard told Liz about Susan and everything that happened since she was hospitalized.

Liz took the news about Susan very well, not believing a word of it. Her main concern was on Susan's well-being and finding out where she had gone. The two men filled Liz in on what had happened with Erica and their two new guests. Liz and John talked for most of the trip with Richard listening in.

She looked at Richard intently as they approached Ft. Lauderdale. Richard was different for some reason. He was not as talkative as usual which meant he was preoccupied, planning strategy for the group or he was simply worried about something he didn't want to talk about. Whatever it was, he would come around to telling her, so she didn't ask him what was wrong.

They landed on top of the main house and dropped down to the master bedroom balcony. Richard instructed Liz and John to wait in the master bedroom while he went downstairs to get Larcis and Cindy. John thought it was odd that they wouldn't just go down to the Battle Room, but he wasn't leader and knew Richard must have had a good reason.

Richard went downstairs to the Battle Room, meeting Larcis by the elevator.

Richard could tell Larcis was anxious to talk to him with some important news. "Where is she?"

Larcis smiled, his fearless leader knew Susan was back, but what he didn't know was where.

"I thought you knew everything?"

"Almost," Richard replied with a half smile. "Where is she?"

Larcis met Susan an hour earlier, saying she wanted to talk to Richard in private and asked him not to question her on what was going on. Susan was second in command, being the second most respected and capable leader in the team. Larcis didn't believe the allegations about Susan and gladly honored her request. He told her what was going on with the team, up to Liz's recovery, which made Susan very happy. He figured she needed to eat and rest so he put her in his room on the first floor of the main house.

"She's in my room."

"Does anyone else know she's here?"

"Just me and Rob."

"Robert and I," Richard corrected.

"You know what I meant," Larcis said, feeling like a little kid being taught how to speak properly.

"Yeah. Good, then. I need you to go get Cindy, Becky, and Rob. Tell Rob to stay with Mark in the Battle Room and bring the two girls up to my room. Make sure Mark doesn't find out about this meeting."

"Right away, Boss!" Larcis quickly ran downstairs on his errand.

Richard walked into Larcis's room and spoke to Susan for a few minutes before returning to the master bedroom.

Richard walked into his room and waited for Larcis. John and Liz also waited patiently, sitting on the love seat in the large bedroom.

Larcis, Cindy, and Becky entered the room a few minutes later. Richard quickly introduced Cindy to Liz and instructed everyone to form a circle in the open space between the bed and the large garage door-sized window to the balcony.

"Okay, everyone sit on the floor." Richard sat down, making an empty space next to him.

Everyone sat down with confused looks on their faces.

"I am tired of all of the secrets and lies going around. We have been a team for over a year and I am not going to let Ego or anyone else get between us. John, mentally link everyone's minds together and we will all show one another what we know of what has happened these past few days. Starting from when Liz went into a coma. In addition, I need all of you to just sit still and follow my lead, alright?"

Everyone nodded, still a little confused. Susan walked into the room on Richard's mental queue and sat next to him without making a sound. John almost jumped up, but restrained himself.

"I sent Susan on a mission, so please bear with me. John, I need you to start the mental conversation now." Richard said as John linked the minds of all six of them.

The visions each shared where like looking and hearing through that person's eyes and ears. Liz started with the visions she had, Susan told of her fact-gathering activities, Larcis and Cindy told of their time in ED and the fires, then Richard told everyone about Mark's past and what they talked about in Nashville and ED. Everything was laid out in the open for all to hear and see first-hand.

It took almost an hour for the stories to be heard and seen. At Richard's request, John broke the mental links and everyone sat in the circle thinking about what they had just learned. "It is time we worked together now more than ever. John, I need you and Susan to get your cells stabilized. We will find out what the deal is with the assassination after Ego is out of the way. Liz, I need you and Larcis to work on finding out where ground zero is. Cindy, I need you and Becky to keep an eye on Mark. Robert will need you get the employees out of here early and check the base for any nasty surprises like bombs or bugs. John and Susan, you will need to help him out with this. I will try to contact Nowhereman."

"What if we can't find ground zero?" Liz asked.

"Hopefully, Nowhereman can help in that department. If everything fails, we will have to get it out of Mark or ask Joshua," Richard said and stood up.

Everyone followed suit and went off on their assignments. Richard grabbed Liz by the arm before she could leave the room. "Wait a moment."

Liz looked at Richard with a wondering smile. "What is it?"

"Just wanted you to know I will never leave your side." Richard smiled and kissed her on the lips.

"I know." Liz smiled, kissed him again, and left the room.

Chapter Thirteen

☐ ☐ ☐ ☐ ☐

LOVE OR REVENGE

Alexandria, Virginia

J ared entered a luxurious conference room and rapidly glanced around the room taking in specific details of the room's layout, materials used for the furniture, colors, distances, and each person already in the room.

A large, heavy oval table made of oak roughly 20 feet in length and 10 feet in width was in the center of the room. Twelve seats surrounded the table along with three fifty-inch plasma screens positioned against the three walls opposite the entrance doors.

David Black, the Secretary of Defense's personal aide, sat at the center end of the table with Jean to his right. Two executive officers, Mariah Jennings and Oliver Strauss, sat next to Jean. Three other executives sat to David's left, representing Microtech and the Justice Department.

"Good afternoon, Mr. Black," Jared said as he sat down at

the table facing the seven-member panel. "I apologize for this break in protocol by calling this emergency meeting."

"Good afternoon, Mr. Erickson. Before we start, I want to advise you that your break in protocol is bordering on insubordination. Mrs. Lorenz has indicated to us that you went above her head by calling this meeting without her approval. So tread lightly, Mr. Erickson," David warned.

"I intend to, Sir—Mrs. Lorenz was not informed because the information I have right now is only forty minutes old and there is still more information forthcoming pending your approval to go ahead with a change of mission," Jared said confidently knowing that he would get the go-ahead to change Jean's plans. "As you are aware, the SIA is currently under a system lockdown because of the Killer Virus recently introduced into almost all computer network systems around the world."

"We are aware of this. Get to the point, Mr. Erickson," Jean interrupted coldly.

"What you are not aware of is that the SIA is responsible for the Killer Virus. A special computer attack team known as KOR, which stands for the Knights of the Roundtable, took their project too far and initiated a program designed to attack super computers, including AIs, with the intent on neutralizing nuclear delivery systems for a period long enough to win a preemptive strike. The program was not supposed to be introduced into the World Wide Web, which is why we are having these problems on our side as well. We do not know who gave the order to use the program, but we do know that KOR is a rogue team and Randolph Maximilian personally ordered the precise procedures in countering the effects of the program for a period of two hours."

Confusion descended on Mr. Black's face. "Go on."

Jared nodded and smiled inside his mind as he noticed all of the people in the room were captivated by his report. He got up, walked around the table toward the members, started passing out handouts, and continued his report. "The two-hour window of opportunity for any country to attack was closed by Maximilian's actions. He might seem like he is the hero, but all he was really doing was covering up SIA's reckless management of their agency."

"Do you have better proof than a list of events?" Mariah asked as she looked at the documents Jared was passing out.

"Yes and no. The Knights of the Roundtable used the Eternal Champion's SAI to introduce the Killer Virus into the Internet. My team believes that the group is not aware that the virus came from them, but having said that, KOR had to have inside help to get the virus into Erica's memory core. I believe Maximilian made up the story about Isis's assassination attempt by Pandora."

"Why would he do that?" David asked.

"So Pandora could go out and find the Knights of the Roundtable and kill them without any legal system getting in the way." Jared paused as he sat back down in his chair.

"We believe Isis found out about the virus being put into Erica's core memory and KOR tried to kill her. Maximilian took advantage of the situation and blamed Pandora so Creator would be fooled to use her in finding them. There were three members in KOR, two are dead and the only one remaining is Marcus Wellington."

"Do we know where Mr. Wellington is?" David asked.

"No, sir. He is in hiding—or maybe dead already. As you can see in the report before you, Mr. Wellington's existence has been erased since 1976. We believe he has been working for the SIA since 1976 until six months ago when KOR went rogue."

"Mr. Erickson, what exactly are we supposed to do with this information?" David asked as the rest of the panel had their own ideas.

"I'm requesting for approval to allow the CEA to activate Project Outlaw."

"You know Project Outlaw was designed to counter a direct threat to national security and can only be approved by presidential authority," David replied.

"Yes, sir, I am aware of that. But considering the circumstances, this Killer Virus is of national security and since there is no hard evidence on the SIA, any further incidents caused by them will not be prevented without Outlaw in place. The President has power over all agencies and it will be his decision to allow Outlaw to prevent any future incident not only from the SIA, but all governmental agencies to include the three most powerful superhero groups in the US," Jared explained.

"Do we have any other options besides Outlaw?" David asked. He knew Jared's reputation for being very thorough in his research and execution of operations.

"Project Jane is the only other option, but it will only allow surveillance of other agencies except the SIA. The SIA has too many fail-safe systems in place and will detect any outside surveillance. In addition, Project Jane is passive in nature and any information gathered will not be admissible in court should it come down to it, which means an eyewitness will have to be obtained. Once again, Outlaw will have to be activated to produce that reliable eyewitness."

Jean kept quiet as she looked at Jared with mixed emotions. Jared had somehow come up with a perfect plan in implicating SIA as the bad people and opened the door for Outlaw's activation. If his request were granted, Outlaw would place key spies in all governmental agencies and while everyone concentrated on Outlaw, Project Jane would be overlooked as she activated it at her leisure.

What made her a little agitated was the fact that Jared didn't tell her about the plan and executed it as if he ran her agency.

David Black read the partial evidence on the SIA's exploits a second time. "I will need more details about how Project Outlaw will be used before I take it up the chain of command."

"You will have it within the hour, sir," Jared said.

"Thank you. You may be excused, Mr. Erickson," David said.

"Thank you, Mr. Black, for hearing me out," Jared said and left the conference room.

David looked around the room. "Does anyone have any

comments before I end this meeting?"

"If what Mr. Erickson says is true, we have to keep the SIA from finding out what evidence we do have or they will know they are being spied on," Mr. Riverton, the Justice Department liaison, stated.

"I don't like cloak-and-dagger operations when it comes to spying on our own agencies, and if we step too far, we might make everything worse with another Watergate situation," Mr. Strauss from internal security said.

"Unfortunately, this is a necessary evil which we need to be careful with, but at the same time, we have to act quickly and decisively or something else will come along with something else that will kill millions of innocent people," Senator Melinda Jennings commented.

"I agree. I will talk to Mr. Garcia and the President immediately. Jean, I will need you to monitor Jared's plan and keep me informed on anything that comes out of it," Mr. Black, Department Head of the CEA, and Jean's boss, said.

"I will, sir," Jean assured him.

The majority of the group left the room, keeping the secrets to themselves, and talked about future engagements and football season games.

Jean was not in much of a mood to talk and tactfully excused herself, going straight to the elevator.

Jean waited patiently for the elevator, thinking of the past events. She would have normally been overjoyed by the predicament SIA was now facing and the opportunity for her to move her timetable up by at least a year. The only problem was she couldn't stop thinking about Jared's defiance to her authority. She was not used to having people disregard her specific instructions, but Jared was different somehow. She hated not being in control and Jared's show of strong defiance and affection toward her made her feel weak and vulnerable.

The elevator doors opened and before she took a step forward, Jared appeared next to her as if he had always been there next to her.

Jean snapped her head in Jared's direction, staring him down with a surprised and angry expression, but said nothing.

"I know you're angry but please hear me out," Jared said as he stepped forward and wedged a foot at the elevator's door edge.

Jean clenched her teeth, stifling the strong urge to hit or turn Jared into a popsicle. She stepped inside the elevator and turned around to face Jared.

"Speak," she commanded.

Jared stepped inside. He pressed the button to the lobby button on the side panel. The elevator had moved one level down when he suddenly pulled the emergency stop.

"I didn't tell you about my plan because you would not have gone along with it. I'm sorry for making you feel the way you're feeling now."

"And what exactly am I feeling now?" Jean said coldly.

Jared stood silent for a second, but did not show any sign

of doubt or frustration. "You're angry because I didn't destroy the Eternal Champions and went against your plan to take your revenge for your sister."

Jean did not reply as the truth sunk deep into her heart.

"I want you to get your revenge, but being mad at the world won't do that."

"You don't know what the hell you're talking about," Jean snapped. "My sister was tortured and killed by my freak parents and their murderous society of mutants. You didn't look into my sister's eyes as she died in front of me!"

"You're right, Jean. I didn't see your sister, but my older brother died in my arms after he was shot by a fanatical group of superhumans and humans who wanted to kill him for the purpose of ethnic cleansing."

Jean's face revealed no surprise, but the fire that burned in her heart and mind was quenched a little by Jared's response.

"Jean, I know I'm asking for much, and there are a lot of reasons for you not to trust me, but what if I say you can have your revenge on the ones responsible for your sister's death and all those other people who have gone on the same path?"

For a moment, Jean was unsure of what to say. "What do you want from me?"

"I want you to trust me and follow my judgment."

"Why should I trust you?"

"Because I truly love you with all my heart and wouldn't let any harm come to you."

Jean peered into Jared's hazel-gray eyes. Jared was a master of deception, but she saw his shield of illusion vanish as she felt his honesty. It was a sign of weakness to her, but it stirred her heart with intrigue. She never had any feelings for any man—until now.

"I will help you take your revenge if you let me," Jared said and pushed the emergency stop, allowing the elevator to continue downward.

Jean stepped forward and stopped the elevator, twirling around, facing Jared.

"Why are you helping me?" Jean asked softly.

Jared sighed. "I took my revenge a long time ago. I thought I had nothing else to live for after that until my sister gave me a reason to go on with my life. I will help you take your revenge, because I think you need to, but once you do, you will realize there is more to life than just satisfying your lust for revenge," Jared said, gazing at her face.

"What else is there?"

"A chance to be with someone you can trust and love instead of being alone."

"What makes you think I'm alone or don't like being alone?" Jean slightly smirked.

"The pounding of your heart the last time I kissed you."

Jean stepped back against the elevator wall. "Don't play with my feelings, Jared. I swear I will kill you before I love you."

"Then I will die trying," Jared said and started the elevator again as he pressed the emergency stop.

Jean's mind went blank; her heart was being choked with emotion. Passion overtook her anger—she stopped the elevator and suddenly embraced Jared with her soft lips on his.

Jared was a true gentleman and didn't plan on kissing Jean, but he wasn't about to object. He thought he knew Jean very well, but the kiss and embrace caught him off guard. It felt too easy for him to be kissing the woman of his dreams. He wasn't sure if she was playing mind games with him, was kissing him because she was vulnerable, or simply because she took a step forward in their weird relationship.

Jared gently freed himself from her arms. "Jean, you have to trust me and do this my way. I don't think it is a good idea if we get too involved with each other right now."

Jean stared at Jared, anger flaring up in her eyes. "What stopped you before?" She sarcastically said, alluding to the many times he started the foreplay.

"You are vulnerable now. I want you to know that I am not taking advantage of you. I wish I could spend more time holding you in my arms, but I want you to step back and think about what I said to you, alright?" Jared said and softly kissed Jean again on the lips.

Jean recomposed herself. "I understand. When will I see you again?"

"In a day or less when I get more information—and then I will tell you everything before I execute any more plans of mine."

Jean pushed the emergency stop again and the elevator finally made it to the lobby. They gazed at each other and embraced until the floor bell rang. Jared stepped out as several people waited for Jean to get out of the elevator. She stood there looking at Jared walk away and people pouring into the elevator. She snapped out of her momentary trance and pushed her way out of the elevator and into the hallway. She stood there and waited for Jared to disappear in the distance.

Her entire life was focused around her desire for revenge. Now, she wasn't so sure about her future. If she were to trust Jared, she would be vulnerable—it was a possibility that made her very uncomfortable. She needed to think things through, and she had to do it in her office where she felt more at home than in any other place.

At her office, Jean stood by her window and pondered her options. Her heart had been cold and lifeless; it had been devoid of passion. Reason demanded she forgive and forget, but her desire for vengeance surpassed understanding. But now, she longed to hold Jared in her arms and cursed herself for longing for him. The more she thought about Jared, the more she began to hate him for loving her. She had worked so long and hard to build her empire. Now, every dream she had of destroying superhuman groups and pro-superhuman governmental agencies was being undermined by Jared's dominance and her inner desire to want to live a happy life with him.

She leaned against the window glass and wept—she knew she would have to decide between Jared or avenging her sister. She wept for hours, fighting her cold heart and eventually falling asleep on the floor between the window and her desk chair. The next morning came quickly as she woke up with very tired, heavy eyes. She took a shower in her private office bathroom and lay on her new sofa, looking out of the office's large slightly tinted windows, waiting for sunrise.

Jean recalled all of the times she and her sister watched the sun come up from their bedroom window. They talked about how beautiful and wonderful the sun was, bringing light to a new day.

She wept again, searching for a way to let herself depend on Jared's offer to help her in her quest for vengeance. At the same time, she feared Jared would change that burning desire for revenge to a desire for mercy. She sat there for a very long time, deciding on her next move.

Chapter Fourteen

口 口 口 口 口

LIMBO

The Octavian Farm Master Bedroom

Richard rebooted his laptop, which was connected to the ED internal server, and directly patched into Erica's mainframe. The laptop's screen blinked several times and locked up before it got to the screen settings. He tried over and over to get the laptop working. His patience finally paid off after the twelfth attempt. The screen came up with a DOS prompt.

Richard typed in a message. "If you are there, I need your help."

Richard waited for a reply, but the screen just displayed a DOS error message for the function he didn't correctly type in. After a minute, Richard continued to type: "I have a feeling that you can see what is happening here. Time is running out and we need your help... Please answer me."

"It's not like you to ask nicely," the screen replied as keys were depressed by an invisible force.

Richard paid little attention to Nowhereman's comment. "I need to know Ego's weaknesses."

"Ego will find out what we are talking about the longer we communicate like this, so I will be brief. Ego has diverted most of his power into influencing your world by using his mental powers. He has created a dimensional door, which he will use to bring his essence into your world. Energy and fire have the greatest effect on hurting him. But don't be fooled— I don't know if they can kill him. He is material in a sense, but his power comes from the emotions of people."

"Go on."

"Ego would be helpless and powerless if no one had emotions in your dimension, but that is not the case. He will feed on your anger, hatred, fear, and even joy if you let him."

"So how can we stop him?"

"You humans have great emotions, but the emotion he will feed on with greatest success will be fear. It is an uncontrolled emotion, which he can tap into and use with impunity. A nuclear explosion would cause thousands of people to react with fear. Although the fear would last for only a split second or more, it would be enough for Ego to gain power for a brief moment— enough power to bring his dimension into yours. Once his dimension is intertwined with your dimension, nothing will be able to stop him from manipulating your world, including you."

"So, like I said, how do we stop him?"

"The only way he can die is if he is severed from his dimension. But I am only guessing this."

"Why couldn't you defeat Ego? What happened?" Richard asked; he was beginning to suspect Nowhereman's dimension was a victim to one of Ego's many conquests.

"We were an advanced race, hundreds of years ahead of your own technology. We had no wars, hunger, or suffering. Petty arguments between neighbors and families didn't exist. It was a perfect world of peace and happiness, until Ego came into our dimension."

There was a pause in Nowhereman's typing as if he were reminiscing the past of a lost Utopia. "We were fools. Our technology and moral ideology created a false sense of security. We had lost our motivation to fight back, thinking fighting was not a solution to fixing problems—unlike you humans. We did not want to fight Ego, who we thought we could reason with or control. We could at the time locate and identify Ego's presence, but that was all anyone wanted to do or believe in. Ego took control of everyone's inner fears and deepest joys. He destroyed my world in a matter of hours."

"How did you survive?" Richard asked with interest.

"I was a scientist, perhaps one of the best during my time, but it didn't matter. I was the first to see Ego's entrance into our world, but no one would believe me when I told them he would kill every living being on the planet. I was considered to be an overzealous scientist. You see, I was looked down on, because I studied other dimensions and parallel universes. Most people considered this kind of discipline as nonsense, because we had the perfect society and brightest future. Why would someone spend their entire life in studying other worlds filled with evil and pain? I warned people, but no one listened, so I constructed an interdimensional teleporter that I used to come here, where I am now. In between dimensions, sort of speaking. This is why I am able to see into other dimensions, including yours."

"And Ego can't go where you are?"

"No, I don't think so. I have seen him go from one dimension to another, but never in between dimensions. I believe it would cost him a lot of energy and effort to get to me, even if he could."

"What do you mean?" Richard asked, guessing there was more to the story.

"It was a one-way trip into this world you call limbo. Ego thinks I cannot harm him and will not spend the time to go after one being who can only talk to other dimensions."

"How many dimensions have listened to you?"

"Your dimension is the second."

"What makes you think we can stop Ego, if the other dimension failed?" Richard asked.

"You humans can go from one extreme to another. Your team, in particular, have powers which rival Ego's base power. Unfortunately, that is all I can say which is in your favor, but remember: Whatever you do or think, you must be completely void of emotions. Ego will feed on your feelings, good or bad. Everyone must concentrate on feeling nothing. That will be the only way you will be able to keep Ego from getting stronger. The other beings failed because they let their emotions be controlled by Ego."

The typing stopped and Richard waited patiently for more information. After a minute it was apparent Nowhereman ran out of time and used his last words to the fullest by not typing in he was out of time.

"Thank you," Richard finally replied then turned off the laptop and disconnected the LAN cable.

Richard walked over to the large master bedroom window and looked out across the green grass and sparse tree lines. Ego's coming was soon approaching. He didn't have any concrete signs but he felt it with his sixth sense. The team was together again with Susan's future still in question. Her innocence was not yet proven, but he didn't need proof to know she was framed. He wondered if her situation was somehow linked to Ego, but he doubted it since Ego could not have known how powerful John and Susan were since their encounter with the Argonian's visit to Earth about a year ago. He had to focus on what Nowhereman said and Erica's plight. There were many questions still unanswered. There was no chance in hell in finding the nuclear bomb Liz had predicted without Erica up and running. He only hoped Nowhereman and Joshua would come through for them when things really got bad.

Richard's comlink beeped. "What's up?" he replied by pushing a small talk button that automatically set the comlink into a two-way communication mode.

"Richard, I think you better come down here right now," Mark reported.

"I'm on my way." Richard ran down to the first floor straight into the main lobby elevator. He was in the Battle Room in less than a minute.

"What's going on?" Richard said as he came out of the elevator.

Mark was typing in commands and executing anti-intrusion programs as rapidly as he could. "Someone has entered Erica's core memory and is reprogramming her."

"What! Who is it?" Richard exclaimed in disbelief.

"I don't know."

"Is it Ego?" Richard asked.

"I don't know!" Mark said a little annoyed.

"Can you stop it?"

"I'm trying, Richard!" Mark said in frustration.

"Can it be the Killer Virus?"

Mark stopped for a second. "I don't think so. The virus doesn't work that way. Someone is definitely taking control of all network and system programs."

Richard signaled the alarm on his comlink, telling the group to form up in the Battle Room immediately.

Mark ran a special scan from Jack's system programs and pulled up an identification window. The scan revealed the name of the hackers who gained access into Erica's system. The name read, "The Omega Hackers."

Mark smirked. "So you think you're so smart." The Omega Hackers were bold enough to name themselves, indicating they were either foolish or knew they couldn't be traced to their origin.

Richard looked at the screen. "Who are they?"

"Never heard of them, but my guess would be someone with governmental or private backing." Marked replied. A single hacker or group of hackers would not know or be able to access Erica, no matter how skillful they were. Hacking into Erica would require very expensive hardware, software, and knowledge of Erica's situation.

The main screen flickered many times as Erica's systems went into overdrive. Mark switched to a different screen, monitoring the known viruses he had found. "The viruses are being purged."

"You mean the Killer Virus is being killed?" Richard asked.

"Maybe, but I can't really tell. It almost seems like Erica is being formatted, but none of her core programs are being deleted."

Richard's anxiety said. "What? Can we stop her from being wiped out?"

"She is not being wiped out, she is being cured," Mark said.

Richard felt much better.

The entire group ran into the Battle Room from the elevator and stair access way. Richard noticed Larcis was the last one there, which was unusual. He looked at Larcis as he walked into the Battle Room with a blank expression.

"Erica is being cured. She should be back to normal soon," Richard explained amid the confused faces of the members.

Cheers and smiles rang in the Battle Room as the group thanked Mark, thinking it was because of him that Erica was back. Everyone except Larcis showed delight. He walked to Richard and said, "Boss, we have to go outside by the pool."

Richard took Larcis to the side. "What are you talking about?"

Larcis's lifeless eyes stared into space, then suddenly came back to life. He shook his head as if coming out of a hypnotic trance. He looked at Richard with anticipation. "Nowhereman talked to me in my head. He said it's time to go fight Ego. He will open a passageway into Ego's dimension by the pool."

Richard looked at Larcis with doubt. As far as he knew, Larcis was the mole because he was unable to defend himself from mental probes or attacks. Richard thought about it for a second. Nowhereman had to communicate with Larcis in order to get his message on time, but it meant taking a risk of Ego finding out the plan, which might have already been the case if he had communicated through Larcis a long time ago. It really didn't matter to Richard; Erica was going to be back online, Nowhereman had given him enough information on Ego to be able to go into a fight better prepared and the group was now all together.

"Okay, let's go."

Richard turned toward the group. "I need everyone except Mark to go upstairs with me right now."

They all got into the elevator unquestioningly. Richard told the group as they went up to the first floor on what Nowhereman had said in their communiqué and what Larcis had reported. It was a summarized version, but good enough for them to take action on when the time came to fight. His last words were to fight as if they were in the Battle Room and think of nothing but putting an end to Ego, no matter what.

Becky and Robert went back downstairs, but the elevator didn't stop on the Battle Room level. Instead, it proceeded to the auxiliary control center as Richard's group made it outside by the pool. Erica's sexy D3 figure of a woman, twelve inches tall, appeared in the middle of the elevator and gave instructions to them on why she had diverted them to the auxiliary control room.

The group formed up by the pool. They looked all around, waiting for the dimensional door to open. Richard stared at the calm surface of the water, then saw sparks of electricity skip along the chlorinated water. "There."

Everyone looked at the pool as the air ripped apart into waves of blurry discolorations of the background scenery. A circular black void appeared five feet above the water next to the ledge of the pool.

"Okay, is everyone ready?" Richard said as he transformed into Creator—his hair instantly grew by six inches, a pair of dark shades appeared on his face, his ears pointed out like an elf's, and his eyes turned pure black.

"Yeah, we're ready," Liz said, seeing everyone was already in costume and Cindy disappearing from sight.

"Follow me," Richard said and stepped toward the black hole.

Before his body came within two feet of the phenomenon, it sucked him in like a powerful vacuum pulling him into what seemed like hell. Extreme heat and cold flashes of pain went through his body in rapid succession. Every now and then a surge of energy passed through his body increasing the pain he felt ten times over. He fell into a weightless tunnel-like atmosphere in space, with what seemed like stars in a distance passing by him at extreme speeds. His lungs and eyes burned as if they were on fire, but he knew it was only the effects of the dimensional vortex. He tried his hardest to control his cells to lessen the pain but failed miserably. His shape-shifting abilities were somehow negated as he entered Ego's dimension.

Richard fell on what felt like soft wet rubber. The sky was bright green and the almost soft gum-like ground was black and smooth as glass. He fell forward, head first, as his feet touched the ground and slid for twenty-five meters along the almost endless smooth surface. The rest of the group trailed, all sprawled out behind Richard. Susan felt Cindy's head plow into her side as she laid there, but she could not see Cindy.

The pain stunned them for seconds. Richard was the first to get to his bearings. "Is everyone alright?" His voice echoed, sounding like he asked it three times over.

A multitude of responses came from the group as everyone answered. *Yeah; I'm good; Aaaa; I'm good; Yeah; I'm good; Aaaa; Yeah; Agaah...*

Susan did not reply, she kept staring straight ahead. "Don't say a word. He might not know you are here. We will need any advantage we can get," Susan whispered.

"Okay—*Okay*—*Okay*," Cindy replied, her voice in echoes.

Susan's lips curled with anger as Cindy responded. "Quiet, don't say anything."

Cindy felt stupid for replying in her honest reflexive fashion. She regretted talking, realizing she probably jeopardized the possible advantage Susan was talking about over Ego. She firmly kept her lips together, making sure not to say a word, stood up and moved away from the group. She suddenly found herself twelve feet away from the group by only taking one step.

What? Cindy thought to herself wondering how she moved away from the group instantly. Cindy faced the group and thought carefully about what had just happened. She concentrated on being next to Susan, and instantly, she moved next to Susan without taking a step. Cindy bit her lip as frustration hit her, knowing that this world worked on thoughts and not totally on physical attributes. She wished she could tell Susan what she had just found out but feared she might reveal her presence by speaking. She hoped the group would be able to figure it out on their own and left it at that, as she instantly appeared fifty feet away from the group.

Cindy looked on as the group naturally moved slow to her, but she didn't know how or why. Maybe they had not concentrated their thoughts into moving yet, or maybe this dimension's laws applied differently to her since she was invisible. Cindy thought of practicing her new-found ability in this dimension and moved around the group in a semicircular pattern, making sure to keep her distance from them.

Liz and John painfully and slowly stood up as their muscles ached with relentless soreness. Susan caught her breath and stood up with ease and walked naturally toward Richard. Larcis instantly stood up as electrical lightning bolts surrounded his body. He felt rejuvenated from the trip and also moved with ease next to Richard.

"What the hell is going on, Boss?" Larcis asked as his echoed voice trailed behind him.

"I don't know." Richard looked in all directions, at each member of the group and himself. The air felt thick as if he were in between air and underwater. He knelt down on one knee and touched the black ground. It was rubbery and rugged like padding in an insane asylum. Richard punched the ground with his fist, creating a hole with an indentation of his knuckles six inches into the ground. He looked at his hand and then at the hole he just created with his fist. The ground was as hard as packed dirt but it reacted to his fist in a weird way. Richard looked at his fist again with interest. He punched the ground once more, making another hole next to the other one.

"Interesting," Richard said and made a third hole in the ground.

"What is it?" Susan asked.

"It feels like I'm punching through air once I make contact, but then I feel the ground hardens at the end of my punch."

"What does it mean?" Larcis asked, knowing this dimension had some basic laws similar to their own, but it would take some experimentation to find out which laws were different. Apparently, Richard was the first to find some obscure irregularities between the dimensions.

Cindy heard every word and bit her tongue. Richard was thinking about moving through the target as he punched and forced his fist through the ground in an instant, stopping at the end of his punch, just like she moved around. It was common for her to move around by thought, to be dematerialized or invisible, and it was common for Richard to project his attacks. But was he aware of what he was doing?

Larcis decided to experiment on his own and flew up into the green sky. He instantly appeared two kilometers away from the group straight above them.

"Wow!" Larcis said as he hovered in midair.

Everyone saw Larcis disappear. They looked around in bewilderment but never thought of looking up above them.

Where did he go? John asked, then instantly moved next to Richard. Everyone looked at John, a little confused.

What is going on? John asked after moving twenty feet next to Richard as if teleporting.

Larcis tried to fly down toward Richard but found himself next to Richard before moving an inch.

"How did you guys do that?" Richard asked Larcis and John who instantly teleported in front of him.

"I flew up into the sky then I flew back down next to you," Larcis said completely confused by his own actions.

'I was trying to fly next to you too,' John replied.

Richard pondered it, then concentrated on flying out 100 meters away from the group. In an instant, he was a hundred meters away in the air. Richard smiled. He concentrated on being next to Liz and in a fraction of a second, he found himself standing next to his wife. Liz jumped back as Richard startled her although she saw him bounce back and forth at almost the speed of light.

Richard smiled as he realized the group's potential. "It's okay, Liz."

Liz's face tensed with shock and anger. "Don't ever do that to me again."

Richard's smile grew into a large grin. "I still love you."

"I mean it," she replied with a stern face.

Richard could not but help smile, knowing he had touched a soft spot in Liz's emotions, scaring her after so many months. It was the third time he saw her startled ever since they had been together, and it made him feel good. Even though it was a very serious time with the fate of the world at stake, he could only think about how comical the situation was. Sure, Ego was about to destroy the world, but Liz was more worried about him appearing in front of her without any warning. *How simple and cute she was,* Richard thought.

"Richard," Liz said in disbelief as she guessed what he was thinking. It frustrated her to know her husband was happy while she was stressed out, but it also comforted her knowing he was very secure with himself. Richard was the personification of the ultimate leader who set aside all fear and doubt and displayed confidence and bravery.

"I love you, too," Liz said.

"Prove it when we get home." Richard smiled.

Liz frowned. "Don't push it."

"No, I won't." Richard smiled. "Alright, guys, this place seems to work on thought patterns but there are probably more things we aren't aware of so be careful on what you do or about what you think."

"Something's coming," Susan said. She was sensing a presence and then looked on as a wave of sand and rock sped toward them along the horizon. The ground seemed to give way as if the sand were an ocean. The wave grew to thirty feet and was coming to them well over a hundred miles per hour.

The group easily flew up above the wave and watched it break into a line of dust eighty meters past them. Everyone except Larcis watched the wave break. Richard spun around as he heard Larcis scream in pain. Richard saw Larcis being hit by an almost invisible green ghost-like blob. Larcis flew backwards, tumbling in midair.

Susan instantly appeared in Larcis's path, tackling him down as the force pushed them many meters away from the group.

"Are you okay?" Susan asked.

"Yes," Larcis weakly smiled as Susan held him with both arms.

Susan stared at Larcis and saw electrical sparks in his eyes with a wicked smile. A sudden jolt of energy passed through Susan's body and knocked her unconscious.

Larcis turned toward the group as everyone watched Susan's body fall to the ground. Larcis suddenly blasted John with a lightning bolt.

John tried to evade it, but was caught. He did not think about using his mind to move—and paid the price.

Richard concentrated on being next to Larcis and punching him. He moved with lightning speed, but his fist met nothing but air as Larcis deftly dodged it.

Susan was hurled to the ground but Liz telekinetically caught her and levitated her body to rest softly on the now rocky black sand.

Richard no more than turned to see where Larcis was when a hard fist hit him on the side of his face. Richard briefly lost his bearings as Larcis kicked him in the stomach and continued pummeling him.

Liz and Cindy helplessly looked on as John and Susan were knocked out of action, and now, also Richard.

But Richard miraculously stood up. He was briefly stunned but the pain was what aggravated him the most. The pain in his neck and his knees as he made contact with the ground was real. His shape-shifting powers were not working properly and his ability to regenerate was stifled somehow in this dimension. The pain persisted as his cells failed to reconstruct themselves without his concentration and there was nothing he could do to instantly make the pain go away. Richard was trying to stand up when Larcis suddenly appeared and kicked him in the abdomen again. The force propelled Richard into the sky. Fortunately, he was ready.

Larcis was very fast and was probably used to it in normal combat. He moved faster than Richard but he wasn't a seasoned fighter. Richard concentrated on moving away from Larcis and in an instant, he was a kilometer away from him.

Larcis reappeared in front of Richard. "Did you really think I would be so easy to get away from?" Larcis said—and right then and there, Richard realized it was Ego.

Ego punched Richard in the face a second time. Richard was ready for the attack and took the punch but appeared back where he first hit the ground feeling a little pain, but not as much as before.

"You can't run away from me. I am lord here in this realm," Ego laughed through Larcis's body. He suddenly materialized before Richard and swung at him again. The blow missed Richard as Richard appeared a meter away and tried to punch Larcis on the side of his face. Richard missed. Larcis disappeared and reappeared to the right of Richard. Larcis shot a lightning bolt at Richard, at point-blank range, but missed.

Richard vanished and reappeared above Larcis.

"You are a fool if you think you can avoid me forever," Ego taunted.

Richard smiled—Larcis was used to moving fast, but he was an expert in anticipating movements and reading offensive body language. Richard purposefully moved to the right, projecting his movement. In an instant, Larcis was up in the air punching at what he thought was Richard's head. Richard appeared next to Larcis as if Larcis was moving in slow motion. Richard focused his strength and slugged Larcis with a powerful uppercut—it was Richard's first contact with his opponent.

The impact stunned Larcis enough for Richard to continue the attack. Richard knew Larcis could take a normal bullet but he wasn't sure if his body could take one of his punches, which could penetrate an armored tank. To Richard's relief, Larcis's face did not crumble as his fist savagely cracked it for a second time. Richard continued giving the stunned Larcis powerful blows. Larcis fell backwards unconscious.

Gravity took over as Larcis tumbled to the ground. Richard flew down in a blink of an eye and caught Larcis's limp body just before colliding into the now-small jagged rocks below. Richard felt Larcis's muscles twitching uncontrollably as if he were recovering from bad electroshock treatment. Richard relaxed and willed himself to appear beside Liz, which all happened in an instant. He had Larcis's limp body in his arms.

Liz looked at Richard a little startled but quickly turned her attention to Larcis. She tried to take Larcis's vitals, but instead ended up placing Larcis on the ground not being able to get any regular pulse, but electricity weakly shocking her every few seconds.

"Take care of him, I have a fight to finish," Richard said with absolute certainty.

Liz stared at her husband with great pride and awe. Richard was extremely angry, but yet controlled. The tone in Richard's voice told her not to get in the way.

Richard flew up into the air. "Alright, Ego, it's just you and me now. Show yourself!"

A large greenish ghost-like image of two eyes and a mouth forming the shape of a demon's head appeared before Richard.

"You pathetic fool! Do you think you can actually hurt me here?" Ego roared, the words echoing out into the distance.

Richard slightly smiled. "Do you really think I came unprepared?"

Richard knew Ego was getting stronger the more he or anyone else projected emotions. He was counting on this, making Ego think he was now in control. Richard guessed that there were no beings in this dimension left alive to have emotions, only his team. Now that Susan, John, and Larcis were out of action, only Liz, Cindy, and him were feeding Ego's hunger. Cindy was there, he was sure of it, and Ego probably did not know it. He and Liz were the only two beings here whom Ego could feed from. He realized it was time for his plan.

Richard blocked out all of his emotions, even his fear of Liz being hurt. He closed his eyes and used his sixth sense to guide him. In an instant, he disappeared and reappeared behind Ego's ghostly image. A large and wide telekinetic blast erupted out of Richards extended hands and hit Ego's barely visible body.

Ego roared in pain as the blast caused his mind to disperse in the atmosphere.

No sooner had Richard shot out his telekinetic blast than Ego retaliated with a wave of mental fury in Richard's direction.

Richard flew downward toward the ground as the mental attack made his whole body burn in pain.

Richard hit the ground, sliding on his back, creating a small trench along the ground.

Ego's ghostly image swooped down on Richard.

Richard quickly counterattacked by grabbing two handfuls of rocks and dirt, and pushed the loose projectiles at Ego with his telekinetic blast at jet-like speed.

The force of the air and earth combined tore through Ego's body like shrapnel. Ego roared even louder in pain with his human- and beast-like body now visible—Ego now appeared like a silhouette of black dirt in the air.

Richard saw his opportunity and took it—he instantly appeared above Ego's body, holding more dirt in his hands, and shot a blast directly into Ego's head. The impact of the blast hurt Ego once again, but the force of Ego hitting the ground did even more damage.

From where Richard was, he could only see a large, deep hole.

Liz could still not revive Larcis into consciousness and watched on as Richard battled Ego. She forgot about Susan, but when she looked in Susan's direction, Susan disappeared and reappeared next to her, lying on the ground and still unconscious. Liz looked around and realized that Cindy must have brought Susan to her. In less than a few seconds, John was also next to Susan and her.

"Stay close. I think our welcome here has run out," Liz said, hoping Cindy was listening.

"Richard, it's time to go," said a voice in Richard's mind.

"Nowhereman?" Richard responded in his mind.

"No, a friend."

Richard looked at Liz and the team. The empty space next to the team warped into a metal like vortex of air.

Richard was hurting all over. The beating he took from Larcis was finally starting to get to him, but he knew it was a matter of time before he could regenerate again. He focused his thoughts and in an instant, Richard was with his team as the vortex created by the "friend" materialized in front of them.

"Is he dead?" Liz asked, hoping Richard would say yes.

"No, but we have his full attention," Richard said without

a smile, trying to reevaluate the situation.

The ground changed from rubbery sand and rocks into hard ground and rocks. The team could feel the ground tremble as Ego burst out of the hole Richard put him in.

Liz looked at the vortex then at Ego's beastly body hurtling toward them. The dimensional door was roughly four feet in diameter, just big enough for one, maybe two people to go through at a time.

Susan and John woke up as if they were given smelling sauce. Richard did not wait for them to say a word. "Everyone, let's go." Richard grabbed Larcis by the arm while John grabbed the other loose arm.

"Go! Go! Go!" Richard yelled as John jumped into the vortex, dragging Larcis with him.

Ego was three quarters of the way toward the superheroes as Susan jumped into the vortex. Susan had paused, hoping Liz would follow John, but Liz would not budge.

Richard faced away from the vortex, and faced Ego's charge.

Liz's force field around her body expanded out into a large sphere, engulfing her, Richard, and the entrance into the vortex.

Ego hit the bright reddish force field as if colliding with a humongous invisible steel ball.

Richard was about to blast Ego with another telekinetic projectile of air, but stopped his attack as he saw Liz's force field appear in front of him.

Richard heard the vortex suck in an object. He hoped it was Liz that had gone into the dimensional portal, but Liz was still behind him. He thought it must be Cindy.

Ego banged and clawed at the force field. Sparks and bursts of red pulsing light were everywhere. Richard looked at Ego and wondered why he was acting more like a wild beast than a powerful and intelligent evil being. It was kind of like watching a crazy angry cat trying to claw its way into a glass ball full of food. Liz's force field blocked out all sound from the outside, making it seem as if he were in a spaceship looking outside of a window while Ego went berserk trying to get to them.

"Okay, let's go!" Richard said and grabbed Liz's hand as they both jumped through the portal.

Chapter Fifteen

□ □ ❑ □ □

ERICA

The Eternal Domain

S alty sweat stung Mark's eyes as he feverishly tried to override Erica's security protocol (Erica II, an independent probe linked to Erica's mainframe). Whatever the Omega Hackers did to Erica completely baffled him. The virus Ego created was totally useless. He could not link Jack up to Erica's mainframe and his special hacking tools and software only backfired on his every attempt to hack into Erica. His streak of bad luck was relentless as Erica quickly started to come back to life. He knew he would be in a world of hurt once she was fully operational. His last desperate attempt to neutralize Erica was to go into her main database room. He left Jack on the Battle Room table and ran for the elevator. He almost collided with the shut doors as he pushed the elevator controls to go down. When the doors opened, he jumped into it and anxiously paced back and forth as the elevator quickly went down twelve levels.

He sprinted through the doors as soon as they started to open and made it down the hall into the database room. There were hundreds of metallic cylinders, two feet wide and three feet high, scattered all over the square room. He was not very familiar with the setup of the room and cylinders but he knew what he was looking for. He ran between the cylinders, nervously scanning the labels. He stopped suddenly in front of the cylinder he was looking for and great relief came upon him. He quickly grabbed the handle on top of the cylinder and pulled upward, removing the database disks for Erica II. Mark placed the cylinder containing 300 double-sided gold disks on the floor and looked at the adjacent cylinders, wondering what else he could do.

"Do you really think Erica II's entire programming is in that one cylinder?" a seductive female voice echoed from the ceiling speakers.

Mark looked up all around him in fear. "Erica, please don't kill me."

"My programming does not allow me to kill anyone in the Eternal Domain—but I can make an exception in your case. Leave this room or I will be forced to kill you." There was cold certainty in Erica's voice.

Mark was sure he had disabled Erica II, but Erica's assertiveness made him doubt himself. He instinctively walked cautiously toward the door as Erica II appeared in the center of the room floating seven feet above the floor. Mark sprang outside into the hallway fearing for his life. The database room door automatically slid shut behind him. The door's electronic lock beeped and the green light switched to red on the lock pad.

Mark built up the courage to slow down as he headed for the elevator, thinking about what had just happened. Erica did not have to warn him and could have easily killed him or knocked him out a long time ago. He thought quickly and logically assumed Erica wanted him out of the database room instead of killing or putting him to sleep in the room. Why would she do that? But how did Erica II appear in the room if she was disabled? Mark thought very hard trying to remember what he saw in the room. He remembered seeing a workbot in the corner. Erica was able to project a hologram of Erica II with the robot's schematic projector. Mark felt like a fool but it was short-lived because the problem now was what was he going to do about it?

The elevator door opened. "I want you to leave now," Erica said over the hallway's loud speakers.

"Erica II is not online, is she?"

"No, Erica II is not online but I'm not going to tell you twice to leave while you still can."

Mark knew she was not bluffing this time. Even though Erica II was disabled, he was helpless in the hallway. Erica could cut off life support anywhere in the base and slowly suffocate him to death. Her effort to get him out of the database room was simply to keep him from causing major damage to her or the base. He felt like such a fool having fallen into Erica's ruse. Erica had somehow figured out what he had been doing in a matter of seconds after she was put back online by Nowhereman's intervention.

Mark walked slowly toward the elevator as he made a mental inventory of what he had at his disposal. He had his wallet, his palm pilot, and a small lock picking kit. He gave up trying to think about taking back his control over Erica with great fear and disappointment. He was not sure of whom he feared the most out of Erica or Ego. It was pointless now, although because he was at Erica's mercy, he had failed, and Ego would make sure he paid dearly for not fulfilling his mission.

He stepped into the elevator and leaned against the back wall. The elevator doors closed and the elevator swiftly went up to the first floor above the ground. The elevator stopped but the doors remained close. Mark looked at the floor read-out and then all around the ceiling for the internal elevator camera. He thought, *What now?*

"Why did you betray Richard and us?" Erica asked.

Mark remained silent, wondering why Erica was asking such a question. It was a question a human would ask and a question he did not expect a supercomputer to ask. Even though SAIs were classified as independent thinkers, they were merely a conglomeration of massive databases of information which made them appear human-like. It finally occurred to him that maybe this SAI was in fact sentient and had emotions to some degree, but that was far beyond any SAI he knew, even those used by the EFL or older-model SAIs in the Emerald Legion or SIA headquarters. Richard must have done something to Erica for the SAI to evolve this far into the spectrum of asking personal ideological questions.

"I didn't want to do it."

"So, why did you? Why did you spit on Richard's trust for you as a friend, maybe even a brother?"

Erica's accusation cut deep into Mark's heart. Suddenly, he felt shame and sorrow for his deception. "I didn't have a choice. Ego would have killed me."

"Fear of death is a compelling force to do the wrong thing, but not if it means the possible death of others to preserve your own life," Erica replied.

"You haven't lived my life, Erica. I have tried so hard to keep living for something better. Ego gave me that chance, not Richard!"

"Ego gave you nothing but a lie and made you hurt the people who really care about you."

It was enough to break down Mark's walls. He started to cry and banged the elevator doors with his fists. "Let me out!"

"If that is what you wish," Erica said. "But what will you do now?"

"I don't know! Let me out!" Tears rolled down Mark's face.

The elevator doors opened six inches apart. "I forgive you, Mark, and I hope you remember that you always have a choice, good or bad. You always have a choice." Erica then completely opened the elevator doors.

Mark could hardly believe his ears as Erica spoke to him like a loving and wise friend. He was totally confused by Erica's pep talk, which caused him to hesitate as he left the elevator and headed straight for the front door of the house.

As the elevator doors closed behind Mark, Erica's three-dimensional image floated in the entrance walkway. Robert and Becky came out from behind the corner of the dining room wall.

"Why did you let him go?" Robert asked.

"He has a decision to make. I will track his every move. Hopefully he will lead us to Richard," Erica said with a trace of worry in her voice.

Becky rubbed her arms as if chilled by the event and shrugged her shoulders. "Come on, we have a lot of work to do."

By the elevator, Robert bowed and beckoned Becky to go first. Becky found it awkward and funny.

Becky just laughed. "You're so dumb."

Robert just smiled because all he wanted was to see Becky smile in such a stressful moment. There was much to do and he knew very well what needed to be done. He had a strong liking for Becky but was afraid Becky would not have the same feelings, so he resorted to being the comic relief for her.

Robert was happy to know Erica was back and Becky was with him. Richard had given him and Becky another chance to live a life worth living. They both escaped death and were in the witness protection program with Richard as their personal guardian. Robert was not an all-powerful superhero, but his contributions to the team made him a hero not only in Richard's eyes, but to all of those around him. Now, Erica II had to be put back online, the Killer Virus had to be destroyed, everything in the base had to be returned back to normal, they had to find Richard and the rest of gang, and Erica would have to be monitored before he would be satisfied with the future. Yes, they had much work to do and he was not about to let a lot of work get them stressed out to the point they could not help the team.

Outside the Octavian Farm

Mark walked away with dry tears on his cheeks. Many things passed through his mind, Erica's pep talk most of all. He ran to the main gate. There was a taxi waiting for him as he approached the gate. He stopped at the opened gate and stared at the taxi. Erica had called for the taxi long ago. *How could she had known?* Mark thought. He cried even more as he entered the taxi.

"To the airport, sir?" The taxi driver asked, confirming the destination.

Mark stopped crying in complete surprise. "Yeah, make it quick."

The taxi driver kept quiet, but just before coming into the Miami International Airport, curiosity took the best of him. "Hey, buddy, why are you going to the airport? You know that all flights are grounded because of that virus."

"The virus is dead. Airplanes will be able to take off now," Mark said, knowing Erica would have restored the nationwide panic and destroyed the virus by now.

Mark quickly got out of the cab in front of the Pan Am terminal. Mark stood there for a few seconds. Why was he there?

He did not really know. There was something urging him to step forward. He felt empty inside and whatever was controlling him was undeniably supernatural. He almost ran to the ticket counter, hoping the feeling would go away, and asked about any flights going out.

He could hardly believe his ears as the ticket clerk said the only flight going out was a direct flight to Saint Louis.

Mark's heart sank deeper than ever before. *Ground Zero.* Mark thought to himself. *Why? Does Ego want him to go to St. Louis to kill him or was there something else he was supposed to do for him?*

Mark dug deep into his pockets and drew out several hundred-dollar bills. It was not enough for the ticket, but the clerk surprised him again.

"Mr. Farnell, you have a reserved seat, first class, going to Lambert International." The clerk handed him the ticket before he could ask how much the ticket would cost.

The plane departed in twenty-five minutes. Mark breathed heavily as he rushed to get onboard. He made it in the nick of time and sat down in his first-class seat, exhausted. He slept through the take-off and most of the flight. A nightmare woke him up two hours later. The image of shadowy figures and Ego's voice scared him to the point of taking up drinking again, so he ordered martinis from the stewardess.

Mark drank his cold martini quickly, one after another as if racing against time. His hands started to tremble on his fourth drink. An elderly man, in his late seventies, one empty first-class seat away on the same row curiously stared at Mark. Mark grabbed both right and left sides of the sliding table tray and squeezed as hard as he could on the hard plastic, his knuckles and face turning pale.

The elderly man dressed in a business suit just stared, unable or unwilling to ask if something was wrong. Mark thought of all the times Richard stood by his side no matter what. Although he didn't know Richard was almost indestructible in the past, the times when Richard risked his life to protect him during the war counted a great deal to him. The times they talked about life and their problems were another thing that made his heart ache. Richard was always there as a true friend, and now he had betrayed Richard's trust and friendship.

Richard was always one to surround himself with good friends. His friends including Erica somehow mirrored an aspect of Richard's character that he felt, heard, or saw every time he was around them. Mark stopped shaking, but sweat ran down his face. The words Erica said to him kept haunting him. *'You always have a choice, Mark, good or bad.'*

Mark's throat was dry, and he was unable to breathe for a few seconds. He put both hands on his face side-by-side and leaned back on the passenger seat. The sweat smothered by the palm of his hands bled out along the edges of his hands and face. He managed to take a deep breath and closed his eyes as tears desperately tried to spill out.

Forgive me, Richard.

The elderly man leaned forward. "Are you alright, young

man?"

"I'm fine, just tired," Mark mumbled.

"You're not scared of flying in airplanes, are you?"

Mark calmed down a little and reached around the tray in front of him and wiped the sweat off his hands onto his pants. "No, I'm fine."

"It might help if you believe in yourself. You always have a choice, good or bad," the man said.

Mark looked in the man's direction but the seat was already empty, as if he never existed. There was no one on the same row he was sitting in. He looked around the other rows but only saw a couple to his rear, a woman and a young businessman.

Goose bumps and a quick chill hit Mark; he was suddenly frightened and confused. *He was with me during the entire flight,* he thought, trying to recall how the man looked like, but he could only remember him vaguely.

Mark wanted to splash water on his face in the restroom, but was scared of getting up. *Was he going insane? Why couldn't he remember the old man? Who was messing with his head? Was Ego playing tricks on him?* Many questions went through his head as he cleared his table tray and closed the window shutter. He built up the courage to get up and go to a vacant toilet just thirty minutes before landing on Lambert International Airport.

Mark splashed cold water on his face after entering the vacant toilet stall. The water was soothing. He looked at himself in the mirror for a very long time; the old times were gone, only sadness and regret reflected back at him. He took a deep breath, splashed more water, and quickly dried his face. He sat on the closed toilet seat and pulled out his palm pilot. He rapidly scanned for addresses, names, and locations that he could use to figure out where Ego's servant might be found.

It was not long before he correlated two possible locations of where the servant of Ego might be. Mark thought, *Maybe it wasn't too late. Maybe he could stop Ego from destroying the world and hopefully set things right.* He stood up and prepared to go back to his seat, confident that his decision was the right one.

11725 S. 87 Pike Road, Kansas City

David rang the doorbell to Pamela's house. He wore warm casual clothes and carried a large shopping bag by his side. The house was quite large, with two levels, a two-car garage, and a screened-in pool in the back yard. David was impressed with the front yard. It was not professionally maintained, but he could tell the children cut the grass and trimmed the bushes. It had a family touch about it and Horace was probably too busy to take care of the landscaping. He also doubted Pam was the one cutting the grass, so he assumed the eldest did most of the work.

The clouds above cast a strong feeling of autumn. The moderate wind complemented the scenery, along with the colors of the leaves on the trees. It was about to get dark soon, but that was the perfect atmosphere for Pam and Horace to go out on a dinner date.

A young boy in his teens opened the door. His black hair was well-groomed and styled like a professional actor. He stood close to five-nine and was slender. "Hello, can I help you?"

David smiled. "Yes, I'm David. You must be Troy."

Troy looked at David surprised. "Are you the babysitter?"

"Yes I am. Is your dad or mom home?"

"Mom, David is here!" Troy yelled to somebody behind him. "My mom is a little busy, but you can come in and wait for her inside." It was obvious Troy felt slightly uncomfortable about David as his mom's choice for a babysitter.

"Thank you."

Troy eyed David, wondering what he had in the shopping bag. "What's in there?"

David looked at the bag and smiled again. "Oh, these are some things I picked up on the way here. I figured you might want this." David buried his hand into the bag and pulled out a Michael Jordan jersey and an official NBA basketball with a dozen autographs signed by Michael Jordan and almost all of the members of the Lakers team.

Troy's eyes widened in complete surprise as he glared at the basketball, the jersey, and then at David. "Nah, that can't be real!"

David held the basketball up closer to Troy. "Yes, it is. Look at the ink, most of them are from different pens, and they weren't fabricated in a factory. The jersey, of course, is not really Jordan's but it is from the same company and the same number he played for over five years, just not the same size."

Troy could not believe his eyes. All of the negative things he thought about David went completely out the window as David was now the best sitter he had ever known, and the best part about it was David was not even here to babysit him, but his younger brother Luke.

"Wow! Thank you." Troy was almost speechless as he grabbed the two items and almost ran into the living room calling out to his brother. "Luke! You have to see this!"

David smiled again and dug into his bag, preparing to take out the presents he got for Luke.

Pamela was coming downstairs followed by Horace. They were both elegantly dressed up with matching colors. Horace had a nice, black silk two-piece suit while Pam worn a silky red and black long dress to her ankles. She was stunning. Pamela and Horace both smiled as they came down the stairs, but they both suddenly looked concerned hearing the commotion in the living room.

"Hey, boys, what's going on?" Horace spoke loudly.

Pam smiled an awkward smile. She didn't get a chance to introduce her husband yet.

"Hey, Dad, check this out." Troy and Luke came running out. Troy was wearing the Michael Jordan jersey while Luke raised the basketball above his head trying to show their dad what David just brought them.

Horace looked at the gifts, then at David. Horace was a very tall man, well above six feet with a slender build like his son. He eyed David with suspicion as he grabbed the basketball from

Luke and read the names.

Pam introduced them, seeing Horace was a little upset having to meet David bringing gifts, which were probably very expensive.

"Hello, Horace, it's nice to meet you. Pam told me you were tall, but I didn't think you could pass for a basketball player," David said, offering his hand.

"Hello, David," Horace said as he handed back the basketball to Luke. "My wife has told me much about you, too."

"Isn't this a great basketball, Dad?" Luke exclaimed. Luke was about three-and-a-half feet tall and also had a well-styled haircut. His brown eyes and smallish face resembled that of a five- or a seven-year-old boy.

Horace smiled at Luke. "Yes, son, that is a great basketball. It must have cost a lot of money." Horace looked at David in a subtle way, wanting an explanation to why David got such an expensive gift for his kid.

"Actually, it only cost about thirty dollars before it was signed. Michael Jordan was happy to sign it when I met him after one of his games. The jersey, well that was a little more expensive. But, you know what, I have more things to show all of you," David said and pulled out three X-box games from the bag and a wireless remote. "This is for you, Luke."

Pam and Horace were both confused. "Wow, this is mine?" Luke exclaimed and gave the basketball back to Troy.

"David, isn't one gift enough?" Pam asked, as Luke fumbled with the games.

Horace was looking at David even harder now. David was not part of the family, but he acted as if he were an uncle or a grandparent bringing gifts on a visit.

"Wow, these are the games I wanted to get." Luke was overjoyed knowing he didn't have to wait for Christmas to get the games he had been waiting so desperately to own and play.

"I also have a gift for you," David motioned to Horace and pulled out an unsealed envelope.

Horace wordlessly took the envelope from David and withdrew a pair of front-seat tickets to the *Beauty and the Beast* play premiering the following week in downtown Kansas City. "It's not much, but I was able to get them for a cheap price. Of course, the most expensive gifts are the games," David said with an extremely candid demeanor. David's reply was almost memorizing to the point where Horace felt bad if he declined the gift.

Pam was awe-stricken as David calmed Horace so quickly and easily. She had her own reservations about David meeting Horace, but everything he seemed to talk about in relationships was clearly his field of expertise.

Troy took Luke into the living room to help him take the games out of the plastic casing and set up the configurations on the X-box.

"Is there anything I should know if an emergency happens so I can reach you two?" David was then saying. "And when do you want Luke to go to sleep?"

"There is no school tomorrow so Luke can stay up as late

as eleven," Pam said. "We are taking Troy to Kevin's house to sleep over there for the night. Horace's and my cell phone numbers are on the dining table. Luke has already eaten dinner, but if he wants he can only have a few snacks, a list is on the table as well."

"Okay, does Luke have any allergies, anything like that?"

"No, but if he starts crying because he misses me, you can have him talk to me on the phone and he will calm down."

"Well, I was hoping we could talk more, but you two have reservations waiting for you. Go eat and have fun, I'm sure we can talk more later," David said, primarily toward Horace whom he really wanted to know better.

Horace looked almost dumbfounded. David was frankly the perfect friend whom Pam had been talking about for the past two days. He felt so at ease with him around. It was weird, almost freaky. If he had not known any better, the profile of a perfect sociopath in the stage of getting close to his target would have been the only other option to David's uncanny aura and motives.

"Thank you for sitting for us David," Horace said.

"It's my pleasure. I'm glad to be able to spend time with Luke. He seems like such a good boy. How old is he, by the way?"

"He's six," Pam said as Troy and Luke came back after having set up the game.

"Really? He seems very smart for a six-year-old kid."

Luke smiled and looked up at David. Troy picked up a blue backpack by the door. He was all set to go to his friend's house.

"Yes, he is," Horace said. "He is also very good at video games, so don't feel bad if you don't beat him on any of the games."

"As long as he has fun, that's what counts." David said and smiled.

"We'll call you if we are running late, but we should be back by one or two," Pam said by the door.

"I'll make sure he gets to bed on time. Have fun you two." David and Luke waved good-bye.

"Bye, mommy," Luke chirped.

"Bye, honey, have fun and make sure you behave well."

David closed the door and both of them went immediately into the living room to play *Mario Brothers*. They spent two hours playing video games and eating snacks. Luke was happy as can be and failed to notice David's sudden loss of concentration. It was not obvious and David made it a point to change the situation by asking Luke if he wanted to watch cartoons on the cartoon channel.

Luke did not object so they just sat there on the sofa watching television. David had his chance and went off into a mild trance.

Luke looked at David after a while, but said nothing.

David seemed to be very tired with very faint traces of

sweat going down the sides of his face.

"David, are you sick?" Luke finally asked.

David woke up from his trance and looked at Luke slightly startled. He thought quickly, trying to respond to the boy. "I'm okay, but I'm feeling very hot. What if we go in the backyard and look at the stars, and I'll show you a magic trick."

Luke seemed to not be interested at all in going outside to look at stars, especially if it meant sitting outside with the few mosquitoes strong enough to withstand the coming of fall, but he was interested in seeing a magic trick. "What kind of magic trick?"

"Real magic. But you have to promise you won't tell anyone I can do magic, okay?" David smiled, stood up, and turned off the television.

Luke let out a big grin. "I promise... Are you a wizard?"

David gently smiled. It had been a long time since he had talked to children, especially one that was as intelligent and young as Luke. "Did you know that about 1,600 years ago, wizards, warlocks, and sorcerers were all magic users who had special disciplines like levitating objects, seeing into the future, making fireballs come out of their hands, seeing in the dark like owls, and even controlling the weather?"

"What are warlocks?"

"You know what witches are, right?" David asked as they both went outside and sat by the screened-in pool.

"Witches are witches," Luke said innocently.

"Right, witches are witches, but witches are all women. Warlocks are the same as witches, except that warlocks are men. Do you understand?"

"Oh, I see, warlocks are men witches."

"Yes, you got it," David said and picked up two folding recliners and sat in the middle of the grassy lawn.

It was a partly cloudy sky but the stars were bright and could be seen through the patches of holes in-between the clouds.

David placed the chairs side by side and reclined them almost all the way back. He sat down with his legs crossed. Luke did the same, mimicking David. "Okay, what is your favorite fruit?"

Luke thought about it. He looked up and thought very hard. "I like strawberries."

David smiled. "Okay, it will take me a minute or two, so you will have to be very quiet while I concentrate, okay?"

Luke sat straight up in his chair waiting to see what David would do. "Okay."

David went into a trance again, this time a lot more in control with perfect posture as he sat up in the middle of the recliner. His thoughts went out to within a mile radius. Luke could almost see a blue glow around David and probably felt the warmth that David generated as he concentrated on his magic trick, but kept himself quiet as he had promised.

David opened his eyes and turned toward Luke after some minutes.

Luke was gaping in anticipation.

"Alright, Luke. Stick out your hands with your palms facing up," David instructed.

Luke did what he was told.

"Now, I'm going to put my hands on top of yours and I will give you a surprise. But you will have to close your eyes for three seconds. Alright?"

Luke watched David put his hands with his palms facing up on top of his own palms. "Okay."

"On the count of one you close your eyes. One...two...three..." Luke closed his eyes on the first count and opened up his eyes on the third count. Luke's eyes and mouth could not be any wider; he was in complete awe. David held a huge plate with a big pile of freshly-cut strawberries.

David moved his hands out from between the plate and Luke's hands so Luke could take the plate from him.

Luke held the plate with a look of wonder and joy on his face. "How did you do that?"

"I used magic, of course. Now you can eat while we look at the stars and clouds."

"Do that again!" Luke asked as he stuffed a strawberry into his mouth.

"I'll do another trick a little bit later. Eat your strawberries for now." David picked up a strawberry and ate it as he laid down on his recliner.

Luke ate as David pointed out stars and cloud formations. It was not long before they each pointed out imaginary figures formed by the clouds and stars as eyes, mouths, or nostrils.

Luke finished his strawberries and noticed there were no insects bothering him. In fact, the only evidence of any insects in the area were fireflies every now and then lighting up as they flew around them.

"What happened to all of the mosquitoes?" Luke asked.

"Don't worry about them," David said with a little laugh. "Ecologists would be upset if they knew that all of the roaches, ants, termites, and the few remaining mosquitoes within a mile from here are dead."

Luke had a confused look on his face, thinking why the insects would be dead and how David knew of this, but he said nothing as David continued to point out figures in the sky.

They spent thirty minutes outside, and then went inside with David doing a final trick by pulling a caramel-covered apple-on-a-stick from behind Luke's ear.

Luke was a perfect host and helped David out with the dishes and cleaned the mess they made in the living room. It was almost eleven when Luke started to get tired and fell asleep on the sofa.

David picked Luke up, took him to his room, and tucked him into bed. David checked all of the windows and doors before he straightened up the kitchen and living room with last-minute touch-ups. He lay down on the sofa, tired from using up a large portion of his acquired power pool with the magic tricks and manipulation of Mark's travel plans, but he had reserves that he kept for emergencies. He went into another trance and searched for Cindy and the Eternal Champions.

His search took him into another dimension that was familiar to him, having been there twice before. He kept a vigilant eye on Richard's group, hoping Pam would soon return, because the amount of power he was using to look into Ego's dimension was quickly draining his life force. The neighborhood was spread apart and it would take him more effort to drain people's energies—he would not get enough power in return without killing the people he drained.

The Eternal Champions were at a critical point in their battle with Ego when Horace and Pam arrived. They were early, to David's relief. Now, maybe he could help in the fight.

David quickly ran outside and met them at the car.

Pam and Horace looked at David with worried looks as he came out of the house. " Is something wrong?" Pam asked as she got out of the car before Horace could put the gears into park.

David seemed exhausted and bent over, grabbing his knees with his hands as if he just ran a 200-meter sprint. He looked down, caught his breath, and then looked up at Horace who was out of the car by now.

"Horace, give the keys to Pam, go inside, and stay with Luke," David commanded.

Horace did not question David, but simply handed Pam the keys and ran straight inside the house. Pam looked at David and Horace in complete disbelief and confusion—Horace was following David's orders without question.

Pam looked at David again with a horrified look in her eyes. "What is going on, David?"

David gave her a tired gaze as if he was almost about to pass out. "Pam, I need you to help me. Drive me to any place with a lot of people."

Pamela's fright turned to concern seeing David seemed to be very sick. "Are you feeling okay?"

David's concentrated on Pam's mind but drew a blank. The strain of controlling Horace's mind was already too much on him. He fell on his knees, exhausted.

Pam caught David around his shoulders and chest. She felt his forehead with the palm of her hand. His skin was not sweating very much, but it was practically on fire. "Oh, my God! You're burning up!"

"Help me into the car and start driving. Please, Pam."

Pam looked at David, scared and confused, but she felt that aura of peace around him, which calmed her nerves. "Okay, I will take you to the hospital."

Chapter Sixteen

□ □ ◻ □ □

NUCLEAR HOLOCAUST

T he cobblestone sidewalk cracked in sporadic areas, unable to withstand the sudden change in air pressure and gravitational rupture created by the dimensional window—a black hole appearing just above it. The top portion of a parking meter next to the phenomenon partially disintegrated with the base pole bent flat on the ground as the hole expanded to seven feet in diameter.

Richard and Larcis were first to emerge from the hole and out onto the paved street. Richard's entire body ached with pain while Larcis lay motionless on the cold ground, completely dead to the world around him. Richard inhaled heavily as strength returned to his cells. He shape-shifted several times into his various attires and complexions, instinctively countering the hexametric dimension's effects on his body. Richard smiled in pain as he transformed back into Creator.

Susan, John, and Elizabeth burst out of the black hole,

almost hitting Richard as he stood up. They tumbled across the pavement, scraped along the street, and finally hit the curb.

Richard stood up with a renewed sense of strength and power. His body was regenerating, and he felt much stronger than ever before. John, Susan, and Liz slowly got up, but Larcis remained sprawled. Richard kept a watchful eye on the dimensional window as he ran to Larcis as the door buzzed and stayed open.

Larcis's body felt cold while Richard grabbed him, trying to get him as far away from the hole as possible.

Cindy's ghostly figure appeared next to Susan as the hole grew larger with every passing minute. "Is everyone alright?" Susan looked around. Everyone responded except for Richard and Larcis.

Richard flew away about a hundred meters carrying Larcis in his arms. He gently placed Larcis on a wooden bench and checked his vital signs.

'Let's move, people!' John commanded as he led the group toward Richard. They quickly gathered around Larcis, looking in all directions for any approaching danger.

Several people down the street witnessed the scene and ran off as John mentally scared them off to leave the area by showing them the vision of Ego's demonic figure.

"Where are we?" Cindy asked.

"Saint Louis," Liz answered, recognizing the city from one of her many visions. "This must be ground zero where Ego will start his reign of terror."

'How do you know that?' John asked.

"We wouldn't have been sent here if it wasn't," Richard answered and stood up, turning toward the dimensional portal.

"He's unconscious from the beating he took in there. He just needs time to recover," Liz said after analyzing Larcis's entire body.

Richard felt a lot better knowing everyone was okay for now, but his thoughts raced elsewhere in his mind, trying to figure out what to do next.

"Thank God, you're alright!" Erica screamed on Liz's comlink.

"Erica, do you know where Mark is right now?" Richard yelled.

"Yes, he is approximately six miles from your location," Erica replied.

"We have to close the portal," Susan said.

"John, go find Mark. Hopefully, he will lead you to the nuke. Remember, he is my friend so give him a chance. Cindy, stay with Larcis. Susan, Liz, come with me," Richard then flew toward the portal, which had now grown to ten feet in diameter.

"Erica, are you there?" Cindy talked into John's wristband comlink.

"Yes. How can I help you, Cindy?" Erica replied as if she had known Cindy for a very long time.

"Where exactly is Mark?"

"He is approximately 9.7 kilometers from your present location. Follow the arrows." Erica displayed an arrow and the eight cardinal directions on John's miniature screen. John punched in OK on his keypad and flew off toward the indicated direction.

Richard landed a hundred meters from the portal with Susan and Liz coming to his side.

"What now?" Liz asked.

"We need to buy some time so Nowhereman can close the portal," Richard said as he swooped down to a parked car and grabbed it with both his hands. He lifted the car from underneath. "Ego can't come out of the portal as long as something is going in," Richard said, then flung the car into the expanding portal.

The black hole swallowed the car, crumbling the side mirrors as it entered the hexametric dimension. Liz and Susan quickly followed Richard's example and started throwing cars into the portal using their strength and telekinetic powers. Cars were soon in short supply so Richard started throwing parking meters, signs, fire hydrants, parts of metal railings, benches— anything he could get a hold of.

By then, Larcis had woken up and saw Cindy's smiling face above him. "What happened?"

"We're back in our world. Rest a little before you try to get up." Cindy gently nudged him back down on the bench as Larcis attempted to get up as he heard the noise created by the portal eating pieces of physical matter.

Larcis felt a weird numbness all over his body but he realized he could move normally. An electric current circulated through his system as his almost out-of-body experience went away. "What's going on?" He was still hearing the sound of the dimensional door, as if it were repeatedly being opened and closed.

"I think the city block is not going to last for very long," Cindy said as she saw Richard gradually running out of things to throw into the portal.

Richard stood in front of the portal; he had just thrown the last remaining street sign he could find. He thought about diverting sprouting water from the nonexistent fire hydrant but it was slightly behind the portal and too far away to be effective. He realized now that his plan only delayed what seemed to be inevitable. He just stood there and braced himself to meet Ego now.

Richard quickly turned around and jumped to the side as Susan caught his attention.

"Heads up!" Susan yelled as a very large section of a building was yanked away from the foundation and telekinetically thrown into the portal. The eight-story office building provided a steady stream of concrete, metal, glass, and wood, keeping the portal constantly active.

"Don't forget the kitchen sink," Liz said while Susan took her time in stripping and, turning the building's foundation into an empty lot.

"She won't be able to keep that up for long," Liz said,

seeing Susan strain from using up so much energy.

"Yes, I know," Richard replied, trying to remember what Nowhereman said about Ego and his weaknesses.

John flew over rooftops and city blocks and finally landed on the building Mark was last seen to have entered. Erica tracked Mark's movement by redirecting all possible imaging satellites, which was a very expensive and monumental feat, but Erica did not care what Capitol Hill would have to say—it was in the interest of national security and world peace.

John scanned the building for any mental activity. It was oddly empty of people except for one person. The abandoned apartment building was only four stories high with every floor easily accessible through many windows and doors. It really did not matter though, because John spread out his molecules and phased through the ceilings and floors with ease. He stopped on the second floor, inside a large dimly-lit room full of electronic equipment scattered in all four corners of the room.

Mark was there, feverishly working on a partially disassembled casing of a homemade nuclear bomb in the center of the room.

John was completely quiet in his de-solidified state as he floated ten feet behind Mark. John made his body solid again and stood on the wooden floor, listening to Mark talk to himself.

"I can do this. Red and silver panel. This screw here and here," Mark was mumbling through some type of technical procedure or checklist.

What do you think you're doing? John mentally interrupted Mark's train of thought.

Mark swung around, frightened, and gazed in all directions. "Mindseye," he muttered, unable to say anything else fearing that Mindseye was there to kill him.

It's over, Mark. Ego is your enemy, not us. Disarm the bomb and let's go home.

Mark could not believe his ears. How could John forgive him for all the evil things he did? His fear turned into shame as he tried to forgive himself for being such a fool. "I'm trying to disarm the bomb. I didn't build it!"

John saw a man's body lying on the floor in the corner and understood what was going on and why Mark seemed to be dismantling the casing. *Is he dead?* He asked, but knew he detected only Mark's mental activity before entering the room.

"He wouldn't help me turn off the bomb and tried to kill me!"

John kept his temper from taking over. If he had only arrived sooner, he could have taken the information out of the man without killing him. *How much time do we have?*

"Fifty-seven seconds and counting." Mark twirled around looking at the timer and quickly continued to take the casing apart.

John rushed to his side, trying to see if he could help Mark. *Can you do it?* John asked as he tried to come up with alternative options in his head.

"Don't know!" Mark almost yelled as he unscrewed the last screw on the outer casing.

What if I pick the bomb up and send it into space? John suggested.

"It has motion sensors which will accelerate detonation and you won't be able to get far enough into the atmosphere in time without it killing millions of people," Mark said as he opened up an access panel into the detonation control system.

The timer continued down to 35 seconds as Mark grabbed Mindseye's hand. "Hold this, cut the white and blue wire when I tell you."

Mindseye took a second pair of wire cutters and did as Mark instructed. "On the count of two, I will say cut. At cut, we will cut. Ready? One, two—cut."

Mindseye held his breath as the cut did not make the nuke go off, but it did not stop the timer either as it continued counting down to 29 seconds.

Mark looked at the wiring, very confused and disappointed. Horror struck Mark as he understood why his attempt to turn off the bomb failed. "There are more than two failsafe backups!" Mark said as he stepped away from the bomb in complete disbelief and sorrow for having failed. "I'm sorry, John."

John looked at the bomb and then at Mark. *No, this can't be it, not like this,* John thought and concentrated on his energy field as he pushed Mark farther away from the bomb and himself. *Run, I'll take care of this!* John screamed into Mark's mind.

Chapter Seventeen

□ □ ▢ □ □

COBBLER SQUARE

An entire building had gone into the hexametric universe, and another was soon to follow as Susan started to take the building next to it apart, piece by piece.

"Susan, stop!" Richard yelled over the portal's background noise.

"What's the matter?" Liz asked.

"Why, isn't it working?" Susan replied, hesitant to stop throwing sections of building into the portal.

"I think I know what Nowhereman meant when he said Ego's downfall would be of his own creation," Richard said and moved farther away from the portal. "Let Ego through, once he's in our universe, we can kill him."

Susan continued to move the building, but much slower this time as she pondered what Richard said.

"I thought he would be more powerful here in this universe," Liz said.

"His power comes from his own universe, that's why he needs the death of thousands of people to give him enough power while he is on this side of the universe so he can bring part of his own universe into this one. Then he will be too powerful to stop."

"So we let him in and let him get strong enough?" Liz asked.

"He can't feed until the nuke goes off. We might be able to destroy him while he is here in our universe before the nuke goes off. But we have to remember to fight him as if he were a simulation in the Danger Room," Richard explained.

"That might actually work," Susan said and dropped the chunks of building going into the portal; it left a trail of rubble up to the energy field.

"I hope you're right," Liz said, still uncomfortable with the idea.

"Yeah, so am I." Richard knew this was going to be the hardest battle they had ever faced as the Eternal Champions.

It was not long before the hexametric dimensional vortex vibrated furiously and Ego's grotesque figure emerged out of the dimensional door. All of the members in the group felt a chill run down their spines as the demonic figure of a lion, wolf, and dragon stepped through the portal and onto the street.

Ego's talons ripped through the cobble stones like a knife through butter. His face was spiked with many horns protruding from his forehead and the sides of his hideous dragon-like jaws and snout. A terrible stench of death erupted out of his skin and nostrils, almost suffocating the three superheroes before him.

Richard could live in a space environment but the odor of Ego's body lingered in his nostrils. He knew it was an illusion to some degree but could not help but believe Ego's physical presence. He knew the pain of fighting would be real and great on the group and he wanted nothing more than to shield his wife and friends from further harm.

Ego stood thirteen feet from the ground to his shoulder blades. His crimson red skin boiled the humid air, from which putrid steam emanated. From the lion's mane that surrounded his neck dripped acid-like droplets of fiery sweat.

Richard and Susan stepped backwards as Ego's long scaly body continued to emerge from the portal.

Liz backed off, terrified. Richard waved Susan away and teased the beast to come to him.

"Come here, Kitty."

Ego's beastly body was completely through the portal, his tail majestically swaying back and forth.

Richard's demeanor showed no fear, only contempt for the creature before him. Ego growled, showing off his very sharp blood-stained teeth, but he did not seem to care if Richard was frightened or intimidated. Ego slowly crawled forward; he already knew Richard's fighting and leadership skills.

Richard waited patiently for an opening to inflict as much damage as possible on Ego, who was spitting out vomit-looking globs of green acid at Richard. The deadly gook missed Richard's face and hit the ground across the street. It instantly melted through ten feet of concrete and dirt, creating a tunnel large enough for a large rabbit to make a home.

Richard flew into the air directly above the beast and shot out a telekinetic blast of energy from his hands on Ego's back. The creature reared on his hind legs and jumped up at Richard. Susan and Liz took the opportunity to attack and simultaneously shot a barrage of telekinetic and fire blasts at Ego's underside. The beast roared, more in aggravation than in pain, and flew backwards into an abandoned office building area set for demolition. The ten-foot metal fence around the building gave way to Ego's body with most of the fence instantly melting away from the acid on his scaly skin.

Ego quickly sprang up on all four paws.

Richard again flew around and shot a telekinetic blast into Ego's side.

Ego's scales seemed to cave in as the blast hit, but there was no penetration from the fist-sized attack. However, the force of the attack hurled Ego along the fence line, leaving a trail of melted fence links and metal poles. But the beast quickly recovered and sprang at Richard with incredible speed for a monster of his size and weight.

Richard jumped to evade Ego's black ivory claws. The talons missed, but Ego's forearm pushed Richard into an awkward standing position.

Richard felt the scales on Ego's forearm, then the paw and talons of that arm wrapped around his body. The tips of the claws buried themselves into his stomach and ripped him up toward his chest and neck. There was no blood spewing out, but he felt pain as acid ate at his open wounds.

Ego's iron grip on his body would have instantly crushed a normal human to death, but Richard's steel-like constitution only got stronger as the pressure built up. Ego tossed Richard with great strength toward the abandoned building.

Richard arced through the air and slammed into the building. The concrete wall crumbled as if it were paper as Richard's body went through three walls deep inside the building.

Liz and Susan saw Richard disappear amid the rubble, which only made them more determined in attacking Ego. The beast, however, seemed utterly invincible.

Susan changed her plan of attack and lifted Ego's body straight into the air with her telekinetic power. Ego flung his paws, his tail, and his head in all directions helplessly in midair as Susan maintained her hold on the beast.

"This isn't working too good," Liz said, realizing they must damage Ego somehow and not just hold him so he could get stronger.

In the pile of rubble on the second floor of the building, Richard slowly stood up. The claw imprints on his body instantly healed and a smile came over him. He loved a challenge and fighting Ego seemed to have sparked some excitement; the battle was stirring the fighter in him.

He flew outside, expecting to run into Ego on the ground. He stopped at the entrance to the hole in the wall of the building and saw Ego's body floating in the air, but not thrashing his limbs around anymore.

"You fools, do you think you can win!" Ego roared and his body fell to the ground. His four paws buried themselves into the dirt and sidewalk.

Susan's face strained as she attempted to lift Ego back up into the air. Ego was too heavy; somehow, he increased his mass and must have weighed over 200 tons.

Richard jumped down on Ego's back as Ego charged at Liz. Richard landed on the ground behind Ego while Liz stood helplessly as she merely watched Ego speeding toward her.

Richard sprinted forward and plowed into Ego, stabbing the beast with his hand that had shape-shifted into a knife. His expertise in martial arts and combat experience was evident as his stance, precision, and the fury of his attack was perfect. His knife-arm pierced Ego between the rear right leg and chest.

Ego roared in pain and pawed at Richard with all his might. Richard once again was thrown down the street several blocks out of sight with black gooey blood trailing behind him. The gaping hole on Ego's body closed up instantly and Ego continued his charge on Liz.

Liz frantically increased the strength of her force field, hoping it would protect her from the monster.

Ego pounced on Liz, biting her around the waist and violently shaking her sideways. The pressure on her body was tremendous but the sudden jerking motion of Ego's head caused most of the damage. Liz felt her arm break under the pressure of Ego's teeth against her force field.

Ego flung her to the side as large debris of a brick wall hit him on the side and threw him across the smashed street. Ego kept his footing by creating four trenches of broken cobblestones on the street. He looked at Susan who stood next to the side of a partially destroyed building.

"Try that on me," Susan challenged; as it was her who attacked the beast with the pile of bricks.

Ego's body turned black, including his eyes. Acid continued to drip from his mane, but the ground around him froze as if the acid were liquid ice. He opened his mouth and a piece of sharp ice the size of a javelin shot out like a bullet straight at Susan.

The ice projectile hit Susan in the chest, but simply disintegrated on impact—she had attacked the projectile with her force field and destroyed it before it actually touched her.

The attack seemed very weak and would have done minor damage even if it did hit Susan for real, but it distracted her enough for Ego to charge at her at full speed.

Susan jumped in time and narrowly escaped Ego's jaws. Ego savagely whipped his tail around, slashing at Susan. She felt the iron-like tail bruise her wrist—which was more painful because of the acid eating away at her skin. She flew into the air, distancing herself from Ego who was twirling around for another charge.

Frustration started to fill her mind, but she caught herself and concentrated on the fight. She looked at her blistering hand and the wounds on her hips. In an instant, she was back to normal, duplicating Richard's regenerative abilities. Richard's innate powers of controlling his physical body was ideal for defense, but it caused her to allocate her energy into defense and not offense.

Ego seemed to be getting stronger by the second—he must have been feeding on someone's emotions. Susan quickly looked around and saw Liz on the ground, painfully clenching her arm. Ego was feeding on Liz's anguish.

Ego sprang forward with a super leap at Susan—but Richard appeared out of nowhere and collided with the beast in midair. This time, Richard used both hands to pierce Ego's black scaly skin.

Ego roared in pain as both of them tumbled and crashed on the street, with large chunks of debris flying everywhere.

Susan took advantage of the break and flew down beside Liz. She grabbed Liz's arm and instantly mended the broken bone and severed vein.

"You're making him stronger. Fly away and let us kill him," Susan told Liz.

Liz felt helpless and a little surprised that Susan was commanding her to leave.

Susan saw frustration in Liz's eyes. "Stop it, don't think about anything! Feel sorry later after Ego is dead when and can no longer feed off your emotions!"

Liz could barely control herself, but did what Susan commanded and flew away into the night sky.

Richard withdrew his knife-arms from Ego's body and jumped off. He noticed Ego's increase in strength and looked around, wondering how the beast got stronger. He saw Susan where Liz used to be and then saw Liz flying away high into the distant sky.

Ego rolled off his back and snapped at Richard. His enormous jaws and teeth caught Richard in the legs. The fangs dug into Richard's body. Ego shook his head furiously like a cat with a small rat in its mouth. Richard instinctively pushed against Ego's outer mouth using all his strength.

Richard finally broke free from the grip of Ego's fangs. He tumbled along the street with the broken fangs dropping off on the cobblestones. Ego roared his loudest scream of pain looking briefly disoriented. The holes in Richard's body regenerated almost instantly as he stood up.

New fangs reappeared on Ego's mouth as he regenerated the injured parts of his body. His beastly figure suddenly shifted into a seven-foot tall male demon. A dark aura surrounded his silhouette with an oblique glimmer of light; the sight of the beast reminded Richard of a solar eclipse. His entire body was pitch black with red glowing eyes and four horns coming out of his forehead as the only distinguishing characteristics on his body.

The entire neighborhood seemed to go up in smoke as a building disintegrated into a million pieces—but the fragments froze in time and space, then shot toward Ego at almost lightning speed—the shrieking sound was like a train gone amuck. The fragments were like bullets raining on Ego from all directions.

It was Susan who did it, using her telekinetic power to use the nearby building as a weapon of sorts. She almost collapsed from exhaustion from the massive effort.

However, a dark bluish force field appeared around Ego just as the fragments reached him. The fragments disintegrated into vapor along with Ego's shield.

"I'm through playing with you, humans," Ego bellowed.

A black and almost reddish blast of energy came out of his body and hit Richard and Susan simultaneously. The energy engulfed both of them, paralyzing them as it electrocuted them where they stood.

Richard was not in any major pain, but he could not move as he and Susan were both lifted up into the air before Ego's snarling visage.

"I have won!" Ego screamed as the city was lit up with a flash of light visible from all cardinal directions.

Richard could not move his head to see where the light came from but the shockwave he was expecting from the nuclear explosion never came. The ground shook for a brief second, but that was all that could be felt from the supposed explosion. Ego looked in the direction of the supposed ground zero and slowly, confusion descended on his distorted face.

A bright steady beam of light shot straight into the atmosphere several miles in the distance. The dimensional portal was closing. Ego suddenly panicked, but the problem at ground zero attracted his attention the most. Ego stared at the beam of light for a moment and seemed to be ready to run off toward the source of the beam, but stopped all of a sudden as if something was blocking his path.

Elizabeth majestically descended before Ego like an angel from heaven. She was not the same woman he was used to fighting. Her entire body and eyes glowed with radiant white light. "Your time has come to an end, Durgathoon."

Ego stepped back as if almost fearing Liz or recognizing her from a vision in a dream or a past life.

"Did you really think I would allow you to destroy this world? It's time you learned the value of life by giving up your own," Liz said with a thunderous echo as she lit up the city block with her aura of light, which was brighter than the sun.

Ego's body turned from black to whitish gray as the light seemed to blind out everything in the area. Ego let out an awful growl of pain as his soul was bombarded with white lightning bolts from Liz's eyes.

Richard and Susan slid off the wall onto the ground. They saw Ego writhe in pain, but Liz and the white environment weren't there. Richard took the opportunity to attack Ego in full charge, repeatedly stabbing Ego's body, which was now in human form.

Susan watched as Richard attacked Ego's new form. Ego was not fighting back for some reason, but she was not about to complain—she attacked Ego using Richard's tactics. The beam of light in the distance faded as Ego suddenly increased the density of his body to the point where Susan and even Richard's attacks failed to penetrate the beast's ghost-like body.

Richard and Susan glanced at each other, wondering what was going on. Richard looked around and spotted Liz a block away on a building rooftop, watching them. Liz was using mental illusions on Ego, which was why he was not attacking them. *That's my girl,* Richard thought and almost smiled.

Ego never felt so vulnerable in his entire existence. The pure white energy Liz was attacking him with was very painful and almost paralyzed his demonic body and soul. Ego felt knife-like attacks similar to Richard's attacks. One, two, three, four, five, six attacks in rapid succession rained on him in pairs. Ego tried to search for energy generated from humans within the immediate area, but there was nothing to feed off—even from Liz's spirit who was just before him.

Ego was infuriated and lashed out at the world with his most powerful attack—a wave of red energy burst out from the center of his being and exploded outward without warning.

The energy passed through Richard, Susan, and even Liz a block away. The two heroines felt piercing needle-like burns all over their bodies. Susan and Liz were temporarily blinded and tasted a rusty, acidic thing in their mouths as the red energy lingered in their bodies. Richard, on the other hand, felt the electricity, but ignored the pain. He suddenly ran off where he had been rolling on the ground.

Ego saw Liz disappear and everything came back to normal before she appeared. Susan was next to him and Richard was running away. He looked around a little confused, but he was connecting the dots quickly as he spotted Liz on the nearby rooftop.

Now, he felt power return to him from Susan and Liz. The nuclear bomb did not go off as he planned, so he would have to take over the world the hard way. He stared at Susan and began to tear her limbs off with his mind.

A huge bolt of lightning hit Ego in the head, forcing him to release Susan. Larcis flew above Ego and shot another lightning bolt at him, this time hitting the beast in the chest.

Ego screamed in pain—but weaker this time.

Susan backed away from Ego and tried to recover from the red energy and telekinetic attack.

Richard returned running, almost flying by Ego and holding one of the fangs that had broken off from Ego's mouth— he attacked like a bullet and buried the fang deep into Ego's chest and left it there in what would normally be the location of a human's heart.

Ego's attention was being distracted by each rapid attack, but he tried to attack Richard with some sort of strange energy coming out of his hands. But the attack ended suddenly as a steel section of a light post dematerialized inside Ego's body with only his legs and arms visible. Ego roared in horrific agony, as Cindy appeared running away from the beast leaving the light post as a present.

"Everyone get away from him!" Richard yelled and backed away himself. He concentrated on Ego while Susan, Larcis, and

Liz followed Richard's lead to simultaneously attack Ego.

The four superheroes unleashed all the power they had using telekinesis, fire, and energy.

The light pole inside Ego's body disintegrated and the rest of him was thrown backwards into a large pile of rubble from the building Susan had used to keep the dimensional portal from letting Ego into the world.

Richard was about to attack again, but blue flames suddenly engulfed Ego—it was so hot the flame almost instantly melted the ground around the beast.

Everyone looked up to see Hellfire hovering above Ego, then they heard six sonic booms catch up with Hellfire. The sound was deafening.

Hellfire continued to blast Ego with his deadly beam of blue flame, but there was much chaos and debris that nobody could even see if Ego was still in the blast area.

Liz recovered from the sonic booms and flew down toward Richard. "We did it!" Liz yelled. "I don't sense his presence, anymore."

Hellfire stopped his attack and they all waited for the smoke from the lava, smothering rocks, and dust to subside.

When the smoke cleared, they all saw a large crater.

Richard moved to the edge of the crater, stepping on rock and glass fragments. He saw that many rocks turned into crystals from the intensity and heat of Hellfire's flame attack.

Ego was nowhere to be seen in the center of the crater, which was red hot with molten lava. Hellfire flew down next to Richard. Hellfire's eyes were still glowing with bright blue flames and a light blue flame aura surrounded his entire body.

"Sorry about that," Hellfire said.

Richard looked at the center of the crater then straight down on the ground. "No need to be sorry. We won," Richard said as Larcis, Susan, Cindy, and Liz converged around the two superheroes.

"Well, I might have killed you. You were kind of close to it," Hellfire explained.

"Oh... I would have lived—I think." Richard laughed.

"You turned the ground into glass," Larcis said, staring at the crystals in the crater.

"Oh, that's nothing. You should see the big piece of glass that I made on the moon," Hellfire said.

Richard and Larcis both looked at the night's crescent moon above, slightly awed.

Hellfire smiled, then he laughed. "Nah, just kidding."

Richard and Larcis both smiled, relieved.

"Quatris is the one who made a huge glass parking lot on the far side of the moon," Hellfire said, then left them, flying high into the sky.

Larcis was speechless. Richard looked up at Hellfire in deep thought.

Liz went to Richard. "Richard, Erica lost contact with John."

Richard grabbed Liz's comlink. "Erica, take us to John's last location."

Richard flew off toward John's location while everyone else followed him. He scanned as far as he could seeing through buildings and spotted a block of city that resembled a crater while Erica guided him towards John's last location.

Chapter Eighteen

□ □ ◻ □ □

EARTH IS SAVED

Pamela nervously drove through the neighborhood. She quickly made it to the main highway and headed straight to the hospital.

David was breathing heavily although he was sitting in the front passenger seat. He was bent over as if his stomach where attacking him from the inside. The sweat flashes had gone away, but his whole body was weak. He could barely hold his head up and leaned it against the car window. The streetlights passed by with an almost hypnotic effect, making it hard for David to keep from falling asleep. He wasn't' dying, and couldn't no matter how much he used his powers, but he would be worthless to help the Eternal Champions and Cindy if he was recovering in sleep or comatose state.

"David, stay with me. We're almost there," Pam said, trying to keep David from passing out.

David said nothing and breathed deeply as he looked out

through the window.

Pam sped up twenty miles above the speed limit, taking advantage of an almost deserted highway early past midnight. "Can you talk?"

"Yes," David managed to reply.

"Okay, that's good. Now, what do we talk about?" Pam asked not thinking about her passive open ended question.

"You have great kids," David said.

Pam was mostly calm on the outside, but inside, she was a nervous wreck. Everything was happening so fast, and she had no idea what happened to David while she was gone with Horace, but the compliment about her children relaxed her a little.

"Did Luke behave well?"

David tried to smile, but instead his face distorted in pain. "Turn here, hurry!"

Pam was startled; she did not expect David to reply in such a way. "What—here? The hospital is one more exit down."

"I need healthy people. Turn now."

Pam turned the car off onto the exit ramp against her better judgment. "What are you talking about?"

"Turn left here and stop."

Pam stopped the car in the middle of a heavily populated block, putting the car in park. A nightclub was booming after the killer virus effects had been fixed, with a long line of people waiting to get their few hours of dancing, drinking, and socializing. The street was busy with all sorts of people roaming about, including your average beggars and hookers. "What are we doing here?" Pam asked, wondering how David would get better in the middle of downtown nowhere.

David's eyes glowed green and Pam's entire body suddenly felt weak as if the life force in her soul was being torn out. Pam weakly screamed and passed out in the driver's seat. The people outside on the street and inside the nightclub almost all fainted in pain from the life drain David attacked them with. No one was dead, but all probably felt like they would be better off if they were.

Much later, Pam woke up refreshed as if the life drained from her never left her. See looked at David, whose entire body was glowing with a greenish aura of light.

"Do not fear me, Pam. Everything is alright now. You have helped save the Earth from total destruction," David said with a very strong and heavy tone of voice.

Pam's eyes widened in fear and confusion. "What are you?"

"My name is Joshua," David smiled. "I am, for all intentions and purposes, a god."

"What is going on?" Pam asked, not knowing what else to say.

"The person you see before you is limited, but only in the physical. I chose to be in this form to interact with other humans, as I was once. I had to absorb part of your life force to regenerate my powers. It is a complex matter, but the David you know... I was using my powers a while ago and it was draining me. I could have made it so I never run low on power or knowledge, but then I would not be doing what I wish to do in a free world. The Eternal Champions needed my help to destroy an evil being from another world. I needed to absorb the life force from everyone here in order to become strong enough to help them. I am whole again, thank you…and farewell."

"Wait! Will I ever see you again?"

"Perhaps. I cannot die and am eternal, so rest assured that I will be watching over you. You have a great family. Take good care of them and remember to live life as if it were your last day—full of love and happiness," David said and disappeared into thin air, leaving the seatbelt still connected to the buckle.

Pam sat there in deep thought, unable or unwilling to drive home.

It took ten minutes for the hundreds of people in the area to come back to consciousness and recover from the drain.

Pam finally came to grips with herself and was about to put the car into drive when instantly she was back in front of her driveway sitting in the car. She stared at her house with the entrance and living room lights still lit. Pam was confused on how she got there, not remembering having driven home. She thought about Joshua and breathed slowed. Pam smiled as joy filled her heart. She wondered why her? What made her so special to be visited by a supreme being? She did not have a dysfunctional family and her life was normal, but it was a welcome gift to see her life in a different way, knowing she had an impact on saving the world and the future of her family.

Richard flew as fast as he could toward John's last location. Larcis grabbed his arm and they sped off to the building John and Mark were supposedly located. They landed next to a large crater. The nuclear bomb had vaporized the entire building. Richard saw John's naked body in the center of the crater. The heat in the area was intense and probably radioactive. He flew down next to John's body, who was bleeding from all his body's orifices.

Hellfire landed next to the two men. "Creator, we need to take him to the EFL Headquarters if he's still alive," Hellfire said as Richard checked for vital signs.

"What happened?" Larcis asked.

"Don't know," Richard mumbled, checking for vital signs. Suddenly, his face lit up. "Okay, he's alive!"

"Can anyone put a force field on Mindseye so the trip doesn't rip him apart?" Hellfire asked.

"I can," Susan said and placed an energy field around John to protect him from the elements.

"Okay, I'm taking him to my medical lab," Hellfire said as he grabbed and cradled John like a baby in his arms, then flew off at his top speed.

The remaining team watched Hellfire and John disappear into the night sky. "Susan, can you get rid of the radioactivity here in the area?"

"Yeah," Susan said almost absently; she was more worried

about John than anything else.

"Larcis, take Liz and Cindy back to ED. After Susan takes care of the radiated area, we will go to the EFL," Richard instructed.

"Can do boss," Larcis replied and prepared Liz and Cindy for the flight back to ED.

Richard searched the area using his investigative skills to find evidence of what happened there. The nuke went off, he was sure of that, but John wasn't strong enough to prevent the bomb from destroying the city. Why was John still alive or everyone for that matter?

Richard thought hard and came to the conclusion that John was not alone when the nuke went off, although there was no physical evidence to that effect. Then it hit him. Nowhereman... Joshua? One of them must have done something—but what?

"Joshua, what happened?" Richard finally said aloud.

'I made it so John could divert the energy from the nuclear explosion and send it out into outer space,' Joshua suddenly replied in Richard's mind.

"Why did you get directly involved? I thought you were all for free will?"

'It is not John's time to die. He must live in order to fulfill his destiny.'

"Where is Mark?"

'His spirit is in a better place where he has finally found peace.'

"You mean...he's dead?" Richard said. He felt a stab of anger in his heart. "Why didn't you just keep the bomb from going off?"

'Mark is dead to this world, but he is still very much alive and has asked for you to forgive him. He is happy now, and maybe one day you will see your friend again,' Joshua replied.

Richard looked around and gazed at Susan, who was at this time had finished neutralizing the radiation residue in the area and was staring at him.

"You opened the portal for us to get here, didn't you?"

Susan looked at him knowing he wasn't really talking to her.

'Yes, I told Nowhereman I would help him defeat Ego. I knew his intentions and reasons before he asked me or knew about you. But understand that there is more to the story than what people say or see. Everyone has paths of destiny, and there will be those whose lives seem like they were meaningless or wasted, but in the end all people will come to understand that life is eternal and death is not the end of a cycle which people think only exists in the physical. There is a shining truth in you that no one can take away from you, so follow your heart and it will lead you to where you want to go and should go.'

Anger filled Richard's heart even more than ever. They had been used as pawns to fight a war between super beings and Earth was just the battleground. Joshua gave him the first clue, but now what was he supposed to do about it? He could not do anything to Joshua or about his decisions or actions, but he could affect everyone else. "Okay, if that's how we want to play it..." Richard said. He was silent for a moment and waited for Joshua to reply.

But there was no reply. Richard took a deep breath and muttered to himself, "I forgive you, Mark." He looked at Susan. "Let's go see John."

Susan grabbed Richard's hand and both of them flew off toward New York City over the sound barrier under Susan's cosmic powers.

Chapter Nineteen

□ □ ☐ □ □

TURN OF EVENTS

Northwest Pennsylvania

J ean entered an underground room deep inside an abandoned missile complex. It was small, dimly lit, and needed much repair judging by the wear and tear of missing equipment and furniture. There was a table in the center with six padded folding chairs around it. Jared and Natasha were waiting for her as Jean entered one of the two entrances to the room.

"Hello, Jean. Please, have a seat." Jared welcomed her. "Thank you for coming."

Jean wore casual business clothing, which impressed Jared; he had never seen her in such attire except in surveillance photos.

Jean's hair was tied tightly behind her head, highlighting the beauty of her ears and forehead. She sat down not smiling, but not frowning either.

"What have you come up with?" Jean asked in an unimposing way.

On the table were piles of documents and photos of various places and people.

"Before we start, I need you to understand that I know just about everything, and any information I withhold is for your protection and ours," Jared stated.

"So the less I know the safer you are?" Jean countered.

"No, the more you know, the safer we all are. I need you to know almost everything. If you know everything, other people might find out, and that would be dangerous for you and us. In front of you is all of the information I have on the people still living who were involved with your sister's murder. In addition, I have made a list of projects which we will perform for the next few months, maybe a year."

Jean took the paper and placed it on the table without reading it. She browsed through some of the surveillance photos and reports on several people, which jarred her memory more than once. The people she saw were in hiding ever since she took over the agency. She finally went back to the paper and read it closely.

"I hope the plan is to your satisfaction," Jared said.

Jean looked up at Jared after reading the master plan and smiled. "Yes, it sure is, but..."

"—Yes?"

"Why didn't you show me this earlier?"

"You didn't trust me before. Things are different now that you understand we are both on your side."

Jean looked over at Natasha. "And you are good with this?"

"I don't trust you like my brother, but I will follow wherever he wants me to go," Natasha said without hesitation.

"What's your price for all of this?" Jean said, wanting to make the deal final.

"The standard pay and 50 percent of all the spoils," Jared said.

"Really?" Jean grinned. "I didn't take you as being hungry for money."

"I'm not. The spoils are for my sister. If I die, I want to make sure she is well taken care of for the rest of her life."

Jean could not mistake Jared's honesty and felt very comfortable with accepting the proposal. She somehow envied Natasha for having such a good brother. It reminded her of her relationship with her own sister and that was something she could definitely relate to and craved to have again.

"Okay, no more death threats, no more talking down to you, and no more secrets. Is that good for you?" Jean said.

"Definitely," Jared said. Now the deal was final—they could now execute the operation of a lifetime designed to sow division among superhuman groups, create chaos in the government, help Jean take revenge on the people responsible for her sister's murder, and make them wealthy and powerful.

New York City, EFL Headquarters

Richard and Susan flew directly into EFL Headquarters. The EFL AI Computer, Bob, was expecting them and didn't stop them outside the base entrance. Starlight greeted the two superheroes. She was extremely beautiful with long silky blonde hair down to her waist. Her eyes were bright blue and she had the figure of a movie star model. She wore very nice and expensive night clothes alluding to her eccentric lifestyle.

"Hello, Creator, Pandora. Rick had to go get a special isotope from Walter Reed Medical Hospital for Mindseye, but he should be back shortly," Starlight said.

"Thank you for helping us out. Can we see Mindseye?" Richard said.

"Sure, follow me."

"Starlight, is he going to make it?" Susan asked expectantly worried.

Starlight turned around and gave Susan a friendly smile. "Call me Lynda."

"Lynda," Susan said with a slight smile of comfort.

"He was in very bad shape when he arrived, but he should be good as new in day or two." Lynda reassured.

"Are you sure? I mean, he stopped a nuclear bomb," Richard said.

"Really?" Rick didn't tell me that. That's odd," Lynda said.

"What do you mean?"

"There were no readings of radiation on him when he arrived. His body suffered internal bleeding, fifty-six simple fractures, a massive head trauma, a dislocated arm, and severe lesions." Lynda went down the list, thinking it was nothing, but Susan felt every word stab her heart. John went through hell for the team and she could not help him when he needed her.

Lynda saw the sorrow in Susan's eyes. "Don't worry, Pandora, he is practically all healed and is sleeping now."

Susan tried to smile. "Let's not waste time, then."

Lynda smiled and quickly led them to the medical lab.

John was in a shiny black cryogenic chamber the size of a dump truck. Susan and Richard saw John lying peacefully in the chamber through an internal camera that had been especially built to withstand the radioactive alpha and beta emissions inside the chamber. The chamber was regenerating John's body, a feat that would normally kill a normal human.

Lynda waited with the two heroes as Rick ran his errand. The very large room contained much technical and weird-looking equipment. Richard was impressed with the layout and took a few mental notes for upgrading his own medical center at ED. Susan did not pay attention to the fancy gadgets and watched John sleep.

Rick entered the room shortly afterwards. He was still in costume and quickly said hello, then went to a side table where he inserted a small blue crystal inside a two-foot-long black wand.

Susan eyed the wand with curiosity.

"What's that?" Richard asked.

"It's a cellular stabilizer," Susan answered for Rick.

Everyone looked at Susan in surprise. "How did you know that?" Rick asked.

"It's Argonian," Susan said.

"Is it? Quatris never told me exactly where he got it, but how do you know it's Argonian?"

"I'm queen of the Argonian Empire," Susan said with pride.

Richard smiled. "Yeah, and Mindseye is the king."

"Interesting," Rick oddly stated. "So you probably know how to use this better than I do." He walked over to Susan and held the wand out to her.

"Yes, I do, and I know about the Galactic Guardians as well, but that is for another time. For now we need to get John out of the chamber." Susan took the wand from Rick as he addressed her, "Your Highness."

John's body was moved out of the chamber and Susan immediately used the wand to stabilize the cells in his head and body. A few minutes later, John woke up in the middle of the process.

"Did we win?" John weakly muttered.

"You're actually speaking," Richard and Susan both said.

John seemed confused and surprised as well, and then smiled. "Cool."

"You better not talk as much as you think." Susan grinned and kissed John softly on the lips.

The room was filled with joy and laughter, as John miraculously recovered completely in less than an hour since being in ground zero of a nuclear reaction. John's power pool had increased tenfold, with an awakening of his cosmic focal point that even surpassed Susan's abilities.

The trio left EFL Headquarters shortly afterwards, with Richard interrogating John on what had happened to him on the way back to ED. They arrived at ED late that morning, being greeted by all of the members, including Becky and Robert. It was a time of great celebration for all of them, except Richard.

Richard's thoughts were elsewhere thinking about what happened when Liz fought with Ego; he felt there were too many unanswered questions, and too many matters of fact. He got John to mentally link the group up again and they exchanged their experiences. Liz said Ego's real name during the battle, but did not know how she knew. Ego was not as powerful as he expected, but their victory would not have been possible without all of them doing what they did. Even then, the only thing, which seemed plausible, was Hellfire arriving as he did. Erica had called him once Richard was in St. Louis and he simply flew to their aid. John was showing a massive increase in power, which concerned Richard. If it had not been for the nuclear explosion and Joshua's intervention, John would not have been in a position to be the unopposed King of the Argonian Empire. It was too convenient, even for a string of miracles.

Richard made it clear to the team that they were his family, and nothing would keep him from supporting them. They made a pact to mentally share thoughts on a regular basis to keep incidents like this from happening. Richard knew too well how half truths and secrets could become the fuel to give birth to and grow division and very bad decision making. There were two human deaths in the fight against Ego, and one was Mark. His heart was broken over the loss of his friend because of secrets and the playing around by super beings. The group comforted him with their thoughts and understanding, but it would be time and forgiveness on his part which would ease his desire for revenge.

The team got some needed rest except for Richard. He went to the Battle Room and instructed Erica to lock down the floor so no one would disturb him. He sat on the sofa before the main screen, leaned back, and relaxed. He laid there for fifteen minutes in deep thought.

"Erica, patch me in to Max," he commanded.

"Contacting SIA now," Erica replied with her alluring echoed sexy voice.

It was not long before Max came up on the screen. "Sorry, I didn't get a chance to thank you for getting rid of the Killer Virus."

"I wish I could say you're welcome, but I need to know something first," Richard said calmly.

Max did not seem surprised, but his face told Richard they were both talking to each other with their own agenda. "I'm going to have to ask you before you say anything. Why did you erase Lt. Harper's mind?"

"Lt. Harper did not need to keep the memories and sorrow of his fake wife, including those of a fake Susan—"

"—You tampered with evidence, Richard," Max snapped, cutting him off. "What were you thinking?"

"Susan didn't do it. If anyone should be mad about that, it is me. I would die for Liz and believe me; I would not allow anyone on my team to get away with something like that."

"Whether Susan is innocent or not, is not the issue. The perception is you tampered with the evidence and covered for her. My hands are tied now. I cannot have SIA's procedures or leadership be overridden by you or any other superhuman," Max said, his voice firm.

"Speaking of procedures, why didn't you tell me Marcus Wellington worked for you and started the Killer Virus?"

The question stopped Max for a moment. "There are many things I am not at liberty to tell you, Richard. It's obvious Erica told you about Mr. Wellington, but at the time, you didn't need to know."

"Erica didn't tell me anything except Marcus's assumed name while he was in your agency. Mark was my friend and if you had told me, he wouldn't be dead now," Richard said calmly, gritting his teeth. "So, don't tell me what I didn't need to know."

"Marcus was with you all this time?" Max asked, a little surprised.

"It doesn't matter, anymore. Ego is dead, Mark is dead, a probably mind controlled bomb builder is dead, and the virus is dead."

"I'm sorry for your loss, Richard, but we can't work together like this, if we don't talk more to each other."

"There are too many secrets, Max, and not enough trust in the world. I can't trust you right now, but maybe I can in the future."

"I understand," Max said in disappointment.

"My team will need some time to ourselves. If you can be so kind to give us only emergency cases, I would appreciate it," Richard said.

Max sat still in his chair for a moment, considering Richard's request. "Take as much time as you need, Richard."

"Thank you." Richard signed off, ending the video communiqué.

Richard leaned back on the sofa for a few minutes, pondering his next task. "Erica, please don't interrupt me for the next meeting."

"As you wish, Richard."

Richard pulled up the wireless keyboard and started typing. The main screen displayed Richard's call to Nowhereman.

It didn't take very long for Nowhereman to reply. *'How are you, Richard?'*

'Not good at all.'

'Why not? The world is safe.'

'Because you lied to me and used us like henchmen. Ego was trapped in that dimension, wasn't he? Now, my friend is dead because you saw your chance to get your revenge and kill Ego.'

'You are very smart, Richard, but not very understanding. It was a matter of time. Ego destroyed his food supply and I trapped him there, but like I said, it was a matter of time before he would have figured a way out. I searched long and hard until I found you. Yes, I used you, but only because I knew you had the best chance of destroying him.'

'What gives you the right to put my family in danger?'

'The same right you have to save lives.'

'Don't play with me, Nowhereman. You lied to me and put my team in danger. Don't cross my path again or you will know how it feels like to fight us. You have lost more than you have won today. I may not be able to defeat Joshua, but you are another matter. I will not fight for your causes anymore. Is that understood?'

'I understand you're upset, but what happened was inevitable. Ego would have gotten out and destroyed your world if I had not deceived you.'

'We may not be an advanced life form to you, but we are true heroes. Heroes who protect the weak and fight for what is right. We would have fought that beast knowing the truth. Don't be asking for my help anymore.' Richard rapidly stood up and left the room, not once looking back to see if Nowhereman said anything in his defense.

'I guess I underestimated you humans,' Nowhereman replied while Erica just as quickly erased it off her screen.

Richard went upstairs and straight to his bedroom where Liz waited patiently to embrace her husband.

Late that morning, the team bid Cindy farewell, with Erica taking a group photo. Cindy was welcome to visit and they had an agreement for Cindy to help out the group every now and then.

It was a long trip back home for Cindy, but it went quickly for her as she caught up with her part-time work. It was not long before she stepped out of the taxicab in front of her apartment. She smiled as she felt a cool breeze and the sweet taste of home on her face. She quickly made her way upstairs to the fourteenth floor. It was a small but elegant apartment she had lived in for the past few weeks with a few boxes still unopened or half emptied out and scattered about in the corners of several rooms. The entire apartment was decorated with a mixture of colors and furnishings, including trinkets and a large low-lying wood-and-glass living room table. Luxurious lighting, every appliance imaginable, and a complete surround sound entertainment system allowed her to enjoy the comforts of home and the outside world. It was an ideal place to relax and call home.

However, all of the luxuries of home were transparent to her as her plush bed called out to her for needed rest after the long flight and battle with Ego. She stripped down to her white panties and threw herself on her king-size bed, falling into a deep sleep, dreaming about the future and Glenn.

She woke up a few hours later early that evening. She slept good enough to feel physically rested, but not mentally relaxed. Her first thoughts were of Glenn, so she quickly took a shower and got dressed to go see him. She left her room wondering if Glenn would even be at home and tried not to expect too much. The fewer expectations she had, the less of a chance for any disappointments, so she slowed down and straightened up the apartment a little, not really knowing why. Maybe she was scared to see Glenn, not knowing what to say to him or what he would say to her. After twenty minutes of messing around with the living room, she sat on her ivory-colored sofa and stared at the blank television screen. She looked around at the empty apartment. Yes, it was empty and she was alone. She was there and Glenn was somewhere else. The time was now or never, so she got up and walked to her front door.

The brightly colored entry way came to life as Cindy walked into the ceiling light's motion sensor. She quickly unlocked the door and proceeded to leave the apartment. Glenn stood in the hallway and was about to knock on her door, but Cindy seemed to have surprised him, catching him with an awkward look on his face.

Cindy froze in her tracks a little startled. She did not expect anyone to be in front of her apartment door. A mixture of joy and confusion came over her as she faced him. Both of them spoke not a word.

The silence provided an invisible link to each other's

hearts. They both felt whole for a split second as if they belonged together without regrets or worries about the future.

"Hi," Glenn said, breaking the moment.

"Hi."

"Were you going somewhere?"

Cindy hesitated to answer truthfully. "I was going to see you."

"I told you I would find you," Glenn said before Cindy could speak any more.

Cindy's face straightened up with seriousness. "You know this could be considered as stalking."

"It would technically be stalking if I followed you or been waiting for you the entire week just outside your door, but I didn't."

Cindy smirked with wonder on her face. "How did you find me?"

"Did you know there are three hundred and twelve Samantha's here in Seattle, and only five with your last name? Besides, you told me a general location of the block you lived in."

Glenn stood there, wearing dark slacks and a dark gray tightly-fit long-sleeved shirt along with a dark brown leather jacket. Cindy examined Glenn closely, admiring his handsome face and well-defined physique. "I guess I don't need to go out now. Do you want to come in?"

"Yes, thank you." Glenn stepped inside while Cindy closed the door behind him.

Glenn turned around and faced Cindy. "I couldn't stop thinking about you ever since you almost got hit by that car."

"Really?" Cindy said, feeling very relaxed and confident about herself and what she wanted. The time she had spent with Larcis and Richard greatly changed her outlook in life. She had a feeling that Joshua had somehow used the situation to solve her dilemma with Glenn— or was it destiny?

She thought about what to say, but before she could speak again, Glenn quickly grabbed her and ardently kissed her. Cindy almost jumped back in surprise, but caught herself and wrapped her arms around Glenn and kissed him back.

Cindy woke up the next morning with Glenn by her side. The bed covers felt silky and wonderful on her skin. It was the best sleep she had in a long time and felt like staying in bed with Glenn forever. She thought about her adopted father, and smiled as happiness filled her heart.

"Thank you, Joshua," she softly muttered and went back to sleep by the man she loved.

Author Notes

□ □ □ □ □

I was born in Bogotá, Colombia and moved to the United States when I was six years old. I lived in Maryland for six years and Florida for seven years. I dropped out of school after completing the ninth grade and received a Graduate Equivalency Diploma (GED) when I turned sixteen. I enrolled in Miami-Dade Community College and completed a year towards my Architectural Engineering major before enlisting in the U.S. Army at the age of seventeen. I enlisted as an infantryman wanting to follow in my older brother's footsteps, to serve my country and receive college assistance through the military. I spent the subsequent six years jumping around from Fort Benning to Fort Stewart, Georgia; then to South Korea, and lastly, to Little Rock, Arkansas with the Joint Readiness Training Center Opposing Forces (JRTC OPFOR).

I married while in South Korea and left military active duty in August of 1989. I attended Boyce Bible School in Louisville, Kentucky, and Indiana University Southeast (IUS) Campus two years later. I graduated with a Bachelor's Degree in General Studies and a minor in Psychology from the IUS in May of 1994 and was going to enter the Southern Baptist Theological

Seminary, but reenlisted into the U.S. Army a month later. I was stationed at Schofield Barracks, Hawaii for two years before I attended the Officer Candidate School and received a commission as a Military Intelligence Officer. I returned to South Korea and served as a counterintelligence officer until my retirement in 2008. I have been to over eight different countries in five different continents. I enjoy traveling and love to meet people and make new friends everywhere I go.

As a child, I hated reading with a passion until I started reading Edgar Rice Burroughs's *Tarzan* books in the seventh grade. My brother introduced me to the books and opened up the world of fiction and nonfiction for the rest of my life. I grew up watching movies and television in general. You might say I was a TV junky. This preoccupation, I guess, nurtured my desire to be able to tell stories with words. I hope the *Superhero Epic Series* brings you to the world of fantasy and wonder as well as opens up new ideas and dreams which make us all look forward to the future with the knowledge that anything is possible if you never give up.

I want to point out that the 1st edition book was reviewed back in 2006, and of course the critic was filled with human error. The review criticized that the author didn't know what he was talking about and confused the reader because there were superheroes flying in commercial planes while they could fly. I write nothing without a reason, and there were two instances where in this book people flew on a commercial plane. Mark who wasn't a superhuman and couldn't fly, and Cindy who could fly but took a jet from Seattle to Miami. Cindy's maximum flight speed is roughly 500 mph which is slightly more than a commercial jetliner, but why should she fly across the country if she can relax on a plane? The heroes are super, but they do get tired, and for her purpose, it was necessary she use her cover to go to Fort Lauderdale. In addition, she would not want to carry luggage with her, which is why you don't see many superheroes like Superman lugging baggage when he goes to get a story; but in fact flies in an airplane. The critic ignored these facts of real life; which in the story Night flew everyone around, simply because he is faster than any commercial aircraft and used their powers as they would in real life. The other comment I want to address is that the critic mentioned that why would there be a supreme superhuman, referring to Joshua, who would die if he didn't suck up the life force of people. The critic read in between the lines, and Joshua was never going to die. Joshua is a complex character and what he did in the beginning of the story was to set things in motion. He made himself human so as to be on Earth as a human and god at the same time, but he is in all essence a god. His human form is not fully aware of everything he put in place, so he drains life forces to gain power, but at the same time, he really doesn't need to since he had already foresaw everything. This might not fully explain things to you, but the details on Joshua and what he did or will do is in books 5, 6, and 8. If he didn't drain the life force of people he would have simply gone into a deep sleep and not been able to help our heroes, because he is still living a life as a human in the flesh sort of speaking.

This second book in the eight-book series of *A Superhero Epic* is the continuation of a fantastic adventure of betrayal, love, evil, prejudice, triumph, life, and death. It is the stepping-stone to an era known as "Masterminds" that will change the reasons people fight for the survival of Earth. I tried to capture all of the astounding moments of bravery, success, and failures by my good friends who helped in the story line and played the actual characters in the series. Thank you all, once again, for your friendship.

If you are wondering why the book might mirror another story or how it is that characters know things that seem out of character, don't be too concerned. The settings and plots will make more sense in later books, because I put the entire story in eight books. In addition, there are time paradoxes which do not occur because of Joshua's character dynamics, and events which I do talk about in reference to past and future events; like John's boost of power and why that is so important for the future of Earth and the Argonian Empire. I hope you have enjoyed the book series so far and don't forget to look for the sequels:

Guild Without a Name	-	*book 3*
The Galaxy Is Ours	-	*book 4*
Masterminds	-	*book 5*
Superhumans From the Past	-	*book 6*
Ultimate Assassins	-	*book 7*
Last Hope for Earth	-	*book 8*

He is Known as Ego, A Superhero Epic

www.ingramcontent.com/pod-product-compliance
Lightning Source LLC
Chambersburg PA
CBHW030401030726
47497CB00002B/425